Bayfield's Secret Notebook

by

David Fabio

This book may not be transmitted, reproduced, or stored in part or in whole by any means without the express written consent of the author except for brief quotations in articles or reviews.

Photographs by David Fabio

Copyright © 2012, 2017 by David Fabio
All rights reserved.

ISBM:
ISBN-13: 978-1973883845
ISBN-10: 1973883848

David Fabio

Contents

Chapter		page
	Author's Notes	iii
	List of Characters	iv
1	The Message	1
2	The Invitation	11
3	The Notebook	26
4	The Visit	33
5	The Civil War	42
6	Inquiries	48
7	The Trip Home	52
8	Man the Cannons	55
9	Piecing the Story Together	61
10	Connections	71
11	Barrels	77
12	Shipping Orders	91
13	Homeward Bound	97
14	Shipping Out	103
15	Ships a Comin'	116
16	Cruisin' on the River	129
17	Paducah	137
18	Up the Mississippi	143
19	Preparations	146
20	St. Louis	149

21	Shallow Waters	156
22	Fire in the Hole	159
23	The Shot	164
24	Calming the Nerves	174
25	Rapids	178
26	Celebrations	184
27	Minnesota Bound	189
28	St. Croix River	193
29	Stillwater	198
30	Family Greetings	200
31	Waiting	208
32	Directions	214
33	Supervision	218
34	Seasons	231
35	Fire	237
36	Big Events	242
37	Biding Time	250
38	Trains a Comin'	259
39	Time to Ship	263
40	Bayfield	266
41	The Trip North	274
42	The Crossing	280
43	Missing	287
44	Final Good-Byes	292
45	Last Visit	295
46	Islands	308

David Fabio

Author's Note

In writing Bayfield's Secret Notebook, I spent considerable time researching what might be to the reader "trivial information." Sometimes, it would take a full day to verify a single fact. Whether it is the distance a paddlewheeler would travel in a day, or the days they traveled, these facts bring life to the historical fiction and make the story real. Occasionally, I found that history was not as good as it could be to the historians. Specific dates and information have been lost or smudged into vagueness. I hope that all my information, which became the basis of the story, is accurate.

The main characters in the book are fictional. The places and facts are as close to real as one can make them 150 years or so from the actual happening. As I placed the characters into the settings, I tried to do so in such a manner that I did not disgrace the real people and actual places described in the book. Any similarities of the fictitious characters to real people are totally by coincidence.

I hope you enjoy where the paths in this book attempt to lead you. The stories of Confederate gold have been the tales of fortune seekers and the hidden scrolls to historians.

List of Characters

Stan Moline – Writer
Jane Moline – Stan's sister
    Nate Duncan – Jane's husband
Barbara Fontaine – Stan's fiancée
Vivian Jacobs – Barbara's mother

Miss Jean Larson – Innkeeper/owner Lamp Post Inn – Bayfield
    Olivia – Jean's friend
Gilbert Miller – Bayfield County Deputy Sheriff

Boone County Distillery – Mr. Snyder – owner, Petersburg, KY
    Appleton – Brother-in-law

Johan Volker - Brewmaster
Wilhelm Volker – Johan's brother
    Josh and Horace – Johan's partners

Mr. Langer – Banker

Colonel Jack Travis
Sergeant Pettit – 1st band
Private Scruggs – 2nd band
Private McCoy – 3rd band
Robert Louden – Confederate conspirator

David Fabio

Lewis Patterson – Confederate treasury officer

Captain Harris – War Eagle
Sergeant Fry – Roommate of Johan Volker
Thor – War Eagle Fireman
    Kathryn Bell – War Eagle traveler
Josephine Kane – War Eagle traveler
Geraldine Lyons – War Eagle traveler
Sergeant Stoltzman – Soldier from Wabasha

Gerhardt Knips – Knips Brewery
Norbert Kimmick – Kimmick Brewery
Frank Aiple – Kimmick Brewery
Sandy McDougal – Lumberjack
Victor Lawson – Guard
    Mrs. Arlene Olson – Co-owner of alterations store – Olson's Sewing
Arnold Simley – Stillwater resident

Bayfield's Secret Notebook

Chapter 1

The Message

It was early morning, **Thursday, July 20, 1865**, when Colonel Jack Travis and his men were met by an unnamed rider on horseback at Travis's temporary camp, located in the protective hills of eastern Missouri, near the Missouri River. The rider's distinctive cloth hat was a signal to the band that he was a messenger from a group of Southern loyalists that refused to honor the end of the war. Except for the gray hat, there was nothing about him that could distinguish him from the average farmer. The messenger had put the hat on just before approaching their camp.

It had been a hot summer. To Colonel Travis and his band of men, it had been a typical southern summer, hot and humid. Even though the Civil War had officially concluded months earlier in April of 1865, several bands of former Confederate soldiers, including Colonel Travis's group, roamed the hills seeking revenge on the North for the severe beating the South had taken. General Ulysses S. Grant's and General Sherman's final marches through the south in an effort to cut all supply lines, was an all out effort that forced the South to give up. It left bitter memories in the minds of many of the returning Confederate soldiers who had been held prisoners in the north.

David Fabio

The folklore of Quantrill's Raiders in Kansas and Missouri a few years earlier, served to give other small bands of rebels the idea to dish out revenge on those who had participated in the Union forces. These unofficial bands of rebel renegades had just enough structure that they could get communications about the local movements of the Union armies.

Now, as Travis and his visitor walked along the grassy ridge high above the Mississippi River, the misty haze was just starting to lift off the water. The sun was climbing in the sky, and the morning rays of sunlight were warming up the moist air that had been hanging overnight in the river valleys.

To protect the information carriers, their names were never used in front of the men. However, the visitor was no stranger to Colonel Travis. The two men had met many times during the course of the war. It had been a brutal war. Both men had been prisoners of the Union forces under General Grant, during the time he reclaimed the river ways throughout the South. As the war concluded, slowly, each side released their prisoners, who had been held in rather secluded and primitive camps. Many years would pass before the resentment and nightmares of the war would be erased from their memories.

After they exchanged greetings, they talked about the health of old friends, neighbors and colleagues in their past. Many of the soldiers and officers who survived the war went home in poor health, only to find their homes no longer existed. For those not shot and injured in the war, months of poor sanitation in prison camps left many with dysentery and other diseases. With homes and families broken up or totally missing, once they regained their health, revenge was their only thought. The stories Travis and the rider traded that day on the ridge about coveted friends only fueled their hatred of the war and the North. Life had not returned to normal as most southerners had hoped once the war was over.

Bayfield's Secret Notebook

The coded message that had been telegraphed from a Confederate partisan, Robert Louden, to the messenger, and relayed to Colonel Travis was simple: A steamboat had left Cincinnati, Ohio on July 14th, heading down the Ohio River. Amidst its cargo were some barrels of whiskey as partial payment to the State of Minnesota for sending troops to the war. The next day, the steamboat "War Eagle" had stopped in Louisville, Kentucky, and was now carrying part of the Minnesota 1st Regiment, that had just been discharged from the Union Army, and was heading home. They had been decorated in Washington before being discharged. Those on the boat included some that had been injured in the war, including a few coffins of those that died in the final actions. It also included the officers of the regiment. The Minnesota 1st had been engaged in fighting many of the important battles during the war.

The message to Colonel Travis was simple, and to the point; **"Burn it."**

"Tell Louden we will take care of it," he answered. "Time for another damn Yankee boat to have a small accident on the way up river. This eagle will go down with its tail feathers in flames."

The two men shook hands, and with a strong pat on the back, parted company. Both men knew the part they needed to play. The men were simply taking orders, just like in the war. All of them felt that the North needed to feel the misery that had been dealt out to the innocent families in the South.

When Jack Travis walked over to talk to the rest of his band of renegades, he outlined a plan to his fellow ex-Confederates, showing how he wanted to make it look like an accident. For years, the Confederate Army had perfected several methods of sabotaging boats that were assisting the Union forces. Now, the plan was simple, sink it. To accomplish the task, they would split into three groups of men.

David Fabio

The first band of men would be led by Sergeant Pettit, a strong, stern, sawed-off looking person, whose body reminded you of a tree stump. If you ran into him, he would not budge.

This group would meet the steamboat War Eagle when it pulled into the levee at St. Louis, Missouri. From their location near St. Joseph, they would have to cross the Missouri to get to the levee. The men would look into getting jobs as shoremen, and attempt to assist the crew that hauled coal on board for the next leg of their journey.

The second crew would be stationed fifteen to twenty miles north of the junction of the Mississippi and Missouri rivers. As the boat rounded a sharp bend along the Illinois side of the river, they would attempt to board the paddlewheeler.

The third group was the enforcement group. If the other two teams failed, they would force the steamboat to shore, and throw dynamite in the boat.

Colonel Travis was as harsh with his men as he had been in the war. "This boat must not make it past the hometown of the Union generals, at Galina, Illinois," he told his troops. "If it does, I guarantee you there will be a few responsible people swinging from a tree. Only, the rope will not kill them, the fire under their feet will. So, think about it, burn this damn boat, or I'll burn those that do not get the job done. No damn Yankees are going home celebrating on Southern whiskey."

Galina was located along the river in northern Illinois. It was the hometown of nine generals that served during the Civil War. The most famous general was Ulysses S. Grant. That knowledge burned even deeper in the hatred held by Colonel Travis. He wanted to send a strong message. He only wished that he could send the boat to the bottom within eyesight of the docks at Galena, with Grant aboard.

His men knew that he meant what he said. The threat was real. He had been a rock-solid Colonel in the Confederate forces. People that retreated after he shouted "attack" were shot. His troops found that

Bayfield's Secret Notebook

following his orders was the way they had been successful. Many times, Colonel Travis had personally led the advances. It was his tight relationship to his men that caused his capture. When met by overwhelming forces in a narrow valley in eastern Tennessee, after losing half of his men in less than one-hour of battle, Colonel Travis realized the certainty of defeat. As a result, he and the thirty men that were left standing were forced to surrender.

The men sat down at their morning campfire. While heating up their coffee, they discussed the individual missions in as much detail as they could. Most of them had gone through this before and had a good idea as to how it was going to happen. Each group had full knowledge of the plans of the other groups, and knew what part they played in the final sinking of the boat.

Colonel Travis told Sergeant Pettit, leader of the first band of three strong men, "I want your group to ride out by horseback this afternoon. Take the trail that follows the Missouri River. The ferry will get you to the other side, and then travel on to St. Louis.

"You need to spend the next week finding work loading riverboats. Use your ragged clothes. You need to fit in with the other roustabouts. Since they do not use colored folk as roustabouts on the Mississippi above the Ohio, you should be okay.

"The War Eagle is expected in about eleven days from now. She will be heavily loaded to the gun rails with cargo and Union soldiers returning from the war. Heading down the Ohio River will be easy for the steamboat. The current will carry her down at about three to five miles per hour, almost all by itself. My guess is that the captain will be running the boilers at half-steam, saving on fuel as it floats down river.

"When she makes the bend and heads up the Mississippi, the boilers will be fired up to maximum pressure. With the river extremely high this year from all the rain, and the strain of a fully loaded paddlewheeler heading up-river, it will require all she has in her until she reaches the wider stretches of the Mississippi. Most boats that come down the Ohio, and do not fuel up in Cairo, will stop at the next location for fuel. That will allow them to make St. Louis for their next cargo stop. The boat could stop early and pick up wood for the boiler, but my guess is that it would prefer to stop for coal, since space is a premium on that fully loaded boat.

"As a result, Cape Girardeau, Missouri is the logical stopping point for riverboats heading up-river into the current to drop-off or load cargo, and top off the coal bin. They should have a supply of coal because as many as five or six boats stop to change cargo there each day."

Sergeant Pettit nodded his head. "I agree. Cape Girardeau is where she'll stop. Too bad we can't get her there. We could probably get there about the time the boat arrives. It would be a long ride, especially, if the boat gets there early and we miss her. So, I think you are right, we should meet her in St. Louis. It will only take a couple more days for the boat to make St. Louis. Want us to send her up in a cloud of smoke when she docks there?"

"No, too many witnesses. However, with all the commotion going on with all the boats and cargo, it will give us better cover to prepare the boat. We will sink her in the shallow waters north of St. Louis, where there are a number of reasons the boat could run into trouble. Here's what I want you to do..:"

Their mission was simple; some of the larger chunks of coal that were destined for the War Eagle would be drilled and plugged with explosives. Then, the hole would be covered over with softer pieces of coal to hide the "surprise." As the boat traveled up river with the boiler pushed to the limit, a few extra charges from the stuffed coal in the fire box, would cause the boiler to fail, causing a fire that would rapidly sink the ship. All the men had to do was find the load of coal that was destined for the War Eagle. Working on the dock should give them the information they needed. If possible, the team would make sure the explosive coal was located just below the top of the coal pile in the boat. It would let the steamboat head up river a ways, before the explosions lit up the boiler room.

The Confederate Army had used this method to near perfection close to the end of the war. Several ships carrying soldiers had been sunk on both the Mississippi River and along the Atlantic coast. Since the poorly designed pressure boilers on the ships was one of its weakest links, an explosion in the boiler was usually blamed on poor welds or bad pressure gauges. In reality, many steamboats had tried to carry loads beyond the design of the ships, and raced to see how many trips they could make. The wear and tear of the high pressures on the boilers was a disaster waiting to happen, and happen it did. Every year, it was common to hear of several boats that blew a boiler, or sunk, after hitting a snag in the river.

Earlier that year, Travis's men, working with Robert Louden, were responsible for the sinking of the Sultana, just north of Memphis on the Mississippi. The Sultana was carrying 2,300 Union prisoners of war who had just been released from Confederate prisons. When the coal bombs went off, the boat, crew and Union prisoners found the bottom of the rushing Mississippi River. The current broke apart anything the boiler explosion failed to disintegrate or scald. It was the largest loss of lives in US maritime history. As many as 1,900 died as a result of the accident.

Travis's second band of men listened to their instructions from Travis. It was led by Private Scruggs. In the war, Scruggs's brother fought for the Union side. He never returned. Somehow, Scruggs felt responsible for not preventing his brother from entering the war.

"Private, I want your band to ride out by horseback in the morning," Colonel Travis told them.

David Fabio

"Your job is to find one of the tight bends on the river, located on your map, where the deepest part of the river is tight to the outside bend of the river. There needs to be trees on the shoreline. The final requirement, find a spot that the boat would reach near dusk. Somewhere just before it finds a safe area to tie-off for the night. My plan is to have one or two of your people wade out into the river's shallow water, before the boat comes by, and throw a small grappling hook on the deck as it passes them, without the passengers noticing it. Hopefully, the noise of the paddlewheels and steam system will hide any sounds. Also, since they are heading home, most of the soldiers will be celebrating and not paying attention to the shoreline. The side walkways should be full of wood even if they have burned some from the front deck. Most of the passengers should be up on the top deck or inside.

"In the areas where the riverbanks are over a mile wide, the main channel will only be slightly over neck deep. This will allow the men to wade well out into the channel. With all the tree stumps that wash downriver each spring, in low light the men standing motionless in the water will just look like another stump from a distance. This late in July, the water temperature is up in the mid 70's. This will allow them to stand quietly for a long length of time as the paddlewheeler slowly approaches.

"Heading upstream near dusk will mean that the boat would be lucky to be travelling at about three miles per hour. By hooking the deck or railings, your men should be able to let the hooked rope glide them next to the boat, where they can climb aboard the low-slung hull, pulling themselves up by the railing. Once aboard, quickly throw a couple sticks of dynamite, from your oil soaked, waterproofed backpacks into the boiler room, and then dive into the water. With luck, you should be able to make shore before the boiler lights up the sky.

"If the first crew is successful in loading charges, you will not be needed. The boat may never reach your area and the sound of the explosion, if she goes, will be heard miles away, along the river."

Bayfield's Secret Notebook

The men remembered that the Sultana only made it seven miles north of Memphis before she blew.

"We'll make sure they never see it coming," one of Private Scruggs's men told Colonel Travis.

Colonel Travis turned to the third group. He had saved the most experience men for the last. The group would be comprised of the rest of Travis's men led by Private McCoy; a very seasoned soldier who had a history of making extra-certain that the enemy was destroyed in each battle he had been involved in.

When Private McCoy returned from the war, he discovered his entire family had burned in their farmhouse. As a result, his hatred for Union soldiers was very severe.

"I would like your band to head out in the morning as well.

"The five of you will travel up-river, and position yourselves ten to fifteen-miles or so, upstream of Scruggs's band. Find a location where the main channel of the river is narrow, about 200-300-feet wide between the islands and shore, even though the river valley is over two miles wide. Here, you need to pick an area where the current runs tight to the wooded, Missouri side of the Mississippi. Position two men on that side of the river. The other three need to be on the opposite shoreline.

"As the boat approaches, the object is to shoot flaming cloth wrapped arrows dipped in fuel oil, at her wood piles. If we can start a minor fire, the War Eagle will be forced to the other side of the river to put the fire out and keep the passengers safe. On that side, your three people will be waiting with dynamite to finish the job. I don't even want to see a piece of wood more than the size of a toothpick," he instructed them.

They were aware that their job was the final attempt. It was their responsibility to make sure the boat did not pass that point. If anyone survived, the men could start rumors that Injuns burnt the riverboat.

David Fabio

"It will be finished," Private McCoy replied.

Colonel Travis told them he would monitor the action from the hills overlooking the river.

Travis was a tall, lanky person with premature gray hair and a short gray beard, for a man of only thirty-seven. The onslaught of his grey hair was probably assisted by the stresses that prevailed in the war. During his final battle, a rifle shot broke his left leg, slowing down his participation in the post war action.

When the ill-trained doctors were finished with the seriously injured, and had saved the lives of those they could, they set his leg. His left leg had lost some of the muscle support it had before he was shot. Now, he had to assist the leg to get up into the saddle. Because of this, he was limited to the planning and supporting of his troops.

Now, as he slept in the hills of Missouri, the visions of the war replayed every night. Most of the nights, he would wake up in a full sweat, his pistol in hand, ready to shoot the first thing that moved. Try as he might, the war was not going to leave him alone. The only thing he could do was use his ability to get revenge on those that destroyed his life and the lives of his family and friends.

* * * * *

Chapter 2

The Invitation

Jane and Nate Duncan decided to use the wedding present Jane's brother Stan had given them, as soon as the weather warmed up in northern Wisconsin. Stan Moline had purchased a gift certificate for two nights at the Le Chateau Boutin, or the Chateau as everyone called it, in Bayfield, Wisconsin. When they got married, they took their honeymoon in the Caribbean where it was a lot warmer in February, than in Minneapolis, Minnesota. Now that it was warming up, they were anxious to use the certificate.

Jane had heard all about Bayfield from Stan, while he was up there researching the new book he was writing. On top of that, it was where he met Barbara, his fiancée. All the stories about the town and the inn sounded like something Jane wanted to see for herself, and enjoy with her husband. They made plans to stay at the inn over the Memorial Day weekend.

When Stan called Jane, to give her his weekly update on what was going on in his life, she told him that she had made the reservations at the Chateau.

"Oh, fantastic!" he replied. "I can give you a list of all the exciting things to do in town, or, you can go searching on your own. What's your preference? What room did you request?"

"I asked for the South Suite at the inn. They thought we would like it very much. Since you spent all those days up there, maybe you could email me a list of the places you think we might be interested in. That way, we can pick and choose as time permits, without realizing later that we missed something. Remember, we only have a couple half days, and one full day to see everything. Unlike you, some people have regular jobs and have to get back to work."

"You must have been talking to Barbara again without telling me. That was her favorite room up there. I think it had to do with the Jacuzzi, and fireplace in the room. The view of the lake and town was not too shabby either. Barbara is going to be envious of you. She keeps reminding me of how much she enjoyed staying there. I told her it wasn't the place; it was the guy she met up there."

"In your dreams," Jane told him.

"Okay, maybe it was the quaint town and beautiful scenery. Anyway, I can send you a list of places to see, and good restaurants in the area. Your reservation is less than two weeks away. I'm going down to visit Barbara that weekend. I'll try to send you the list, or drop it off, before I get started on my next project and forget all about it."

"Thanks! Try not to put your foot in your mouth when you see her. Good thing love is blind. So far, she thinks you are perfect. I wouldn't want you to screw up any plans for that wedding you have planned for next spring. I'm not sure you will be able to find anyone else that can put up with your need for free time."

"Hmm! Did I tell you about that 3-hour cruise around the islands?" Stan asked. "If you are not a little nicer to me, I will make sure Gilligan is the first mate. We'll find you in November."

"Okay, I can see where this conversation is going. Have a great weekend. Give me a call when you get back."

Bayfield's Secret Notebook

Stan put together a list of the interesting things for Jane and Nate to see while they were in Bayfield, including a meal at Maggie's restaurant. He labeled it as a must see. When he sent it to Jane, he put a note on the bottom: "If you get some free time, please stop in at the Lamp Post Inn. That's the bed and breakfast I stayed at when I was in Bayfield. It is nice, just not as deluxe as the place you are going to be staying. If you get there say hello to Jean, the owner, for me. If you mention my name, she will know who you are."

Jane and Nate drove up to Bayfield early Saturday morning for their romantic get-away. The past week had been hectic at work for both of them. It felt good to get a good night's sleep, and get up early in the morning to drive the 4-hour drive to northern Wisconsin. If they had driven up the evening before, the 4-hour trip would have probably taken over 6-hours, due to the traffic jams of everyone leaving town for the three-day weekend.

They arrived just before noon.

Stan's list of things to do included several places to eat. He had put an asterisk on Maggie's, so Jane figured Stan really wanted them to try that place. They decided to stop before checking into the inn.

When Nate drove down the street and saw the sign for Maggie's, he turned to Jane, "Are you sure your brother is not trying to get even with you for not being up here with us? I was thinking of a quaint little place looking over the water."

Jane had heard Stan talk about Maggie's before and knew what to expect. However, she thought she would surprise Nate. "Oh, you know Stan. He loves to go to different places. I think we should give it a try."

Nate pulled into the parking lot and checked out the metal flamingo sculpture. They matched the pink flamingos in front of the pink with yellow trim restaurant. "If this is a joke, I'm burning the rest of Stan's list," he told Jane.

When they went inside, Nate was impressed with the flamingo decorations all around the bar. "Someone went to a lot of work making this place unique. You pick the booth."
Jane picked a quiet table, and they sat down and looked at the menu. Nate was impressed. The selection was very good.
"Stan told me there was a reason this place was very popular," she told him. "It's the food. He said that most of the locals eat here, especially in the off-season."
"Proof is in the pudding. For now, Stan is back on the maybe list. What would you like to do after lunch?"

The food was far better than Nate had anticipated. Both of them had sandwiches for lunch instead of a larger dinner selection. They figured they could eat a bigger meal later in the evening.
Neither of them left hungry. The plates had enough food on them for two people. It made them wonder what the dinners were like. If they had a chance, before they left town, they would come back and try the dinner menu. After a great meal, they stopped off at the boat terminal and purchased tickets for the 4:30 pm cruise out to the islands. Jane decided she better not tell Nate about Stan's joke, about having Gilligan for their first mate.

The restaurant and harbor were at the base of the hill, where the picturesque town of Bayfield had been built. Much of the town was developed in a manner that they had a fantastic view of Lake Superior and the Apostle Islands. The islands provided the barrier for the sheltered harbor area, giving the boats a break from the wind and waves that made Lake Superior famous.

Bayfield's Secret Notebook

When Jane and Nate looked up the hill, they could see the Chateau. It sat in a location where it had a great view of the harbor. They drove the two blocks up to the inn to check in and drop off their luggage. When they arrived, they were shown to the South Suite. It was up on the third floor of the old mansion that looked as though it had been preserved from the day it was built.

While Jane was admiring the room, Nate took one look at the Jacuzzi and queen size bed, and turned to Jane and said, "I have a feeling the view is going to be even better when the sun goes down."

"First things first," she told him. "We have one hour until the boat leaves. You might want to find a jacket just in case that wind comes over the cold water."

Nate would have preferred both of them sitting in the Jacuzzi with a few less clothes on.

The 4:30 pm boat ride to see the lighthouse and tour of the islands was enjoyable. The winds were light and the temperature was moderate, at 65-degrees. As they got farther out into the islands, the breeze got cooler from blowing across the 39-degree water temperature of Lake Superior. They were glad they brought jackets.

The tour of the islands was a good learning experience. It gave them a better understanding as to how far apart the islands were and how remote the outer islands were from the mainland. The tour included seeing the old lighthouse on Raspberry Island and the deep sea-caves cut into the rock cliffs on Devil's Island. When they approached the outermost islands, they could see a large ore boat traveling down the lake. It reminded them how big the lake really was. The 1,000-foot ore-boat looked like someone's toy bobbing out on the horizon, while navigating Lake Superior.

When they got back to the harbor at 7:45 pm, Nate got his way; they found a restaurant along the harbor with a view of the water. The Pier Restaurant gave him the view he was looking for, even though the sun was heading over the horizon. They sat and watched the boats in the harbor by moon light before heading back to the Chateau.

Jane told him that she had enjoyed the day and all the scenery. Nate hinted, "I think the scenery is about to get better."

They spent the next hour at the Chateau relaxing in the Jacuzzi, and then cuddling in the queen-sized bed. That night, after the long drive, the wind and sun of the cruise, and relaxing in the bubbling water, both of them got a great night's sleep.

* * * * *

Stan Moline and Barbara Fontaine were enjoying a weekend in Chicago, at a marina where Barbara kept her boat. It gave them a chance to be alone and Stan enjoyed every minute of staying on the boat. The 45-foot Sea Ray was as nice as staying at any hotel room in town. Barbara had not given up the boat, even though she had temporarily abandoned her oceanography career in favor of helping manage the family apple orchard.

They spent some of the time discussing the plans for their wedding in the spring. The invitation list was almost completed and invitations were ready to put in the mail. Now, it was time to consider the menu, and make sure everyone had places to stay. Barbara seemed to be enjoying the planning. She had missed all the small details, when she and her first husband had eloped in Las Vegas. Her mother, Vivian, was enjoying the planning stages as well. She made sure that her friends were up to date with everything that the wedding couple decided on.

Bayfield's Secret Notebook

On Sunday, they took a cruise up the Lake Michigan shoreline, enjoying the warm temperatures. It was 78 degrees with only a slight wind.

Stan looked at Barbara. Her blonde ponytail was blowing in the breeze as they traveled. She was wearing a blue bikini, and was trying to soak up the sunshine. He just sat there and admired how easily she could turn a man's head, when she went by.

Stan joked, "Think your mother will ever go out on your boat again?"

The trip last summer, from Chicago to Bayfield and back, had shown Vivian that she was not a very good sailor, especially in rough water.

"I think mother is quite pleased to be back at the orchard this weekend, making sure the trees don't bob up and down, thank you. Actually, I think she would enjoy a couple-hour trip in calm water. She really did not like traveling long distances."

Stan put his arm around Barbara and squeezed her tight. "Well, I really don't mind having the day for just the two of us."

Barbara was not going to argue. She found herself missing Stan between visits, even though they talked by phone daily. With Stan living in an apartment in Minneapolis, Minnesota, and the Fontaine Orchard about 60 miles northwest of Chicago, visits were limited to a few weekends a month.

* * * * *

Jane and Nate found a local church to attend Sunday morning. After church, they planned to head out and check the hike to Houghton Falls that Stan had mapped out for them, about 10 miles south of town. They had found that both of them loved hiking and exploring new places. The hiking was good exercise to keep them in shape. At 29-years old, they wanted to look like they were in their 20's for the next 20-years.

David Fabio

The drive along the main road to the falls was brief. As they came close, they saw a small sign, saying Houghton Falls, on the side of the road pointing east along a dirt road. Down the county road about a mile, they came across a parking lot with signs showing a map of the trail and information about keeping the park natural.

From the parking lot, it would be only a short hike, which was fairly flat, from the point they reached the creek, until it meandered through the woods to Lake Superior. The map indicated that it was about 2-miles along the trail to the lake. As they approached the creek, they could hear the gentle sound of water rushing down a small set of waterfalls.

The view was amazing. The water had cut a 20 to 30-foot deep ravine into the limestone. The sharp cliffs made the small creek more enchanting. There were two small waterfalls, which sounded like they were much larger due to the reverberation of the babbling sound of the water as it echoed off the cliffs. Thanks to the constant rain the past week, the water filled the small creek.

Stan's "to-do" note, had warned them that the creek tended to dry up in-between rains.

Jane and Nate hiked along side the stream to where it emptied into Lake Superior. It was a wonderful hike. The woods along the creek made it so silent that they could only hear the birds and the creek. A pileated woodpecker, high in a dead popular tree, sounded like someone pounding on an old war drum. It was amazing how their senses picked up as they walked through the forest. Even the smell of the woods and ferns seemed stronger than normal. When they reached the lake, it was as if the world had just opened up to this wonderful blue body of water.

So far, they had been the only people on the trail. It was as if they were in an enchanted forest, made just for the two of them. The only thing they forgot was to pack a picnic basket. If they had one, they would have stayed there until evening. What a place for two newlyweds. Nate took several pictures of the two of them standing in the creek, near the falls. He set the timer on the camera to try to get some pictures they could use for a Christmas card.

Finally, as hunger pains started to exceed the desire to be alone in paradise, and before they headed back to the inn, they made a detour and picked up a sandwich in Washburn. They purchased take-out, and ate it at a small park, right on the lake, watching the sailboats out on the water.

As they drove back into Bayfield, discussing the wonderful time they had experienced in the area, Jane spotted the Lamp Post Inn. "Nate, we have to stop a minute," she told him, "I promised Stan I would stop at the inn and say hi to the owner."

Nate parked the car and went in with Jane to meet, Jean Larson.

When they walked in the door, an older woman, with gray hair greeted them. "Hello, can I help you?" she asked.

"Well, actually, my brother asked me to stop in and say hi to Jean. Is that you?"

"It is indeed. And who might your brother be?"

"Well, let me step back and introduce ourselves. I am Jane and my husband is Nate. My brother is Stan Moline. I believe he stayed up here last summer. He asked me to stop in and meet you, while I was in the area."

"I'm very glad you did. Last I heard from him, he was chasing some good-looking gal from Illinois. Did he ever catch her?"

"He's planning on getting married next spring," Jane answered.

"Well, tell him congratulations. Please come in, and sit down at the table." Jean instructed them. "I want to hear about this romance and get to know both of you. Jane, Stan mentioned your name a couple times while he was at the inn. Where are you staying?"

"Stan gave us a present of a couple nights at the Chateau when we got married in February," Jane told her, watching to see if there was any sign of disappointment that they were not staying at her inn.

"Oh, marvelous!" Jean exclaimed. "What a great present."

They talked for almost an hour, while Jean got the lowdown on Stan, and now, Jane and Nate. She told them that Stan had been instrumental in figuring out the disappearance of Barbara's husband. Her husband had rented a sailboat with another person, when it was still real cold on the big lake at the end of April. One day, they failed to come back in.

She said she used to sit in the kitchen and listen to the discussions between Stan and the authorities, which they had every morning during breakfast at the inn.

Jane remembered Stan mentioning how Barbara and her mother, Vivian, had asked him to help pilot their boat when Barbara was looking for any signs of the missing sailboat on the shorelines. Vivian had seen all the waves she wanted to see for this lifetime and the next.

It was how Stan and Barbara met.

Just before Jane and Nate were going to leave, Jean asked a favor.

"Is Stan still writing books?"

"Yes, he is just finishing the one he was researching when he came up here last summer," Jane answered.

"Good," Jean said, "do you think he might be interested in writing a historical mystery?"

"Perhaps," Jane replied. "What do you have in mind?"

"Well, I have this information I came across in the past month or two. If you could have your brother give me a call, I can give him a hint what kind of information I ran across."

Nate spoke up, "Knowing Stan, he'd probably drop everything just to have an excuse to come up and see what you have."

Bayfield's Secret Notebook

"That would be just fine as well," the soft-spoken innkeeper told them. "I miss the talks we had."

Jane and Nate thanked her for sitting down and talking. Jane promised she would give Stan the message the next time she talked to him.

They drove back to the Chateau for another dip in the warm Jacuzzi, and snuggling time.

The next morning, they had breakfast at the Old Rittenhouse Inn. It was as good as Stan had suggested. The French toast and fruit was just what Nate wanted. Jane had the omelet with fresh baked muffins. When they finished breakfast, and checked out of the inn, they started their drive back to Minneapolis. Jane decided it was a good time to call Stan.

"Well, did they kick you out of town already?" Stan answered his phone looking at the caller ID.

"Nate wanted me to see if you two had such a hot weekend that the boat burned?" she shot back.

"So, how was Bayfield? Did you find it as interesting as I thought you might," he asked.

"Yes! In fact, we are considering going back there this fall if we can find some time. The hike to Houghton Falls was spectacular. How did you find it?" Jane asked.

"Just a tip from an expert on the area," he replied. "How about the restaurants?"

"Nate thought you were playing a joke with Maggie's when he first saw the place, and could not understand why we were supposed to eat away from the lake. He said to tell you that you were back on his good side after the fantastic meals we had there, the Pier, and at the Rittenhouse. Is the wedding still on, or did Barbara kick you overboard?"

"Nah! She just pulled me behind the boat on an anchor rope until I agreed to everything she wanted. It was either 'yes dear' or drown. Would you like to talk to her? She is right here jabbing an elbow in my side."

"Sure, put her on."

"Barbara, I still can't understand how you can put up with him," Jane told her.

"I'm hoping he might be trainable," she answered. "I have a few more months to see. How was Bayfield?"

"We had a great romantic get-a-way. You were right about the South Suite. Thanks for the suggestion."

"Glad it worked out. I know I sure enjoyed staying there. My mother enjoyed her room there as well. In fact, once she hit dry land, I had to tie her up to get her back on the boat."

"Well, Nate and I just wanted to thank the two of you for a wonderful weekend. Everything was as good as both of you told us. Oh! I almost forgot; we met Jean at her inn. She asked me to have Stan call her. Said she had something that might be interesting for one of his future books. Can you let him know?

"Thanks again for everything."

When they hung up, Barbara told Stan, "Jane really liked the weekend in Bayfield. We need to do that again sometime. They want to go back again this fall. Think we can join them up there?"

"What about the orchard? Don't you need to be there?" he asked. "Besides, what about all your wedding plans?"

"I was thinking more like before the fall rush; say the second week in September, before it starts to get real cold. It would give me one more chance to see if I really want to put up with you permanently. Mother can take care of things for a weekend."

"I'll talk to Jane and see if she can handle the cool weather," he told her.

Bayfield's Secret Notebook

"Oh, before I forget, Jane said to call Jean. She had some information that you might like for a book."

Stan looked puzzled. All the information from last fall was complete, he thought. Did Jean hear something else from Deputy Miller? "Okay, I'll call her later. Right now, I have plans that we cannot do in the middle of the day back at the orchard."

For the next hour, the heat was rising from the vents of the boat. When they were tired out, and popped their heads topside for some fresh air, Stan called Jean to see what she had discovered.

"Stan, it's good to hear your voice," Jean answered. "I assume Jane gave you my message."

"Well, actually, she told Barbara that you had some information and wanted me to call. What's up?"

"I think I have found something you might be interested in. I was helping an old friend move last month. When I opened a box, I found an old leather notebook. She said I could read it if I wanted. She just wanted to get rid of everything."

"Did you stay up all night reading it?" he joked.

"It was hard to read. It talked about her great grandfather's life at the end of the Civil War, and hiding things."

"What did they hide?" Stan asked.

"The Confederate treasury," she replied. "Interested?"

"Is it for real?"

"I'm no expert. You might want to talk to her and see. She is getting old and starting to lose some of her memory, so if you are interested, you might want to do it sooner rather than later."

"Who else knows about it?" Stan asked.

"I mentioned it to Deputy Miller at breakfast one day. He suggested I call you. He said history was not his jurisdiction. You are on your own. Interested?"

"Can I call you back in an hour? I need to clear this with someone."

"Okay! Tell Barbara there is room for two." Jean told him.

Stan hung-up and turned to Barbara.

"Jean might have run into something important, or it might be a wild goose chase. I think I may have to go up to Bayfield for a couple days."

"All by yourself? I'm not sure I can trust you with another woman. Besides, you get sidetracked by every woman with a ponytail. What did she find? Is it that important?"

"I'm not sure. If it is for real, it could be what I need for another book. I need to look at a notebook she found and talk to its owner, while I can. If you are worried about me, you could tag along for day or two. Just make sure the chains are loose enough around my legs and neck so I can still chase the best-looking blonde ponytail I find, when she goes for a run."

"Do I get to stay at the Chateau?"

"No!" Stan laughed. "I think this time we need to stay at Jean's place. Since she found the information, it would only be right."

"What's it like? Does it have a Jacuzzi in the room, like I had at the Chateau?"

Stan looked into her green eyes. "Well, it is extremely clean. Jean watches over it like her own house. Actually, it is her house. The rooms are slightly smaller than you are used to, but the bed is comfortable and there is an attached bathroom. She does a great job of decorating the rooms. Each one is decorated in the Scandinavian colors of a different country. She also makes a great breakfast every morning. Besides, you keep saying, 'all you need is me.'"

"When are we going?"

Bayfield's Secret Notebook

"I'll call Jean and see when she has time. Is next week okay with you? I have a meeting in Minneapolis I have to be at later this week."

Stan called Jean back and set up a day in which they could stay at the inn. Hopefully, all of them could go meet Jean's friend.

Chapter 3

The Notebook

Stan and Barbara drove up to Bayfield to see Jean at the Lamp Post Inn, Bed & Breakfast.

Barbara had let Stan know that there was no-way she was going to let Stan go up to Bayfield by himself. She wanted to see what this new information was all about, and was looking forward to seeing Bayfield under better circumstances. It was a great chance for a romantic get-away. Even though they were not staying at the Chateau, she was looking forward to seeing what it was like for Stan to investigate leads for his books.

They arrived in Bayfield at about 3:30 pm. The town looked just the same as last summer; tourists were walking all over town and the ferry was making its scheduled crossing of the channel to Madeline Island. It was as though the town had hibernated all winter just to spring to life as the summer season broke into full stride.

As they walked in the door of the Lamp Post Inn, Jean spotted them at the door and shouted from the counter, "Well, it's about time you brought this good looking gal with you. I was beginning to think you were just a name set aside for one of his books. I'm Jean Larson," she said as she held out her hand to Barbara.

"I've heard a lot about you as well," Barbara replied. "It is really an honor to finally get to meet you. Stan has talked about you and your great cooking ever since last summer."

"Well, you know men. As long as it's on the table and it's warm, they think it's the greatest thing since sliced bread," Jean joked.

"Stan, I've got your regular room all set up for you if you want to haul your things upstairs. Later, when you have time, I can try to fill you in a little more on my friend Olivia. I think you will be pleased to meet her tomorrow. By the way, I really enjoyed meeting your sister and her husband. We had a long conversation about the two of you."

Stan gave her a smile. Barbara glanced around, and noticed all the decorations in the lobby area and dining room. Just as Stan had told her, it was definitely Scandinavian. There were orange Dala horses and straw goats on the window ledges and above the windows were flags of all the Scandinavian countries.

Stan and Barbara went upstairs to the Sweden room, which was a corner room on the second floor. When Stan opened the door, Barbara smiled. Once again, it was just as Stan had described it to her. The medium size room was decorated in the Swedish colors of yellow and blue. It had a nice view of the town and harbor from the curved window in the corner of the room. There was a queen size bed with a high pillow top mattress, covered by a quilt with yellow and blue colors.

"Think this will do for the next couple days?" he asked her.

"As long as you don't snore. If you do, I get to move to the Chateau with my own private Jacuzzi," she jested. "It is great. At least we have a private bath. Besides, we are here to talk to Jean and her friend. I'm looking forward to getting to know her and see if all your stories are real."

After putting away their clothes, they wandered down to talk to Jean.

Jean was relaxing in a chair in the dining room when they came back downstairs. The long, antique, oak table looked bare without food on it. There was just a vase with flowers in the center. "You want to talk now or after you head back from dinner?" she asked. "I figured you might be hungry after that long drive."

"Still watching out for me," Stan replied with a smile. "Do you have a lot of guests coming in today?"

"No, I have only one other room rented. They came in last night. Why, what do you have in mind?" she asked.

"I was just wondering if you would like to join us for dinner. You could put out your 'back–in–one–hour' sign, and I could treat you to dinner," Stan suggested.

"Wow! That's the closest thing to a date I've had in a few years," the 70-year old innkeeper replied. "Won't Barbara be a little upset if you dumped her for an older woman this quick?"

Barbara had all she could do to keep from laughing. "Maybe I should go along just to keep the two of you from getting thrown out of town!"

"Sure, let's do it. If anyone breaks in and takes anything, it will give Deputy Miller something to do tomorrow. Life has been awful slow for him since the two of you left town. Let me put up a sign and we can sneak out while the boss isn't looking."

Stan drove down to the Pier Restaurant, where they got a corner booth overlooking the harbor and ferry.

"Bring back memories?" Barbara asked Stan.

"Yes! Do you want to try falling off the dock again this year?"

Bayfield's Secret Notebook

Last summer as Barbara was trying to untie her boat at the marina, she tripped on a plank that was sticking up and almost fell into the water. As she tried to regain her balance, she dropped the ropes, causing Stan and her mother to be sent adrift into the harbor on her boat.

"Careful, I might push you in this time," Barbara responded playfully.

"Jean, what's good on the menu here?" Stan asked, as he decided to change the subject.

"I like the whitefish," she answered. "I prefer the fish while it is in season. I think you will find all the other dishes good, also. Barbara, what are you going to have?"

Barbara was still looking it over. "I think I'll try the whitefish as well," she answered. "How about you, Stan? Got a preference?"

"I'll try the lake trout."

Stan was curious about the information Jean had, and so far, she was content to just sit there, until he asked. "Okay, Jean! Give me the lowdown on this story you dug up for me. You said it might be the information I need for another book."

As they were relaxing at the table, Jean proceeded to tell them the story about her friend's notebook, speaking softly enough that other customers would not be able to hear the discussion.

"You see, I have this old friend, whom I have known for over fifteen years. She used to run a bed and breakfast here in town, like mine. She sold her B&B about five years ago and moved into a small house in town. Well, a couple months ago, she decided it was time to move to Washburn, into a townhouse. She was not able to keep up a house by herself anymore. She needed help getting rid of everything, except for the few pieces of furniture she needed for the new place. A couple of my friends and I helped her go through all her things.

"When we started to go through some boxes downstairs, I noticed an old notebook and asked her about it. She said it was just some old notes that her grandfather had kept as a journal. She was not too interested in it. Well, I was fascinated and perhaps a little nosey. I asked her if I could read it. She said, "Sure, just pitch it when you are finished."

"I took the box home, and a few days later started to look at the pages. It was hard to read. It took me an hour to finally realize what I was reading. It was the story of her great-grandfather, not a journal of her grandfather's. The time-line started out in the 1860's. I didn't realize it, until I saw a lot of references to the Civil War. Her great grandfather wrote in pencil. Some of the writings were smudged, and in other places, he erased something, and re-wrote what he wanted to write. The binding was coming apart, also."

"Well, there are a lot of stories that have surfaced about the Civil War," Stan told her. "Were there other things in there that stood out – like shooting at General Lee as he rode by?"

"If it was that simple, I'd have given the book to the historical society," Jean told them. "No, it was his story. I was shocked when it talked about hiding the Confederate gold from the Union forces. I think he really did it."

Stan's demeanor became more serious. "He wrote all about it in this book? In detail? Jean , you might have just earned yourself a piece of pie for this one. It took a long time for the Union forces to try to uncover all the treasures of the Confederacy. They were not very successful at finding most of it."

"Yes! There is a lot of information in there; some names, places, and even how they did it. However, you are going to have to do a lot of research to see if all this is true, and not just a made-up story. That was the reason, when I met your sister a couple weeks ago, I asked Jane to have you call me. I figured you might want to see the information I had, and talk to my friend before anything happens to her. It would be a

Bayfield's Secret Notebook

shame if all the additional information she might know, regarding the story, is lost."

Dinner was served. As great as the food and view out the window was, Stan could only think of one thing – he wondered if it was true. Several times Barbara had to remind him to eat his food. Stan's mind was in full gear – just not inside the building. He was making a list in his mind of all the things he could ask Jean's friend, even before he had a chance to read the notebook. Somehow, the food had taken a back seat.

Jean told them a few things she found in the notebook, and promised to show it to them when they got back to the inn. She said the notebook talked about the sudden need to get the gold out of the South, so that it would be available for a later time, or shipped back to where it came from.

Barbara was fascinated. "You mean they actually hid their gold for another chance at the North?"

"That's what it looks like," Jean answered. "I always heard southerners telling me that they really never lost the war, they were just resting. Maybe there was some truth to that statement. Wouldn't it be something if the leaders were actually planning a comeback.

"Still want to meet my friend tomorrow?" she asked.

"Absolutely!" Stan answered.

When they got back to the inn, Jean found a note on the front desk: "Looking for a room. Please call us if you have a vacancy. We'll be at the restaurant."

Jean chuckled, "Always happens that way. I can sit here all day, and the door never opens. Walk away for a minute and someone shows up. I guess we may have another guest for the night. You think they were eating at the Pier, sitting next to us?"

She opened a drawer and gave Stan two old, worn-out looking leather notebooks. "I forgot to tell you, I discovered the other notebook, after we talked on the phone. It had a different cover, so I missed it at first. I was taking some of her reading books to the library when I spotted it. I'll bet you are glad that we didn't send it with the others. Don't forget to set the alarm for breakfast. I would not want you to be late and get cold food."

Stan turned and told her, "Not a chance. Unfortunately, we probably will not be able to talk about the book in the morning. I think this information needs to stay quiet until we can sort it all out, too many ears with all your guests.

"See you in the morning," Stan told Jean as he took the notebook, and along with Barbara, went up to the room.

Jean was wondering, which would get top billing that night – romance or the notebook.

Chapter 4

The Visit

Stan and Barbara spent the next five hours, in the room, reading the notebooks and asking questions. If Barbara was hoping for a quiet romantic get-away, tonight was not going to be the night. By the time they were done reading and asking questions, they were so exhausted that they fell asleep.

It was not one of those restful sleeps either. Their minds were racing all night. It was as though they were still awake asking questions – is this really true? Can we prove it? What happened to the gold? Where is the gold now? Who else knew about it?

When the alarm went off at 6:00 in the morning, both of their thoughts went immediately to the black tattered notebook lying on the table.

"Darn, I wish Jean didn't have guests this week," Stan told Barbara. "I'm not sure I can sit still and eat, without asking her questions."

Barbara laughed. It was fun to see how involved Stan had gotten into his research this quickly. She was also a little nervous and anxious about the visit with Jean's friend, later in the morning. She was amazed how quickly her thoughts had gotten away from the management of the orchard back home.

The pair went down and had breakfast with the guests from the other two rooms Jean had rented last night. The morning light coming through the windows glimmered through a couple of the red glass flower vases. The reflections on the walls made a good point for starting conversations. There was a couple from Milwaukee and another from Madison. Both were in Bayfield for the first time, and were interested in sightseeing. Barbara and Stan suggested a few places around the area that they might enjoy visiting. Stan told them, "Jean is the local expert on everything in the area. Just ask her if you have a question."

Jean brought out orange juice, sourdough biscuits, jelly, scrambled eggs, and sausages. Barbara took one look at the food and understood why Stan wanted to stay at the inn. It was for Jean's food.
Jean told Stan, "My friend is available at 11 am, if that is okay with you."
"Great! That will give me a chance to check a few items on the internet before we go," he told her.

After breakfast, Stan and Barbara looked up as many items on the internet as they could spot from the notebook. So far, the more they checked, the greater the possibility that the book might be authentic and not a made up story. It was definitely something that Stan and Barbara wanted to clarify directly with Jean's friend. The most intriguing thing, they felt was that the actual story was nowhere on the internet. It might not be a copy of someone else's story.

At 10:30, Jean knocked on Stan's door. "Interested in taking a ride?" she asked. "All the guests are out checking out the town. Time for the mice to come out and play."

Bayfield's Secret Notebook

Stan drove as they travelled the 16 miles south to Washburn. There, Olivia was living in a townhouse near the lake.

As they approached the house, Jean reminded Stan and Barbara that her friend was starting to show the advanced signs of old age. Her memory was not as good as it used to be, and if it looked like she was getting tired out, they might have to come back another day.

Olivia was waiting at the door as they approached.

"Oh! I am so glad to see you," she told Jean. "It has been too long since we were together. And, who might these two people be?" she asked.

Jean spoke quietly, "Olivia, remember I called you yesterday and told you I had a couple friends that were in town. This is Stan Moline and his friend Barbara Fontaine. Stan is a writer. I met him last summer when he came up to Bayfield to research a book."

"Well yes, I remember. Glad to meet both of you," she acknowledged.

She invited them into her house. Jean had packed some rolls and jelly for all of them to have. It supplied a good icebreaker.

As they sat around the table sampling the goodies Jean brought, Jean asked, "Olivia, do you remember the notebooks your great grandfather wrote?"

"Yes! I remember you saying you found one when we were packing. Was it fun to read?" she asked.

"It was indeed," Jean answered. "Can you tell Stan about him? What do you remember about the stories of his life? You remember, he was in the Civil War."

Olivia sat there a while, thinking. Then, as if the twinkle in her eye was the memories coming back, she answered.

"Oh, yes! I remember my father talking about his father; or was it his grandfather? Oh well, he used to tell me stories at night when I was young. He was in the Civil War, you know. He used to tell me about the war. It was terrible. Brother killing brother, just because they had a different opinion on politics and on slavery. He told me that my grandfather was on the side of the South. Or, was it the North? I'm not sure anymore.

"Apparently, he was not involved in the actual war. The companies he worked for remained neutral during the war. Although, my father said my grandfather would deliver messages to the generals of both the North and South. He actually met General Grant.

"He worked for a whisky distillery. He was their 'brewmaster.' With all the fighting, somehow the whiskey industry was off limits to both the North and Southern troops. I think both sides realized that if they attacked a distillery, they would cut off their future sources of whiskey and disinfectant for wounds. From what I hear, whiskey is fairly pure alcohol, compared to beer and other products. Even the grains that were needed for the fermentation were unofficially protected during shipments. When towns were going hungry, the grains shipped to the distillery for whiskey were off limits. You know, my father told me that they would ship the final product in kegs and casks to both sides. Did I tell you he met General Grant? They say he really liked his whiskey.

"Apparently, just before the war, the distillery my grandfather worked for was the largest in the whole United States. Much of their product was shipped un-aged to other breweries to finish aging and to be distributed. A lot of it went by rail to Cincinnati. The rest went by rail or by steamboat on the Ohio River, to other large cities.

"When the war broke out, his boss fell into hard times with collecting bills. Eventually, he sold off most of the estate, leaving the brewery to his son-in-law. After that, his boss moved to Tennessee. My grandfather said the move was an attempt to get further into Confederate territory. Anyway, I think they started up another distillery somewhere, just a lot smaller. They would get some product from the old distillery, plus make beer to complete the line."

Bayfield's Secret Notebook

"So, your grandfather did not own the distilleries?" Stan asked, noticing that Olivia was starting to look a little more distracted with all the conversation.

"No, my grandfather and his brother were 'brewmasters.' They were the people in charge of the process. They knew the exact times to mix and ferment the mash. In fact, as I recall, his brother moved to Minnesota to escape the war, just before it started. He started a brewery somewhere along a river."

So far, everything Olivia had told them matched the log in the notebook. Olivia had filled in some of the details that were missing.

"Do you remember more?" Jean asked. "It is really interesting to hear about your families."

"Yes! Did I tell you that he met President Jefferson Davis? I rather forget whether we talked about it or not. When he was with the first brewery, he delivered some casks directly to the inauguration of President Davis, all the way down to Montgomery, Alabama. To prevent contamination, they wanted him to accompany the load and guarantee the quality. He said he met President Davis personally. That was where he met many of the other important leaders of the South.

"I told you that he used to carry messages to the leaders of the North and South, didn't I? Since his business was protected by both sides, they felt he was the safe one to carry discrete messages, like agreements on prisoner of war exchanges. Do you think that was why they protected their business?

"Well, sometime after they moved to Kentucky or Tennessee, one of the Confederate generals asked him for a favor. He wanted to ship some things to Canada. He asked my grandfather to ship them in barrels of whiskey, with false bottoms, so that no one would find out about it. My grandfather had the special barrels made, and went with the barrels to make sure they arrived. You see, people trusted my family. They still do. They also told him that the Union forces were heading toward his area in Kentucky, and it would be wise to travel north for safety."

"Do you know where the barrels went?" Stan asked.

"I suppose to the breweries," she answered.

"No, I meant the barrels which he had made with the false bottoms," Stan replied.

"I do not remember. Maybe it is in his book. Did you look in there, Jean?"

Jean answered, "I was wondering, do you remember if any of them were delivered up here?"

"I remember there was some reason that my family moved up here from Minnesota. However, I do not remember exactly."

"All this is just getting confusing. It was just too long ago. I guess I'm starting to forget all the stories I heard when I was a young girl. Jean you are getting up there in age too. Don't you have problems remembering your childhood?"

"Yes, it is often hard to remember things a long time ago," Jean told her. "Do you remember anything else about your relatives?"

"I'm not sure. Sometimes I think I do, and sometimes I wonder if I am just remembering a dream. Just like right now, my head starts spinning when I try and remember a lot of things from so long ago."

Jean told her, "We should probably go and let you take your afternoon nap. I'll call you tomorrow and see if you remember anything else."

"Thanks! It was so nice to have you stop in. Please come back again."

As they were about to leave, Barbara asked Olivia about a beautiful set of eagle bookends on a shelf that she had been admiring. "These are lovely, did you purchase them in Bayfield?"

"Thank you. My parents gave them to me when I was a young girl. I used to read a lot. I guess I need to find some more books, so that they look like they have a purpose. Jean, maybe you could find me some good books somewhere. You know, I used to have shelves of books. I'm not sure where they are anymore."

"I'll check the next sale at the library," Jean replied.

With that, Stan, Barbara and Jean left to head back to Bayfield.

When they got into the car, Jean turned to Stan, "Well, what do you think? Is the story for real or just a story?"

"Jean, I think you have opened the door to an amazing quest. Where it will lead, I cannot tell. You forgot to tell me, when we talked over the phone, that they did not just hide the treasures, they actually took it. I only wish I had a crystal ball to see the whole story as it happened. It is hard to believe that a Northerner made up a story like that about someone from the South. It makes me believe there is something here that needs a lot of examination."

Barbara sat silently. Finally, she responded, "I have a feeling that you are going to be staying up nights for the next month trying to put this story to print. Don't forget you have a wedding coming up in a few months that you are supposed to be concentrating on."

"My, my! I hope I haven't caused a problem," Jean said.

"No, this is an opportunity to re-write history," Stan told her. "It may take years to put all the pieces of this puzzle in place. When the off-season comes at the orchard and the wedding planning is over, Barbara and I can spend some time together looking at the pieces, and see if we can find the real story. Each of us needs to find time for the other person in our lives. This may be something exciting for Barbara; she can help me find answers."

Barbara gave him a smile. She wanted to be reassured that she was still the important part of his life. Somehow, deep in her thoughts, she knew that Stan would not be able to put this away until the off-season.

The rest of the way back, they talked about the significance of Olivia remembering additional details about her relatives; more than what was in the book. The fact that Olivia was confused about whether it was her grandfather or great-grandfather really did not matter. They could sort out the facts and dates, later. Now, finding names and businesses that matched the descriptions would give them a starting point. It was interesting that Olivia never mentioned the word gold.

When they reached the inn, Stan and Barbara thanked Jean for all the help. Without her, the story would have never come to light. They promised to keep her up to date on anything they found.
Jean told them she would keep talking to her friend, and, if she revealed anything new, she would let them know.

When they got to their room, Stan could see that Barbara was still concerned with the effort Stan was going to put into this project. She did not have the experience to know if Stan could put a balance in his projects or not. This one looked like something a team of researchers should be working on.
Stan turned on his computer and spent the next three plus hours doing research. By 6:00 pm, Barbara told him it was time to take a break and go out for dinner. She suggested the Rittenhouse. She wanted some time away from the project to talk. This was supposed to be a chance for the two of them to get away, and relax on a romantic outing. After her last marriage, she still had a slight gun-shy feeling in her gut about anything she did not know.

Both Stan and Barbara decided that they needed the exercise, so instead of driving, they walked over to the Rittenhouse. It was a pleasant evening and the short walk to the Rittenhouse felt good. Barbara enjoyed eating at the historic bed and breakfast with its three dining rooms and the grand old oak staircase. Since she could not stay at the

Bayfield's Secret Notebook

Chateau, she figured that Stan could at least take her to eat at their dining room located at the Rittenhouse. Dining at the Rittenhouse was an elegant affair. This was what Barbara had been looking forward to as soon as she heard they were heading to Bayfield.

Barbara ordered the Lake Superior lake trout, while Stan indulged in the apple glazed pork porterhouse. They ended their feast by ordering the chocolate cake with the molten chocolate center – to go. They could enjoy it later at the inn. It was smoldered in raspberry sauce, and chopped with Venezuelan chocolate – included, two forks. This was Barbara's one-time break for the week, from her normal low calorie diet.

After a pleasant dinner away from the computer and notebook, and some one-on-one time, they returned to the inn. With the big dinner, they were glad they were walking. They had to help the digestion process before sitting in front of the computer once again. Back in the room, they talked about the project the rest of the evening.

About 9:30 pm, Barbara told Stan, "I guess one of my problems with this story is that I really don't know very much about the Civil War. Why was it so important, other than the slaves were freed?

"I was never that interested in wars, except for trying to map and locate some sunken ships," Barbara told Stan. "You have to remember, I majored in oceanography. Perhaps you could explain to me a little more about the history, and why these people in the notebook are so important. Then, I might be able to understand why people get so excited about it."

"Fair enough. Let me give it a shot. See if I can explain, in one evening, everything you do not know about the Civil War."

"No, that is not what I meant. Just give me the reasons that all of this, after all these years, is still important."

"Okay, I understand. Let me think where I should start. My knowledge is not perfect, but I remember quite a bit from my history classes." Stan responded.

David Fabio

Chapter 5

Civil War

Stan began his short history lesson.

"You see, the Civil War officially began when the Confederate army opened fire on Fort Sumter on April 12, 1861. Only one day earlier, the Confederacy demanded the surrender of Fort Sumter located on an island, in the entrance to the Charleston Harbor.

"To their surprise, the Union troops surrendered on April 13th after only one day. To many people that observed this, the war was going to be a short war with a quick arbitration of differences.

"The real planning for the war began years earlier. The flames of war were kindled in rhetoric for a decade prior to its formal start. It was just a matter of time before some event would occur to ignite the formal flames of the war. Even the final arguments that were shouted at the Virginia convention on April 4, 1861, where a test vote on secession was held, did not reach an accord. The state's vote was to remain with the Union. Most people felt that someone would back down and an agreement could be reached.

"The North was heavily industrialized. It had the industry and money to sustain itself through the war. The South lacked the heavy industry. Hot summers with no air-conditioning in the 1860's, lent itself to the slower activities of farming in the south. As a result, with war on the horizon, strategic alliances were formed with some of the European countries to help with the finances and heavy machinery needed.

"England was still rustling over losing the Revolutionary War slightly over 80-years earlier. The mending of the ways had not been entirely successful. In fact, you may not remember, but in the War of 1812, England sent its ships to attack and burn Washington D.C. It was after England blockaded the United States, trying to prevent us from trading with France at the end of the Napoleonic War.

"When the emissaries of the South came courting the leaders of England for support, they looked at it as revenge. If the United States split in two, it would not be the major force in the New World. England could keep its dominant position in the New World with Canada and now a sympathetic South to trade with. The North would be squeezed in-between. If the North lost the war, they would have to deal with England in a new manner. England would have the upper hand."

"I forgot that it was only 80-years after we fought the English," Barbara inserted. "I guess if countries hold grudges for centuries, 80-years was still fresh in their memories."

"Yes, losing the United States put a real damper in their colonization efforts. Until then, England felt it was invincible. That was why France came to the aid of the 13 colonies," Stan reminded her.

"France was the other country that supported the South. Just as France had helped finance the Revolutionary War between the United States and England, France wanted to re-establish its interests in the New World.

"The Louisiana Purchase of 1803, transferred France's entire holdings in the New World to the United States. Napoleon had been at war with Europe. When President Jefferson sent James Monroe to

France to try to purchase New Orleans to protect the mouth of the Mississippi River for shipping, Napoleon refused the offer. Then, to the surprise of James Monroe and President Jefferson, he offered to sell the entire territory to the United States. Napoleon had seen the handwriting on the wall. The wars in Europe had been costly. With the advances in America, it was only a matter of time before the settlers would be starting to move into the Louisiana Territory. As a result, 828,000 square miles, beyond the Mississippi River, were purchased from France for only $15 million. All of France's domination in the south and central United States was gone.

"When the South started talks with France for financing, France saw one last opportunity to gain a favorable position with the South and perhaps control some trade with the southern ports. As a result, France joined its old archenemy England in secretly financing the armament of the Confederacy. Where the North and South both thought the war would only last a few months, the European countries who were more experienced in wars, realized it might go on for some time."

"I thought the war was about slavery? Didn't England and France care about slavery?" Barbara stated.

"No," Stan replied, "they only cared about trade and power. Just like today. Wars are usually fought over economics. It is just hidden in the background.

"The Europeans were correct, the Civil War turned out to be one of the bloodiest political wars in history. The issues – states rights, and the right to keep slavery. It split families; brothers fought brothers, and the war was fought in over 10,000 locations across the states. It was not until long after Gettysburg that the direction of who might win the war started to become apparent. After winning the battle at Gettysburg in 1863, where 95,000 Union troops faced off with 75,000 Confederate soldiers, the nation realized they had witnessed almost 50,000 men killed

Bayfield's Secret Notebook

in the fields over a couple days. Winning the battle at Vicksburg, on the Mississippi River, in the summer of 1863, started to give the Union forces momentum. The Union forces had started to seal the fate of the south. Under the guidance of General Ulysses S. Grant, the Union gained control of the Mississippi River, all the way from New Orleans north. The South was going to be slowly strangled into submission as the North started to control the supply lines at the ports.

"Prior to the battle of Gettysburg, both England and France must have been getting worried. To the observers from Europe, the South was making significant advances on the North. The average citizen of the Northeast apparently felt it was just a short skirmish that would be ended quickly. If the South would have advanced quicker, they might have been able to take Washington, D.C., while the North's army and citizens were taking the war as something that was happening only in a few locations. People actually came out to Gettysburg to watch the war, as if it was a spectator sport. Any chance that the South could put a strangle hold on Washington was not what England or France wanted. They preferred a split in the United States. They wanted to see two distinct countries. If the South would have won the battle and taken Washington, the North might have been forced to give in to all their demands.

"Somehow, the armies of the North were finally summoned to that bloody field in Gettysburg, to make a stand. Did the army suddenly develop better leaders, or were they tipped off to the movements of the South? Was it the scouts from the North, or was there someone else?"

"That's the point at which I start to lose interest," Barbara said. "All those battles and all that bloodshed, it is just not my cup of tea. All I can think of is all those soldiers lying in the field dying."

Stan encouraged her, "Hang in there for a couple more minutes. I'm getting closer to the reason for our mystery writer's part in this drama, along with some of the other people mentioned in his notebook."

David Fabio

"Armies from all the states were mustered. The request was sent out to all the states for 1,000 troops. Minnesota was one of the first states to send 1,000 volunteers. They sent two companies of sharpshooters, and five regiments of troops. The 1st Regiment from Minnesota played an important role in the Civil War including, apparently, a role in the notebook's story. I checked it out last night on the internet to see if it might be true. There were a number of stories in there about the call to action.

"The Minnesota troops had been called to action in April of 1861, and signed up for what the Federal government insisted was a three year enlistment. Actually, many men thought they were volunteering for only 90 days until they looked at the bottom line. These men were seriously involved in the war by July of that year. They found action in the Battle of Bull Run and continued all the way to fighting in the Battle of Gettysburg. They were so well trained compared to most of the Union forces, that when the generals told them to charge the Confederate forces with bayonets at Gettysburg, they helped hold the Union lines even though most of them lost their lives.

"The Minnesota volunteers that re-enlisted after their three years were up, and stayed in the war along with new volunteers, were decorated in Washington at the end of the war, and were released back to Minnesota from Louisville, Kentucky. I think that is where the information in the notebook picks up."

"Stan, you mean we are talking about the notebook starting up after the war?"

"Yes, Barbara. There are a few items that are mentioned prior and during the war. However, the most important things in the notebook start with the end of the war. That's the part that makes this interesting. The notebook is not about the war, but what happened right after the war.

The second book appears to be a continuation of his journal.

Bayfield's Secret Notebook

"Okay, I guess I'm a little more curious now, than I was before. Let's talk about it in the morning. That is if you can get to sleep without dreaming about the South."

"Fine! Just give me an hour to check out a couple leads on the computer before I get caught in the middle of your arms, all night long. Besides, you might roll over in the middle of the night and punch me, while you are dreaming about the bloody battles."

"If you don't get to bed at a reasonable hour, you might need your army hat," she chided him.

David Fabio

Chapter 6

Inquiries

Stan woke up in the morning and looked in the mirror. So far, so good. No black eyes from any nightmares Barbara might have had last night, while dreaming about the war. She had not awakened with swinging fists.

She saw him looking in the mirror and told him, "You lucked out last night; I dreamt that I turned you over to the Chicago mob."

"I think I would rather have the firing squad," he joked back.

Barbara asked him, "Where are you going to start on this investigation?"

"Well, we need to start the investigation on both ends. We need to find out all we can about Olivia and her family while we are up here, and then start looking back into the history, which is written in the notebook."

When they went downstairs for breakfast, Jean told them, "We are on our own this morning. Both guests packed up and left early. I gave them a snack to eat on their way home. My new guests are not expected until later tonight. Mind if I join you at the table for some breakfast? It will give us a chance to talk, and I can get to know Barbara better."

Jean brought out a huge breakfast, staged in three parts. They had fresh out-of-the-oven rolls with juice. When they had finished that course, she brought out scrambled eggs and sausages. Finally, to finish off any spare room left in their stomachs, she topped it off with a fruit bowl that included bananas, apples, oranges, and strawberries. Stan figured that Jean was trying to keep them at the table as long as she could. As long as the food lasted, they would stay and talk about her friend.

"Jean, what do you know about the background of your friend Olivia? Did she ever talk about her family in the past?" Stan asked.

"No, it is interesting that she never mentioned anything about her family history. I have known her ever since she purchased her bed and breakfast fifteen years ago. We used to talk every week about the events in town that might draw visitors. I'm sure she told me years ago where she lived before then. However, to tell you the truth, I do not remember talking about it. Everything we ever talked about seemed to relate to business or tourism. Oh, there was the usual discussion about the strange visitors we both had, but in this business, that's the excitement you get."

"Jean, did she ever seem like she was hiding something?" Barbara asked.

"At the time, no. However, now that I think back in time, the fact that she rarely talked about her childhood or family might have been intentional. Do both of you think she was finally letting the cat out of the bag?"

Barbara nodded. "I think Stan thinks there is definitely something there. Everything he tried to check on the internet, which we found in the notebook, appeared to be possible. I'm not an expert on Civil War history, but my research on shipwrecks have told me where we find this much written history, there is usually a strong possibility something is there. The problem is finding it."

Stan suggested, "I think Barbara and I will spend a little time at the Bayfield Historical Society, trying to pull up some records on Olivia and her family. If we can pull up some records on the purchase of the B&B, it might have some background information on her. I would like to trace her family history back to her great grandfather. Something in her past might shine the light we need to solve the question – fact or fiction.

"If it is fiction, someone had a fantastic outline finished many years ago looking at the aging of the notebook. Heck, this thing was written in the days of Samuel Clemens and his Mark Twain series. Tomorrow, I think we will head back. I'm not sure that there is a lot more we can do here until we find some more hints."

"Please keep me up to date," Jean asked. "I'll keep in touch with Olivia. If she mentions anything, I'll give you a call."

Jean spent the rest of breakfast talking to Barbara. She wanted to know everything about her. When they were all finished, she turned to Stan, "I think I know why you enjoyed spending time out in her boat last summer. I hope you bring her up here again."

The Historical Society was only a couple blocks away. They walked over to the building and tried to find everything they could about Olivia. Using their computer and looking through state records, they had been able to find the date that she purchased the B&B, and when she sold it. In the documents, they found her drivers license information. Records indicated that she had never been married. Digging deeper, they found her birth information in the county register, which also listed her parent's names.

Bayfield's Secret Notebook

Barbara and Stan got so involved with their research that they worked right through lunch. One lead often led to just another set of questions, which usually had to be researched in another spot. By the time late afternoon came around, they were starved.

Barbara was pleased. She had helped Stan find some of the older information in the microfilm. She only wished everything on the microfilm had been up-loaded onto the computers. It would have been a lot easier to do their searches.

Stan had enjoyed the company and the help. It was nice having a working partner.

David Fabio

Chapter 7

The Trip Home

The next morning, Stan and Barbara headed back to Illinois, and Barbara's house. As they were driving, Barbara looked over the old notebook to see if there were items, they had missed. It was hard reading the light print on the pages. Sometimes, she read a sentence one way, and later, when she looked at the words, it seemed like the author's broken English was actually referring to something else. It was difficult to interpret all the thoughts left between the lines.

When they got home, Vivian was waiting for them at the door. "Did you discover any new worlds?" she asked, expecting to hear that it was just a wild goose chase.

"I think we found evidence that Columbus came up the Mississippi River and found the Ohio," Barbara told her. "He left a Spanish doubloon stating, 'I'm lost! If found, return to the Queen.'

"Actually, that might have been easier than figuring out the interesting story we heard. Stan's girlfriend gave him the notebooks she discovered, which appears to date back to the 1860's. It seems to suggest that the Confederacy tried to ship money back to England. The only problem is that we cannot tell if the story is true or just a tall tale."

Bayfield's Secret Notebook

Vivian's eyebrows raised as her daughter informed her that Stan's "girlfriend" gave him the book. She knew from discussions in the past that the owner of the Bed and Breakfast was close to seventy. Something must have led to that comment. She would ask Barbara later.

"Well, dinner is almost ready. If you two gold diggers are clean behind the ears, I might even let you sit at the same table with me, and tell me all about your trip. That is, if I can believe a word you say."

Stan laughed, "I think your mother is making fun of us again. We had better behave at dinner."

While eating, Barbara told Vivian all about the notebooks that Jean had found, and their meeting with Olivia. "It was strange. Olivia didn't really act as though she knew much about the notebooks. When we talked to her, she would comment about things that we knew were in the books, but I'm not sure if it was her early stages of dementia or what it was, she just didn't seem too connected to the notebook. That was the puzzling part. Was the story real, or was it just a good story, written long ago. If she was a little more protective of the book, we would have felt better."

"That was my thought too," Stan told her. "But, when I saw she was having problems remembering if it was her grandfather or great grandfather, I realized that she was really having problems with relational items. Anyway, I am going to do some follow-up research in the next week and see if there is any evidence to back up the story. You can never tell, what might show up, with something like this. I am really hoping that when I am done with some more of the research, Olivia can tell us if it sounds true or not. Jean said she would be seeing her again in a week or so."

The rest of the evening, they talked about the small items of history, referenced in the notebook. It did not help that the writer was from Germany. He was obviously still working on his English, in his early writings. Between his broken English and writing in pencil, they spent the next two hours trying to decipher many of the lines of text, which they had problems reading earlier. This was proving to be a major task. They needed to understand the notebook before they could research the items in it.

Stan headed back to Minneapolis the next morning right, after breakfast. Barbara gave him a big hug and kiss, thanking him for taking her along. It had been fun to get back to Bayfield. She told Stan, "Please call me when you figure out additional items in the notebooks."

"Okay, I'll see if I can remember your number." Since he had called her almost every day for the past month, he was pretty sure he had it memorized by now. "Still want me to come back in ten days?"

"I'll keep the porch light on," she answered.

Stan got into the car and drove out of the orchard. He was not more than ten miles down the road, when he had to pull over and re-read a page in the notebook he had looked at the night before. Stan was not an expert on the Civil War. However, the entries in the book kept triggering things he remembered that his high school American History teacher had lectured them about. Unfortunately, this page referred to a General that Stan could not remember.

Stan knew the first thing he had to do tomorrow morning, after a good night sleep, was to call a friend of his who was a Civil War buff. He could at least tell him if the sequence of events in the book might have been possible.

Chapter 8

Man the Cannons

Stan's friend got a call first thing the next morning.

"Stan, I haven't hear from you in a while, what's new?"
"Ned, how did you know it was me? Oh, I suppose you had my name on your cell phone list. Someday, I am going to surprise you and call from a friends phone, just to catch you off guard.

"I need a favor from you. I got some information about the Civil War and I cannot tell if the items are real, or just a story someone made up. Can you take a look at it and see what you think?"
"Well Stan, I have a meeting with my Civil War Roundtable later today, how about tomorrow? Think it can wait until then?"
"What time is best for you?"
"How about meeting me at the old coffeehouse for lunch, around 11:30. We can grab a bite, and I can look at what you have," he told Stan.
"That would be great, Ned. I'll buy. That will force you to give me an honest opinion. I think it's my turn to buy anyway."

"Well, if you had led with that, I would have suggested the steakhouse. See you tomorrow."

Stan knew from conversations that his long time friend Ned was a Civil War buff. He could recite each battle, and what determined the winner. Stan was hoping that Ned's experience would enable him to say one way or another that the descriptions could have happened, or it was impossible.

He spent the rest of the day with his nose in the notebook. There were so many lines that were smudged. He took them one line at a time. If he could clear up the text, it would make his friend's job a lot easier. To make it easier in the future, he put each line in his computer. That way, he could run a search on any item and find it immediately, instead of searching pages of the notebook and wearing out the fragile binding.

Later that afternoon, he started to check the chronology of the notebook. Since the writer wrote it as a journal, everything in it should be in the correct order. So far, as he checked the history, things appeared to be in the correct chronology.

The next day, Stan met Ned at the coffeehouse. It was a small restaurant, located half way between their places. Ned had gotten there early as usual. It seemed that every time they agreed to meet, Ned would always be early. Stan figured it was part of his make-up. Ned probably worried about getting there late, and as a result, he was inclined to be early at all events. As Stan walked in, he was glad to see that it was not busy. He really did not want to have a lot of other customers too close to ear shot.

"Thanks for coming," Stan greeted him as he walked up to Ned's table.

"Stan, I haven't seen you in months; ever since you started chasing that woman in Illinois. Still seeing her?"

Bayfield's Secret Notebook

"Yes, I was with her the past week. I guess Barbara has been taking a lot of my weekend time."

"I suppose that's the reason I haven't seen Stan Moline on my caller ID lately. To think, I figured you just hated to lose in cards. You know that it is hard to play with only four guys. The others were wondering if you were trying to ignore us."

"Oh, heck no! In fact, we need to get a game together sometime; I'm running low on spending cash. All my petty cash has been going for gas the past couple months."

"I hope you saved a couple dollars for the tab. Remember, you said you were buying."

"Okay, but only if Ned's memory is working. Got your thinking cap on?"

"Well, show me what you've got. I suppose you found an old war button, and want to know which side it belonged to. Was it brass or grey?"

Stan opened his backpack and pulled out one of the ragged, old, leather covered notebooks. "Careful, it is very delicate."

"Well, well, what do we have here?" Ned took one look at the pages and turned to Stan, "We'd better eat first. I'm not sure I want to get any of my greasy fingerprints on this one. It looks like a very old binding."

After gobbling down a turkey sandwich and a coke, Ned took a brief look at the notebook, gently turning the pages. After he got past the shipping inventory and found the journal, his expression changed.

"Is this for real?" he asked Stan.

"That's why I'm paying you the big bucks, buying you lunch. What do you think?"

Ned sat there for the next ten minutes reading the lines. Every once and a while he would moan, "Oh my," then keep on reading. When he got to the part about meeting with the generals to arrange exchanges of prisoners, he stopped. "Either the writer was a real history buff, or this is real. I have seen stories about the exchanges, but this is the first time I have seen a first hand account as to how they had been arranged. It looks real to me. Where in the world did you find the book?"

"Bayfield. A friend was helping to clean out a little old lady's house, and found the notebook. She called me and asked if I wanted to have a peek. If it is real, it is a great find. If not, it is probably good fiction information. What is your interpretation?"

"I think, I want to read the whole book. Any chance I can get a copy?"

"Yep! Just wait until I get it published. Twenty dollars ought to cover it."

"You that broke that you would charge your best friend?"

"Nah, fifteen to everyone else that buys my book at the bookstore. You wanted a copy of the original."

"**DEAL!** I'll even buy lunch," Ned proclaimed.

They sat there looking at the notebook for the next two hours, discussing the various items that were written by the author. Ned was glued to the print. "You realize, you could probably get several thousand dollars for the notebook right now," he told Stan.

"I thought of that. I do not think the price of the book will be going down in the near future. I am just hoping everyone says the story is real. You know, there were some great authors about that time. What if someone just wanted to become a Samuel Clemens, and made up a great story? For all I know, this could be his outline for his book. Until I know for sure, I guess I am just going to have to keep digging into the facts. Just don't count on me putting the book in the pot at the next card game."

Bayfield's Secret Notebook

By the time the two of them left lunch, Ned was drooling over the book. Stan had only let him read the first twenty pages, keeping the full story about hiding the Confederate gold, a mystery.

Ned still thought the author was talking about his role in working with both sides in the war.

Ned wished he could tell all his friends at the Civil War Roundtable what he had seen. It would keep them talking for the rest of the year, and Ned would be the center of attention. However, Stan had made him promise that he would not say anything to anyone, until he gave him permission.

This was one time that Ned wished that he was not true to his word. For now, all Ned could do would be to call Stan and try to pry more information out of him as to what was in the notebook. He would have really preferred to be able to read the whole thing, and be the one that told his Civil War group the story.

The next two weeks passed quickly. Stan called Barbara every night. He had all he could do to keep from talking constantly about the book. He realized that it might not be in his best interest. Barbara wanted a little of Stan's attention, not the attention aimed at the book. Besides, he wanted to keep most of the information a surprise until the next time he could get back to her house for a visit. Stan had a small writing job the next weekend that needed reviewing, so it was two weeks before he could get back to Barbara's.

When the weekend finally arrived, he packed up the notebooks along with his computer and drove to Illinois. Barbara and Vivian were waiting for him.

As they helped him bring his stuff into the house, Barbara asked, "Well?"

"Well, what?" Stan replied.

"Stan, you know; did you find out if the notebooks were real or not?"

"I'll tell you after dinner."

Chapter 9

Piecing the Story Together

Stan arrived just in time for dinner. After bringing in his things from the car, he joined Barbara and her mother at the table for some fried chicken.

Barbara knew that Stan had been working extra hard trying to decipher all the lines of the notebook, while he was home the past week. In fact, he had spent almost all of his spare time working on linking the lines of the notebook, with as much history, as he could find on the internet. Amazingly, there was a correlation that loosely followed the events recorded. If you combined the notebook with recorded history, there were very few conflicts.

Stan waited as long as he could before starting a discussion about the notebooks. He wanted to show Barbara that he was more interested in her than the research.

Finally, after getting a few questions from Barbara, he told them that he had asked a friend, who was a Civil War buff, to look at the book. He told me that the information looked original.

Barbara was a little upset. "You let a friend know about the notebooks?" she asked. "I thought you knew better than that. What if he tells someone?"

"I made him promise that he would not tell anyone about it, until I said it was okay. Besides, to be safe, I only showed him up to 1864. He has no idea where the notebook leads. I only showed him the first part of the first book. I did not tell him there was a second notebook."

Vivian was as curious as Barbara was, about what Stan had found. So far, she was politely waiting for Stan and Barbara to bring up the real story.

Barbara told Stan, "I have a feeling you have a lot to show us. How about waiting until after dinner, you can tell us the story as you have put it together. If it is a good one, Mother said she would serve us some apple pie in the intermission."

"Hmm, apples from the beautiful damsel's mother. Where have we heard that story before? Okay, on one condition, do we get ice cream with the pie?"

Vivian laughed! "Is that your last request?"

After they had cleaned off the table and retired to the den, Stan snuggled into the leather sofa with Barbara and his notebook, while Vivian took the recliner. Vivian warned Stan, "If the story gets too long, just keep on talking. You can pretend my snoring is someone cutting wood." Somehow, she knew this story might be too good to sleep through.

Stan laughed, and started telling the story about the writings in the notebook. As he went along, he filled in the parts of history that were missing, from between the lines, which he had found looking on the internet.

Bayfield's Secret Notebook

"The notebook starts out in the early days of the Civil War. In fact, it appears to start as a log of whiskey deliveries. Then, as the war progresses, the writer, Johan Volker, slowly changes over to a journal of what was happening. It was as though the author realized that history was being made, and he was part of it. It appeared that he was writing it to tell his family at some later date. The more I looked at it, the more I wondered if there had been a third notebook. One that he kept as information about each batch of whiskey they made at the Distillery."

Stan started the story he had collected.

"Johan Volker came over from Germany to be the brewmaster for the Boone County Distillery in Petersburg, Kentucky. He had experience in Munich, Germany where both he, and his brother Wilhelm Volker, had been apprentices at an old established distillery. According to the notes, they had been approached by one of their senior brewmasters, who told them of a letter he had received from the United States, asking for a suggested list of qualified people that he thought might be available to be hired at the largest distillery in the New World. The job was open, and it required the special talents that were not readily available in the States.

"In April 1854, Johan Volker travelled from Germany to Petersburg, Kentucky, to become the new brewmaster at the Boone County Distillery. The "brewmaster" was a title, which carried with it the responsibilities of managing the distillery as though he was the owner. Whatever was done, he was in charge of making all the decisions that ultimately made the taste of the whiskey what it was.

"I found that the writer started the journal about ten pages into the notebook. He must have realized that the story needed to start with his voyage to the United States. The first paragraph appears to be an introduction he added to the journal at a later date, and shows a change in his English abilities from the rest of the first year's entries."

Stan started by reading some of the actual lines from the notebook, which he had finished reconstructing from the missing words.

Johan Volker's Journal

After arriving in Petersburg from Cincinnati in 1854, at the seasoned age of 29, I found that my new job was similar to my old manager's brewmaster position in Germany. It only took a month, or so, for me to adjust to the living style in the States, or should I say, it only took them a month or two to adjust to my style.

Many of de workers are of Irish descent and at least hav a taste for liquor. I have to remind dem dis ist not potato mash dey are distilling. De old recipes from de homeland must be safely guarded, as I look fur better sources of grains. I asked brudder to come join me here in New World. I tink he has better chance to make fortune here den work as apprentice at distillery.

The distillery owner is stout but honest man. He is willing to work at a distance as long as we maintain clients and grow business. So far, he be in charge of setting up distribution of barrels and kegs shipped out in all directions. In fact, we now have two factories making de oak barrels we need for aging. Dis was one of first improvement I make after taking over job. Whiskey requires charred oak barrels to season taste while aging.

Bayfield's Secret Notebook

Friday, July 18, 1856, brudder arrive from Germany today. I am pleased to see him. So much ta tell him. He like to find a job as a brewmaster as well. I tell him – be patient. He can work here blending the mash until he find good opening. He is a stubborn German. He tinks he be able to find job immediately with his qualifications. He will learn. People here are not as demanding for taste as Deutschlanders. If alcohol content is high, and it does not taste like fresh out of a still, they tink it good.

Tuesday, January 27, 1857. Boss – Mr. Snyder, want me to deliver a load of kegs to Lawrenceburg, Indiana, up river. It will then be shipped to Cincinnati. Coldt this winter. Too much ice for riverboats. We drive a team of horses over ice to the other side. Snow crunches as horses walk on it. Ice sounds like it is breaking, with every move we make. I can hear ice crack all the way to shore. Horses not like it. Very jittery. Regular teamsters claim it is too cold for delivery. Called me a stubborn kraut.

I have words for them too. I would need to write this in my native German to use them. I need practice writing in English. So, I write in English. I do not know why they call this English. In Germany, I learn German, French and English at school, so I can do business with each country. This is not English. The Americans fought to get away from England. Why didn't they call this American. When I cross the Ohio, they speak it differently. Now I learn how to speak three types of English. Stableman is colored folk. He say to me, "Y'all yust ain't speaking Anglish." Maybe there are four types of English. "Who y'all?" I tell him, "It yust me." Can not find ain't in my dictionary I keep by me bed. Today, I tell him, "Sprechen sie Deutsch?" He yust shake his head and walk away. It will take time before I learn the language gooder.

Brudder Wilhelm Volker went wit to Lawrenceburg. We put deer hide covers over clothes to stay warm. Delivered load on schedule. Wilhelm tells me he wants to start his own brewery. We talk all the way back about it. He talks bout new territory in Minnesota. They will need someone like him. Wants me to give him starter. We talk about it. He talks – I listen.

Monday, June 15, 1857. Brudder Wilhelm going by riverboat down Ohio. Will head up-river to Minnesota to town where the logging is done. Long journey. Set up brewery. I tell him to make beer and whiskey. He is ambitious, he will survive.

Monday, September 28, 1858. Letter from Wilhelm. He is settled in wild town called Still Water. Met a man on riverboat from St. Louis. He is also German. They talk. They agreed to become partners.

Wilhelm says he will start brewery, partner will run saloon to sell liquor. Found limestone cave for aging liquor. He says Minnesota has become a state. Many saloons in Still Water and in capital – St. Paul. Lots of Norwegians and Swedes,

Bayfield's Secret Notebook

and many Irishman in St. Paul. He say not many saints in St. Paul. Will make fortune. Everyone drinks. I should come and join him.

Saturday, January 15, 1860. Too much talk about war. Mr. Snyder talks about moving to Tennessee to move away from people that say we should fight South. Ask me to join him. Will see about job farther south. Like job here. Worried about business. Shipping kegs both North and South. Everyone say if there is a war, it will only last over summer. Too cold to fight in winter – everyone go home up North.

November 1860. Lincoln elected President over Douglas. Many people upset. Good for business. Many discussions at saloons.

Got order for 50 kegs of whiskey to be delivered by train for inauguration in March. Will require special seals on kegs. Military will escort kegs on train. Boone County Distillery one of only two suppliers for festivities.

December 1860. South Carolina to leave Union. Tensions are running high. Making sure barrel suppliers will keep supplying us if there is war.

Saturday, January 5, 1861. Got order for 30 kegs of Kentucky whiskey. South electing own President. Wants me to deliver them in person in February to Montgomery, Alabama.

David Fabio

Took a week to deliver to Alabama. Weather was good – not too cold. No snow. Ran two wagons and had four extra people to guard cargo. Loaded on train in Lexington and rode in rail car to Birmingham.

Saturday, February 9, 1861. President Jefferson Davis sworn in as President of seven states called the Confederacy. Attended inauguration. Met President Davis, and several army generals. He was trying to recruit some of them from the North to be part of the new army of the Confederacy. Met a general named Lee. He was trained in a place called West Point along with other generals. I think it is in the state of Maryland. President Davis told me my whiskey was as good as he had ever tasted. I thanked him. I asked them what they thought about war. Might happen they said. Told me they would try and protect distilleries. Alcohol needed even in war times. Hope war does not happen. Too many wars in Germany.

March 1861. Train with whiskey for Lincoln's inauguration arrived three days early. Got telegram today saying it arrived intact. Money to send tomorrow.

April 1861. Got word – War! They just do not understand. They think that it will be over by the end of summer.

Bayfield's Secret Notebook

Snyder is making sure we can still ship to both North and South. Lost several workers this week. Three signed up for army, two jumped a riverboat heading for the west to get away from the war. Hard to find replacements to deliver kegs and pick up grains. Several customers are getting behind in payments. Snyder needs money to buy crops.

Tuesday, September 10, 1861. War going on too long. More customers behind in payments. Mr. Snyder worried. Debts are growing. Confederate army is getting more organized. Moving north. Riverboats are no longer moving up and down Ohio River. Only boats moving troops and supplies. Mr. Snyder still sending some shipments north by boat. As long as we supply army, they let us ship whiskey with boats. Not shipping goods past Kentucky/West Virginia line. River not safe.

Tuesday, October 8, 1861. Mr. Snyder having money problems. Selling business to son-in-law, Appleton, and moving to Chattanooga, Tennessee. I have worked with Appleton for several years. He is okay to work with. Snyder asks me to go with him to set up new business in Confederate territory, away from war. I tell him I will stay to keep current business open. When he gets business started, I can join him.

*****

As Stan took a break, Vivian asked him, "You think this is really a first hand account of the war? This is exciting. If this is a first hand account, you are going to have a number of people interested in what it contains. You could make this into a book, and you might be able to get a best seller out of it. Does he really get involved with the gold?"

"Well, I'm running a little low on my 'southern lightning.' If you could find us some of that apple pie, with ice cream, I might be able to let you know how he gets involved."

"That's blackmail!" Vivian shouted at him.

Stan just winked at her.

"I'll give you a hand," Barbara told her mother. "I have a feeling that Stan found a lot more about the notebook, compared to what I read in Bayfield. Looks like he is playing hard to get. Unfortunately, I want to hear the rest of the story too, or I would show him what hard to get is really like."

They dished up some apple pie, with ice cream, and brought it back into the den.

Vivian told Stan, "You know, you are really pushing your luck. If you don't watch yourself, you may not stay on my good side."

Stan just smiled. "Best pie I have had in a long time," he said as he winked at Barbara. He knew that comment would buy him a little more time.

Chapter 10

Connections

After a fantastic piece of apple pie ala mode, Stan resumed his reading from Johan Volker's journal. He made sure that Vivian knew that he really liked her pies.

As he watched, there had not been a yawn in the group. Everyone wanted to know what the connections were between Johan Volker and the Confederacy. They knew the answer was probably just around the corner of the next page.

*****

Saturday, February 22, 1862. Letter from Mr. Snyder. He has met with businessmen and will start small brewery near Chattanooga later this year. Wants me to come also. Ask me to wait and work with son-in-law until he sees an ending to war.

Thursday, March 6, 1862. While making a delivery to Lexington, I was stopped by three riders in Rebel uniforms on the way back. I thought I was being forced to join army. They asked me to go with them. Tell me, I am not in danger, want meeting.

Met with General Lee. I recognized him immediately from inauguration party. He ask me to be emissary to talk to Union general about release of prisoners. I asked why me. He said he felt he could trust me because I was from Germany, and not from either the North or South. My job would be to convey the messages that went from Confederate Generals to Union Generals. I would not have to talk. They would do the negotiations.

He said if I agree, both sides would protect both me and Distillery. He said it might be one of the most important contributions I can make.

I agreed to carry message.

He said he would send a messenger to me with exchange information. It would come from General Hill. Not sure who he is. If I met him earlier, I do not remember. General Hill will hide a coded set of letters in special place on all messages. If it was not there, I was to tear it up. He left instructions as to how I am to leave a hidden message in whiskey supply wagon for his people to pick up.

The next week, I go to Cincinnati as General Hill requested. Met with Union army, General Dix. Gives me same instructions and guaranty of safety. Union will use different code letters and different hiding place for messages to make sure messages are authentic. First release set for next month.

Bayfield's Secret Notebook

Many prisoners that agree to go home and stay out of war will be released.

I sent reply back to General Hill.

Saturday, May 10, 1862. War is heating up. We get as many orders from armies as from taverns. Army uses whiskey for surgery as well as drinking. Alcohol works as disinfectant as well as numbing the nerves.

Thursday, September 4, 1862. Got message from Union general for another prisoner release. Sent message to Rebel officers. They have new formula for releasing prisoners. General worth 60 soldiers, colonel – 15, lieutenant – 4, sergeant worth 2. Not sure they stay with numbers after first exchange. Too many prisoners to feed.

Riverboats no longer working Ohio, Tennessee, or Mississippi Rivers unless working for government, shipping troops and supplies. Much harder to ship grain or liquor.

Lincoln signed order saying slaves will be free as of first of year. Mr. Snyder has 6 slaves working his farms. Letter from Mr. Snyder said he not sure if slaves will run for Ohio to be free.

Wednesday, December 3, 1862. Confederacy starting to win war. News of battles starting to spread quickly along Ohio River.

David Fabio

Tuesday, March 10, 1863. War still fought. General Halleck now issuing requests for prisoner exchanges for Union army. Confederate general not willing to trade colored Union prisoners for same exchange as white. Many notes being sent before exchanges are agreed upon.

Monday, July 6, 1863. Heard about terrible battle in town called Gettysburg. Too many from each side killed.

Saturday, November 28, 1863. Chattanooga taken by Union forces. They say they have all of Tennessee. Look like war turning back in favor of Union. Confederates running out of supplies.
    Problem with workers at Distillery since still blew up last year killing brewers. Lost three men I trained in. New workers not very good workers. War take all hard workers. Not heard from Mr. Snyder in months. Maybe he flee farther south. I have been told of job available in Louisville. Move there next month.
    Leaving Distillery in good terms with boss. He say I can buy un-cured product and he ship to me.
    I send note to generals, tell them I am moving. They thank me for my service to help those in war prisons.

Monday, March 28, 1864. Set up small brewery outside of Louisville in January. City wants to keep businesses

Bayfield's Secret Notebook

that might cause fires outside of town. Too many people worried about fires burning down whole town. Brick or stone buildings being built.

War appears to be south of us now and commerce starting to pick up. In January, I ordered three barrels of whiskey from Boone Distillery to cure for year, plus ten kegs of seasoned whiskey. Order arrived last week.

Thursday, September 15, 1864. Union forces trying to capture Richmond. War looks like it might come to end soon. Confederate forces falling apart.

I hear that General Grant had stopped prisoner exchanges. Too many Rebels heading right back to the South's lines. I think he hopes for quick end to war.

*****

Barbara interrupted Stan's reading.

"Stan, do you realize what time it is getting to be? It is almost 11:00 pm and we have not even gotten to the part that we wanted to hear."

Stan told her, "I guess we might have to finish this tomorrow. That's if your mother's pie holds up?"

Vivian gave a sigh. "Well, this has been an interesting history lesson so far. However, it is not the information that I was led to believe you found in conjunction to what was in the notebook. So far, this is just what Johan Volker wrote. I usually do not give panhandlers a second shot at my time. I guess I can make an exception, on one condition; if you don't get to the good stuff tomorrow, you have to do the dishes."

Barbara looked to see Stan's reaction. So far, he was playing the game close to his best.

Stan replied, "Tomorrow, I'll show you that this story really does become a story. I have found a lot of information to support what is in his journal. However, without this background information, you would not understand the reason for the story.

"How about getting back to the story after lunch – with pie for dessert? Think you can get the orchard in automatic mode by then?"

Barbara laughed. "Mother can get that done in one hour. This time of year, she has it totally under control. It is when picking time comes that we need to put in the fourteen-hour days.

"I'll make sure we have enough ice-cream to keep you talking."

They headed off to get a good night's sleep.

Bayfield's Secret Notebook

Chapter 11

Barrels

Stan let Barbara slip out of bed early the next morning. Barbara and Vivian had things well under control in the office of the orchard by the time Stan rolled out of bed at 9:00 am.

It was unusual for Stan to sleep in that long. He figured the long drive and talking until 12:30 am with Barbara, had finally caught up to him. He found a note on the kitchen counter when he got up.

Thought you needed some sleep. You were so tired you were snoring last night. There is some orange and apple juice in the refrigerator and fresh rolls in the microwave. Help yourself. We will see you at lunchtime – or should I say lecture time? Love, Barbara

Stan helped himself to breakfast and went into the den, to use his computer and do a little more research before his audience returned. So far, he was getting at least one message a day from his friend, the Civil War buff. He was still trying to get Stan to let some of the information out of his hands.

At noon, Vivian and Barbara came back from the office, above the Apple Barn. Vivian spotted Stan first and called to him, "Stan, I forgot to tell you, the dishes I mentioned are not those in the dishwasher. I had in mind the big kettles and pie pans in the kitchen of the Apple Barn. Hope your beauty sleep has gotten your energy recharged."

Barbara laughed. She knew that her mother and Stan had gotten to know each other well enough that they were starting to see who could stay one-up on barbs.

They had a quick lunch of chicken salad, and moved into the den for what they were hoping would be an exciting tale. Stan asked, "Is there enough ice-cream and pie in the refrigerator to compensate me for all the comments I might have to take?"

"Just keep from putting us to sleep," Vivian answered.

Stan proceeded with the storyline he had written the past week using the information given in Johan Volker's journal accounts, and combining it with relevant information he found on the internet. He had written it as a continuation of Johan's journal from the point they had stopped the night before. As it turned out, it was the perfect break point last night. Now, Stan could start his story.

*****

The Story of Johan Volker

Wednesday, October 12, 1864. Louisville is a bustling town on a sharp bend of the Ohio River separating Kentucky and Indiana. It is much bigger than the town I left in Petersburg. I find that business in

Bayfield's Secret Notebook

liquor supply is brisk. There are a number of taverns in town, along with a number of military people that are heading through Louisville on their way to or from the war.

My new distillery is very small compared to Boone County Distillery. Because of this, I have a very small overhead and am able to make money quickly to pay off the cost of my building. I have a team of horses, wagons, and two partners helping me. I have 51% investment, so I stay boss-man.

Last month, my partners and I dug a cellar in the basement, to store the liquor as it cures. Floor was all limestone rock, which allowed us to dig room that will stay a constant temperature. Once we used our picks to break the rock, it came out in layers four to five inches thick. We broke the rock into pieces twenty inches by twenty-four inches. Made cellar 40-feet by 25-feet. Ceiling is going to be 15-feet high.

Put timbers across top, and laid pieces of four-inch rock, to insulate the room. Should keep it nice and cool even in the hot Kentucky summers. Maybe I should sleep down there, on hot nights.

I ordered an old, heavy, iron door to lay on floor for entrance. After installing steps down to cellar, we cut and cleaned two straight sapling oak trees to use as rails, to roll barrels down steps. Used many of the extra limestone rocks for a wall in front of building. It looks like we have been here long time.

I brought in ten barrels of whiskey and four barrels of rum to keep us in business. Keg manufacturer brought me fifty oak kegs and casks this week. We can fill them to meet orders until our products age enough to sell. We have two stills on top floor. Have to be careful of fire or explosion. Roof is designed to blowout a raised-up roof vent, in case of explosion.

My partners, Josh and Horace, are very helpful. We have purchased grains grown locally and distilling operation is running. By spring, we should be able to supply whiskey, rum and beer to local taverns. I have made arrangements with Boone County Distillery, and another rum distillery to supply us raw product for aging.

Josh and Horace are both married men. They fought for Confederate side, until captured in 1862. When they were released, they came home to find work. Their families kept busy making clothing while they were away. Stories they told me about Confederate prisoner of war camps are not as bad as the stories I heard from some of the Union soldiers that were released. Josh and Horace were in a prison in Illinois, constructed long before the war. Even though their war days were over, they still resented Northerners. The feelings they had from the war and from the prison camp, have stayed with them like flies on a piece of raw meat.

Today, I delivered liquor to several taverns along the waterfront. When I stopped at the bank on way back, there was a short, thin man waiting to talk to me. He was dressed in worn out farmer clothes. I did not know him. He said that Snyder told him where I worked. He figured I would stop at bank at end of my deliveries. I was rather suspicious of the man, and I asked him to wait outside when I paid bank account. I told banker, Mr. Langer, to keep eye on me as I leave. I wanted to make sure the man did not come to rob me. Since I had deposited all the money, they would not get rich if they held me up.

When I came out, he was still there. I stared at him and figured he was probably looking for a job.

"Mr. Volker, you do not know me, my name is Lewis Patterson. I met your friend Mr. Snyder in Birmingham, and he told me he had heard that you have moved to Louisville. He said you were a man that could be trusted."

I told him, "I have not talked to Mr. Snyder in over a year. How did you find me?"

Bayfield's Secret Notebook

"Apparently, Mr. Snyder has kept in communications with his daughter in Petersburg. She told him that you moved to Louisville to start a distillery. Is there a place we can talk in private? What I have to say should not be left for errant ears."

"I have to take the wagon back to distillery. You can ride along and we can talk."

As we started back the short mile to the distillery, Mr. Lewis Patterson told me, "I was told that that you served both the Union and the Confederacy during the war, delivering messages to the generals that allowed for prisoner exchanges. I have another favor to ask of you."

This caught me by surprise. No one other than Snyder knew about it, and Snyder said he would never tell anyone. "I am not sure what you are talking about," I answered.

"President Davis said you might say something as such. He told you, that you made the best whiskey he had ever tasted. You probably do not remember, but I was there also. I had different clothes on then. I did not want anyone to recognize me, while I searched for you."

"I thought you talked a little too good for a person from Birmingham, your accent is from further north."

"Raised in Ohio. Went to West Point for two years. I was recommended to West Point by General Lee. He is a relative. When the war broke out, I left the academy to become General Lee's currier to President Davis for two more years. Can we find someplace quiet to talk?"

"Let's hold our talk until we reach the distillery. Cellar is quiet enough to make the dead speak back to you." They rode the wagon talking about the weather and the countryside until they reached the distillery.

After stabling up the horses, and checking to see that his partners had gone home for the day, I showed Lewis Patterson the cellar designed for storing the barrels. I lit a couple lanterns and we went downstairs, shutting the heavy steel door behind us. I was pretty sure no one would be able to hear anything the stranger had to say down there.

Even if my partners came back to check on the still, they would not hear us under all that rock covering the cellar. It also meant; if I ran into trouble, no one would hear any shouts for help. Was I putting too much trust into Lewis Patterson?

"Well Sir, I think you need to start that conversation back at the beginning, so I can figure out who you are and what you want," I told him.

"Fair enough! As I told you, my name is Lewis Patterson. I have been sent here with a request from President Davis. He sent this letter with me to let you know that my word is good." He showed me a short letter of introduction, signed by Mr. Hancock. It was a letter of reference for getting a job and was addressed to Johan Volker.

When I looked at the letter, I quickly spotted the coded letters in the note indicating the writer knew the code I was used to seeing on letters pertaining to prisoner exchanges.

"As you can see, President Davis did not use his real name. In case the letter fell in the wrong hands, he wanted to protect both you and me. However, he did code the letter."

"So I see. You must understand, I am no longer communicating with the generals," I told him.

"Yes, I was told the same. Before I give you the message, I must ask you some questions. You can stop me as you wish, and I will disappear as I came. You must agree, as I will, that this meeting never happened."

"Okay, I am listening."

"You are from Germany, correct?"

"Yes!"

"Are you aware that other countries often come to the aid of countries that are at war?"

Bayfield's Secret Notebook

"Yes, that is common in Europe as well," I replied.

"Well, as you probably know, the war is not going well for the Confederacy. We are losing the war. It is just a matter of time before our military runs out of bullets. Our navy has not existed for the past year. Our ports are blocked and rail supplies are non-existent. Some people in our cities are eating rats and other varmints that can be found. Our food chain is non-existent. It is just a matter of time.

"England and France advanced the Confederacy certain sums of money and industrial goods to support our cause. If we lose the war, we do not want the money left to fall into Union hands."

"I understand your problem. How does that affect me?" I asked.

"We have tried to ship money back to France and England. However, we have lost a couple ships to the blockade, had a few other attempts turned back, and still need to find a way to move the money. France is impatient. They are still having financial problems, ever since the wars they fought between the countries over there, and want their money immediately. England is a little more patient. They feel that if we can regroup, they can wait for their money a few years to see if there is a possibility of winning. Even if we lose the war, there is always a chance we can make one more strategic strike after restocking our food and ammunitions. If successful, we might be able to negotiate a better set of terms for the end of the war.

"I have spoken with your Mr. Snyder. He says you are an honest man who could deliver money."

"I am a brewmaster. I am not a military man. I only have small pistol to protect against robbers. Why do you ask me?"

"We need someone who can deliver the money to England, in Canada. You do not sound like a Southerner. You speak with many accents. You could hide the money and deliver it to Canada. For this service, we would pay you extremely well. Do I continue or leave at this point?"

"How do I keep from being robbed or caught by Union army?"

"I take that as an answer that you are still willing to talk," he stated.

"You talk, I listen. Then I decide."

"Fair enough," Lewis Patterson answered. "We need your expertise. Here is the plan that we have worked out. We think that with your help, it will be successful."

Mr. Patterson told me about the plan that he had developed to get the money from the Confederacy to England. He did not tell me where the money was currently, or how he was going to get it to me; however, he outlined a plan involving me once it was delivered to Louisville.

"You are brewmaster. You make and deliver whiskey orders. The plan is to have you deliver whiskey to the north. Go by riverboat down the Ohio and up the Mississippi. No one is looking for Confederate gold in the north."

"Gold! I thought you said money."

"Gold is the money of countries. Confederate bills may not have any value in a few months. Actually, they do not have any value now. There is nothing to back our currency. The plan is to have you take the gold to Wisconsin. They started working on a train a few years ago. It leads from a town called Hudson, located on a river called the St. Croix, which connects to the Mississippi, to a town on Lake Superior, called Bayfield. By the time you get there, it should be finished. England has informed me that they have men working in Bayfield that regularly go to and from Canada. The Union blockade will not spot the movement of the gold. They are not looking to the north. It will be safe. If we regroup as we hope we will, the funds will be available again."

"How do I hide this gold?" I asked. "It is not something to put in my trunk."

Bayfield's Secret Notebook

"We thought of this as well. You will hide it in the fake bottom of whiskey barrels being delivered to the railroad in Hudson. No one will question a brewmaster delivering barrels of whiskey."

"What if someone steals the barrels?" he asked.

"We will make sure that this does not happen. When you complete your job, you will have enough money to buy your own business, wherever you like."

"And if I take the gold and disappear?" I asked.

"You did not recognize me. You probably will not recognize someone else accompanying you on the riverboat. We think you are an honest man. You will deliver the barrels to Bayfield."

"I have brother in Minnesota that owns brewery. He could repack gold in shipping crates for railroad," I informed him.

"Yes, we know. We considered this as well. Is he as honest as you are?" he asked Johan.

"Yes! I would trust my life on him," he told Patterson.

"You might have to. Do not tell him until you are there and you are sure he is trustworthy."

As they discussed the smaller details, the two men shared a stein of whiskey. It warmed them up from sitting in the cool cellar of the distillery. Lewis Patterson was surprised that Volker agreed this easily. His only thought was that Johan was hoping to move closer to his brother, and this way he could buy his own business at the same time. He gave Johan an advance to pay for the barrels, kegs, and whiskey using Union dollars that the Confederacy had obtained.

By the time they exited the cellar, it was dark outside. Lewis Patterson left as mysteriously as he had appeared, with no one else knowing why he was there, or who he was.

Monday, October 17, 1864. The next week, I placed a special order for twenty custom oak barrels from my supplier. The details were exact. There was to be a space between bottoms, about the same size as a rough sawn 2" by 3". It was to be framed such that two – 13 inch 2X3's could be snuggly placed in the space between the bottoms. The outer bottom was to be in place but not nailed to the frame. I would also need thirty ten-gallon oak kegs. I told my suppliers that I had a new secret formula for affecting the taste of curing whiskey I wanted to try. I could not tell them what I was placing in the opening that would slowly affect the un-cured whiskey. They did not ask.

I told my partners, Josh and Horace, that I had accepted a large order from a warehouse in Paducah, downriver on the Ohio. They would let us know when to ship it. They were waiting for riverboat traffic to resume.

My partners were excited about the large order. It would help pay off the cost of the new cellar construction. We were to get payment prior to shipping product downriver. I told them that part of the agreement was that I would accompany the large shipment to make sure that it arrived in good shape.

Sunday, November 20, 1864. The last month went quickly, as I awaited word from the Confederacy on how and when they would ship the gold. I was in such a cloud that I did not even realize how much money it was worth. I sent a letter to my brother and told him that I might be coming to see him when the rivers opened from ice.

The barrels and kegs have been delivered and are stored in the warehouse. The plan I agreed to, was to ship them to the Boone County Distillery to be filled with un-aged whiskey in the barrels, and aged whiskey in the kegs, just in time to head north.

All I needed to know now, was when.

Friday, February 3, 1865. On a cold snowy day, I got a shipment of grain that needed to be milled before using in the still. The drivers

Bayfield's Secret Notebook

were not the familiar ones I am used to from one of our regular farmers. When I checked the billing sheet, it stated paid in full.

I realized who must have sent it, and asked them to bring the wagon around back, so we could unload it into the back of the distillery. When we had unloaded 20 sacks of grain, I saw the floorboards of the wagon were very short. In fact, they were six and one-half inch boards on top the regular boards. They almost looked like bricks. When I looked closer, I realized they had been painted the color of wood – it was the gold.

Working with the aid of the flickering light from four lanterns, the two drivers helped me unload the bricks into the warehouse. We spent the rest of the night wedging them snuggly into the compartments made specially to fit the gold bricks in the base of the oak barrel's double bottom. I forgot how heavy gold was. It was a good thing the large oak barrels were very heavy. They hid some of the extra weight that four six and one-half inch long bricks added to each barrel. Each brick was 27.4 pounds, which added a total of 109.6 pounds per barrel. By morning, I was exhausted. The barrels were sealed and stacked in the cellar, and my drivers were gone. I told Josh and Horace that I needed to go visit a tavern owner in the next town. I did not want them asking me questions about why I was so tired. When I got there, I rented a room for the night and went to sleep.

I was extremely restless. Every time I turned over and woke up, all I could think of was all the gold in my warehouse. What if something happened to it? What if the warehouse caught fire, or the still blew-up? What have I gotten myself into? I am a respectable brewmaster.

I cannot believe the way I have allowed my life to go. When I left Germany, I had no idea that I would be anything other than the brewmaster. Now, if something happens, I have a chance of spending my life in prison or worse. Unfortunately, there is no turning back at this point. I hope Lewis Patterson is as smart as he appears, and has this totally thought out.

The next morning, when I got to work, I painted signs on the barrels we had loaded. I marked them with a symbol for a tavern I made up, so that the barrels would not be mixed up with requests for regular customers. Then, I showed the symbol to my partners, so they would save those barrels for our delivery. The only question was; when were we to ship the barrels? We needed to know that to have them filled at the Boone County Distillery.

Saturday, April 1, 1865. I got a letter back from my brother. He is pleased to hear I may come to Minnesota. He says that he sold his interest in the brewery in Stillwater to his partner and is now brewmaster at that brewery and another in St. Paul. He travels between them regularly. He says that both towns are wild and unorganized. Lots of drinking when the men are done working. He is waiting for my letter to tell him when I am arriving.

Monday, April 10, 1865. Word spread quickly, General Robert E. Lee commander in chief of the Confederate forces surrendered yesterday. The war appears to be over. Still no word on my delivery. What should I do if everyone surrendered? Sleepless nights are becoming the norm. Too many "what if's."

Friday, April 14, 1865. Telegraph office messenger ran through town today. He said that President Lincoln had been shot. Was this the quick end and restart of the war they had been talking about? The South has not had time to restock food and ammunition.

Thursday, April 27, 1865. Word has spread of a big disaster on the Mississippi River. Big paddleboat, Sultana, carrying injured Union soldiers that were released from a prisoner of war camp, blew up on river. Most of the passengers feared dead. Telegraph office says that boiler exploded when the ship was overloaded and the captain was trying to push the boat too fast. What a tragedy.

Wednesday, May 10, 1865. Newspaper says that normal riverboat travel on the Ohio is anticipated below Cincinnati, starting in June. This must mean that the Mississippi River is going to have riverboats again. The army has started to release all the boats they requested for supply and movement of troops. Paper claims that they will be refitted for passenger travel as soon as possible.

The boats were stripped of their fancy furniture and carpets before they started hauling troops and supplies for the war. They say it will take a couple weeks to refit each of the boats. I assume that means they will all get a fresh coat of paint after they filled all the bullet holes that occurred on some of them.

Reconstruction, as they call it, is starting. Supplies from the north are coming down, into the south, through cities like Louisville. People up north are getting rich bringing goods to town that used to be available in the south. Because of this, the taverns are very busy, all day long. I had to hire three men to help with deliveries. We may have to buy another still to keep up. We are still purchasing extra product from Boone County Distillery to meet demand.

My partners are very pleased with money coming in. We have paid off all debts from startup. Bank tore up note today when I deposited money.

We all celebrated when I got back to distillery.

*****

Barbara turned to Stan, "You mean to tell me that they shipped the gold to Johan knowing that the war was almost over? And then, they expected him to protect it? Why didn't he just take it and run?"

"That's probably the reason he was selected. Most people would have done just that. With all the training he had in Germany, he was trained to do things exactly as instructed, and they knew it. That had been the structure of his life. They probably figured he would do the same with the gold. He was a self-made man with little connections other than running his own distillery. By promising him money to buy his own business when it was done, it gave him the freedom to go anywhere he wanted, where he did not have competition. He would be both the owner and the brewmaster. That would bring him a lot of prestige," Stan suggested. "That was the one thing that drove Johan, the desire to be his own boss."

"I think both parties took a huge risk," Barbara replied.
"Stan, would you have taken that risk?" Vivian asked.
"No, I guess I'm not driven by prestige and position in life."

*****

Bayfield's Secret Notebook

Chapter 12

Shipping Orders

Friday, June 23, 1865. The paper says that all the Confederate armies have surrendered, including a few groups that had resisted all efforts to have them surrender. The war is truly over.

David Fabio

I received a letter today, with no return address. It stated that my brother is waiting for my visit. In the letter, it explained how the 20 barrels were to be labeled as compensation from the US Government to the State of Minnesota, for the meritorious service of the 1st Minnesota Regiment. It was to be held for use at the 10th anniversary of statehood celebration, in 1868. By then, the whiskey would be well seasoned. The 30 kegs were for the soldiers to have, while protecting the barrels on the way to Minnesota. Enclosed with the letter was a paddleboat ticket for July, heading downriver. I noticed that my ticket was marked from Cincinnati, and not Petersburg.

So, the plan was still in place. Now, I had to put the plan in motion. That meant that I needed to send the barrels and kegs up-river to Petersburg immediately. The order needed to be filled for delivery, and then shipped further up-river to Cincinnati. It seemed like the plan was heading me in the wrong direction.

Later in the afternoon, I went to the telegraph office and sent a wire to the Boone County Distillery informing them that I was sending barrels to fill the order I had previously discussed with them, and that I would personally accompany the delivery. The barrels would require shipping to Cincinnati, to be pre-loaded on the paddlewheeler, the War Eagle, which was scheduled to leave on July 14th.

When I returned, I told my three deliverymen that I would need all of them to deliver the barrels to Petersburg. We would be leaving next week. Josh and Horace would stay behind and maintain the business.

Monday, July 3, 1865. This morning, we loaded the twenty empty barrels and thirty kegs into three wagons. Josh complained that the oak used for the barrels appeared to be wet, and not properly kiln dried, as they weighed more than the empty barrels we filled last week for shipment to a tavern.

Bayfield's Secret Notebook

I confirmed Josh's observation with him. When we loaded the barrels, they seemed heavy to me also. I told Josh that I would speak to the barrel manufacturer. Meanwhile, I asked him to watch the still and maintain the supplies needed. He and Horace would run the distillery while we were gone. I told Horace that I planned to return in a few weeks.

He told me, "If de go'd Lord's willing and de crick don't rise." I am still trying to understand all the sayings of Southern English. This one, I think I am starting to understand.

In the morning, the roads were dry, and the weather mild. I guess you would say that the crick did not rise. Rain in Kentucky makes dry creeks into rivers quickly.

We left Louisville with three wagons loaded with the twenty barrels and thirty kegs. With the extra weight of the hidden cargo in the barrels, I figured that each wagon was loaded with about 2,000 pounds of cargo and a few food supplies for our trip.

The road was good, until we reached a creek bed the second day. Logs had been placed across the creek bed to prevent wagons from getting stuck in the mud. Unfortunately, as our loaded wagon bounced on the logs, one of the wheel hubs came loose. The wheel came loose and the wagon came crashing down on the axel with a loud bang.

We were lucky, the wagon could have easily tipped over and the barrels cracked. My driver jumped off the wagon when he felt the wheel drop, fearing the wagon would roll over on him. Fortunately, he was not injured. Since we were traveling very slowly over the creek bed, the damage was minor. We used a couple of the logs that had been placed in the creek bed to leverage up the wagon, so we could put the wheel back on. It was a miracle that none of the spokes were broken and the wheel was still usable. Had the wheel broke, we might have been delayed by a couple days.

David Fabio

After the accident, we decided to check the hubs more often each day. We could not afford to break a wheel or axle on this trip. The riverboat would not wait for us. We took it slowly each time we crossed a creek bed the rest of the trip.

We made the trip in six days. The minor problem with one wheel was the only problem that slowed us down. If the riverboats were available, we could have delivered our cargo in two days. I thanked my men, and they returned to Louisville.

Friday, July 7, 1865. Mr. Appleton and his wife are kind enough to offer me a spot in the guesthouse, until they can fill the order and ship it out by rail to Cincinnati. They said it was the least they could do. They appreciated all I had done as brewmaster for many years, and now with this large order, they wanted to show me their appreciation.

It felt different staying at the Distillery. For all the years I worked here, I was the boss of operations. Even the owner would honor my requests. Now, I was a guest. I toured the operation thanks to a request by the current brewmaster. He received his training at a distillery in Pittsburg and was proud of his ability.

I am not sure his training would qualify him for a job as senior assistant at a distillery in Munich. Although, he is a very personable man and seems to have the respect of his co-workers.

I inspected his grains. They are not as good as those we selected prior to the war. I did not tell him that they were not fully prepared. It would have been an extreme insult. This explains why the whiskey does not have the full aroma that it used to have when first tapped from a keg.

Staying at the guesthouse, for the first time in years I missed the Distillery. If had not been for the war, I would probably still be the brewmaster for the Distillery, working under Mr. Snyder. It was a wonderful location. It is located on a small hill overlooking the Ohio River. There were several buildings. The distillery, where the mash was cooked, was in a separate building from the storage shed. We made this change when the still blew up years ago. You must learn from experience.

The guesthouse and main house were just down the road. They had a great view of the river, also. The farms Mr. Snyder used to own, where they grew some of the grains for the whiskey, were just over the ridge.

I will be staying here as a guest, for five days. Then, the barrels and kegs will be full, and a train will carry them and me to meet the War Eagle. There is a little time put in the schedule, just in case the trains do not run on schedule.

I was shocked when I heard the name of the paddlewheeler. What an inappropriate name for a riverboat, right after such a devastating war. You would think they would re-name the boat rather than leave such a poor impression on Southerners, as it runs down the Ohio River.

There was a letter under my pillow tonight. I am not sure how it got there, but I am no longer surprised. How someone was able to enter the building without anyone seeing them on the grounds, keeps me wondering.

The letter informed me that the shipping costs for the whiskey, heading to Stillwater, Minnesota, had been paid for in advance. Part of the payment was in cash, and some of the payment was in the whiskey I was bringing. Half of the kegs of whiskey were to be partial payment for the boat. The other half were for the Union soldiers returning home, who agreed to help protect the barrels during the journey.

Even though the war is over, this man Lewis Patterson appears to be able to do things as if he is part of the government. I do not know how he does it, however, I am impressed. For now, I realize that I am just the pawn. He is making all the moves.

David Fabio

In the envelope was some money for me to use on the trip. It is a lot of money for me to carry on my person.

*****

Bayfield's Secret Notebook

Chapter 13

Homeward Bound

As Barbara and Vivian curled up on the couch and settled in for the next round of storytelling, Stan brought them back once again to 1865. He picked up where he had left off, before once again indulging in a well earned piece of Vivian's apple caramel pie. He turned to the next chapter and began reading.

*****

On July 15, 1865, many of the Minnesota volunteers were mustered from Louisville, Kentucky. Most of the men were replacements for the original infantrymen, who were some of the first militias supplied to the Union army. Those men fought gallantly, though the majority of these first recruits were killed in the battle at Gettysburg. Many others had gone home after their official three-year enlistment was up. The outfit had participated in the official recognition parade in Washington, and had been dispatched to Louisville awaiting orders. Now, it was finally their time to head home.

For those who had survived Gettysburg and had re-enlisted, it was an especially joyous occasion. They were heading home as heroes.

David Fabio

The unfortunate truth was that there were a few that were heading home in coffins. Those that were officers, and died in the final days of the war, were being shipped home for burial. Enlisted men who fell were buried in the many cemeteries designated for the war dead. Many of the others returning home were wounded in battles or suffered the effects of poor sanitation, especially those who were prisoners of war in the Southern camps.

Now, all the men were heading home to what they hoped would be a hero's welcome in their hometowns. Many of them boarded the train out of Louisville headed for Cincinnati. From there, after they crossed the river, they would continue by train to get as close as possible to their hometowns.

Someone had made a special honorary gift of passage for up to twenty officers, thirty enlisted, and twenty wounded soldiers on a paddlewheeler that was heading all the way from Cincinnati to Minnesota. The passage was worth $32 each. It was a rare gift that was readily accepted by the regiment commander. It had a request attached to the gift; they were to protect the gift of twenty barrels of Kentucky whiskey sent on-board to the Governor of Minnesota. The boat would dock in Louisville on the 15th.

First choices were given to those who had served with distinction in his regiment. Occasionally someone would opt out and give the opportunity to someone else. The trip by water had some risks, as well as the fact that some of the troops wanted their feet on dry land. There were others, who chose to pay their own way on the boat, even if they did not get a free passage. Approximately 90 of the regiment's soldiers were about to board the War Eagle.

July 15, 1865. That morning, a train loaded with joyous soldiers heading for home, left the depot in Louisville, scheduled for Cincinnati.

Bayfield's Secret Notebook

*****

Three days earlier, on Wednesday, July 12, 1865, a train left Petersburg, heading for Cincinnati. Among its cargo list, were barrels of whiskey bound for Minnesota.

I thanked my hosts for allowing me to stay at the Distillery while waiting for my cargo. In the days I stayed there, while I watched the steamboats traveling up and down river, it gave me the chills. I was leaving a life I was accustomed to, and was about to head into something over which I had little control. The move from Germany to Petersburg, was an adventure for me. I knew what job was in store for me. This was more than an adventure. It contained all kinds of risks that I had no idea existed. Even the boat had risks. I figured that if my brother could do it, I could do it.

When the last of the twenty barrels were loaded safely into the railroad car, I breathed a sigh of relief. No one had realized that they held slightly less liquor, with the false bottom. It was a detail that I would have noticed in the days I operated the Distillery.

The train ride was peaceful, although slow. With the war, the lack of maintenance of the tracks had allowed them to deteriorate. The train proceeded at a painfully slow pace down the crooked tracks. I watched the smoke and steam of the engine puffing by my open window, as we travelled away from the river, through a wooded area. Several times we had to pull over on a siding, and wait for a train traveling the other direction to pass. Schedules were hard to calculate due to the tracks, and many times the opposing train was behind schedule. What was once a set of parallel tracks, in the past three years it had been downgraded to one usable track.

Upon arriving in Cincinnati the next morning, I observed from a short distance, while the barrels were unloaded and brought by wagon to the loading dock. The War Eagle had arrived earlier in the day and was undergoing a cleaning of her three boilers. The river water, which is pumped into the boilers to make steam, plates the boiler with the sediments from the river. This plating in the boiler reduces its efficiency, forcing the crew to clean it. Unfortunately, the Ohio River carries a lot of sediment, so this job had to be completed every couple of days to keep the boilers operating.

The boat looked huge sitting at the levee, even with the other steamboats in town. The War Eagle, with its two side-wheels, is supposed to be 225-feet long and 27-feet wide. It looks like you could load the whole city on its deck and still have room left over. I am told that there are even larger boats due in here in the next week.

When I arrived at the boat, the colored roustabouts, who load the boats, already had a shipping order for the cargo. It was stamped, "pre-paid." The captain had decided they would load the barrels onto the ship before anything else. The barrels would be put in the lower hold, since they would not be touched until the boat reached Minnesota. I was glad to hear that decision. It will keep roving hands from helping themselves on the voyage. The kegs were loaded in the liquor storage room. Later, when I looked at the size of the room, it was obvious that this was where the ship made its money, when hauling passengers. They reserved the prime space for items that were profitable.

I stayed at the ship, watching, as the twenty barrels were rolled up to the deck and lowered into the shallow cargo hold. There was just enough clearance for the barrels to fit below deck.

The crew was preparing for the return trip down the Ohio River, by cleaning the entire vessel. I saw people painting the railings and the pilothouse. The name "War Eagle" is painted above the wooden cover of the wheelhouse that protects the huge paddlewheels on the sides of the boat.

Bayfield's Secret Notebook

Another person was painting the black smokestacks. The stacks are hinged above the top deck, and were lowered for the paint job since the boiler was not operational. He was painting green stripes on the top half of the stack, just below the decorative crown, located on the top of the stack. It must have been something the company that owned the boats requested, as a logo or identification for its fleet.

I would think the soot from the boilers would cover that quickly unless the rain could wash it off.

The man painting the stacks completed the job quickly, and they raised the stack back to their full height – almost 80-feet over the water. It needed this height to keep the sparks and hot embers emanating from the firebox from landing on the wooden vessel and starting a fire that could consume the whole vessel.

The boat, parked next to the War Eagle, blew its loud whistle. It was about to back up and head down river. I watched as it backed out without touching the other boats. This will make it easier for me to watch what is happening on the War Eagle. Within minutes, the other boat was a mile down river. I could still hear the sound of the boat. Billowing out of its stacks, the black smoke easily filled the river valley.

By mid-afternoon, I could see smoke starting to come from the stacks of the War Eagle. The boiler cleaning must be finished. In a short time, they will be heating up the boilers for the trip south. It takes a long time to fire up the boilers after a full cleaning, and loading of the wood in the firebox for the boat. Each boiler has to be hot enough to change over 1,000 gallons of river water into boiling steam before anything on the boat starts working.

Very soon, they will be loading cargo over the steel door to the lower hold. Then, the barrels will be impossible to get to, without unloading the cargo on the deck. As soon as that happens, I will not have to watch the ship.

David Fabio

There are many cabins on the second level of the boat. Tomorrow morning, I will find out which one is mine.

Now, I hope I can start to relax. My heart has been beating so hard that I hear it beat. I found a room at a boarding house for the night that was close to the river. Tonight, I might not be able to sleep, thinking about the adventure.

While I lay in bed with my windows open, I can hear the sounds of the steamboats at the levee. As they keep their fires stoked all night, the banging of the firebox doors coming from all the steamboats, echo all over the river valley, and can be heard all the way to my room.

I am too nervous to sleep.

Bayfield's Secret Notebook

Chapter 14

Shipping Out

Friday, July 14, 1865. It is a perfect morning for a steamboat journey. As I look out my window of the boarding house this morning, I can count six paddlewheelers at the levee. It seems as fast as one boat leaves, another comes up river to dock. After breakfast, I will head down to the boat and claim my cabin.

I grabbed my bag. I have limited myself to one carpetbag. I cannot make it look as though I might not be back. My partners think I am on a short trip to deliver whiskey. If necessary, I will buy clothes when the boat docks in another city. As I carried my bag to the boat, I was surprised to see many men that had been sleeping outside, waiting for the boat. It is a good thing the weather is warm. A few wore clothes that were part of their military uniforms. Some of the men were already boarding the boat. I was worried that my cabin would not be available. They told me to be at the boat by 8:30 am. We leave at 11 bells.

The boat has a long gangplank that is attached to a boom by a set of ropes. It allows it to swing to the shoreline when there is no dock. Men are coming and going on the gangplank. There are men working all over the big white boat. Up on top, I can see the Captain. He is watching, and occasionally shouting, at people on shore, to get all the wood and other cargo onboard. I saw some coal loaded onboard, also.

In-between men hauling wood, passengers are starting to go onboard. There are men standing along the railings of the second deck, and a few men and women up on the roof of the boat. As I approached the boat, I could see a man on deck who was checking passenger's tickets and assigning quarters.

On shore, I saw a group of men sitting in the shade of an old tree. I asked a man boarding the boat, why they were sitting over there. He told me they were "wooders." They travel for a very cheap fare and do not have a cabin. They sleep on the main deck. The boat allows a number of men to travel that way. When the boat needs to stop for wood, it is their job to quickly load the wood onboard and keep the stop as short as possible. It is very hard work.

Bayfield's Secret Notebook

He also told me that some of them will not make the Mississippi River. If they are lazy and do not work, each trip a few end up being thrown off the boat in the middle of the night. Usually, the captain picks a shallow area of the river, just in case they can't swim. Paying the boat's fare does not always guarantee that someone will make it all the way to their destination.

That thought does not make me comfortable. I can swim, but I need to stay with the barrels. I will need to make friends.

As I walked up the gangplank, a crewmember stopped me, and inspected my ticket. "Mr. Volker, we have been expecting you. Your cargo is all loaded. You have cabin seven on the boiler deck."

"Thank you, could you please point to where that might be," I responded.

"Yes Sir! The boiler deck is one deck up. It is the floor above the working deck and the boilers. Room seven, is on the starboard side – that's the right side of the boat. You will be sharing the berth with a Sergeant Fry. I believe he has already boarded the vessel."

"Are there no private cabins?" I asked.

"Sorry, all of the forty-six berths contain at least two bunks. Plus, all the bunks are sold out. We have reservations for the cabins that appear empty, at Louisville, for more soldiers. I am sure you will find Sergeant Fry a delightful companion. I met him earlier and he had a good sense of humor. I did move you from cabin five to cabin seven at the captain's request. Cabin five has the smoke stack next to it, and it tends to be warmer because of it. Dinner will be served in the main salon at five bells. Libations are in the saloon in the meanwhile, along with light food. If you do not mind, the captain asked that you speak to him prior to sailing. He is up on top of the Texas deck – in the pilothouse. Just knock on the door and he will talk to you, while he is supervising the loading."

David Fabio

I climbed up the stairway to the boiler deck and found my berth, second cabin from the front. Sergeant Fry had left his clothes on the floor. I was surprised. Apparently, he is a considerate man, and he is letting me select the top or lower bunk. I picked the top. There are two vent windows on top of the end walls. One goes to the outside and one to the saloon on the other side, which allows air to pass through. The room is small – it is painted white, and is six feet wide by eight feet long, with a door on each end. There is a washstand and a mirror.

As I was admiring how small the berth was, I joked, *"No 'Home Sweet Home' sign."* It is much smaller than the berth I had crossing the Atlantic. It will be home for many days. I hope Sergeant Fry does not snore.

Interior of the War Eagle

From the collection of the Murphy Library, University of Wisconsin – La Crosse

I opened the inside door to the interior of the boat. There was a long, wide corridor, which went almost the entire length of the boat. The floor was carpeted and it had tables and chairs for eating and playing cards on the trip.

The interior was lighted with chandeliers and with skylight transoms that were above the cabin walls. The ceiling used decorated rafters that supported the decks above it. There was also a stove on each end of the long corridor. I was thinking, the stoves better not be needed on this trip.

The gentleman's social hall was at the front, bow end of the central corridor, and there was a small library on the stern end. Looking at the massive corridor, I hope it would not be too noisy with partying at night. The carpet and the decorative rafters would probably help reduce the noise level.

There was also a walkway that went all the way around the outside of the boiler deck. The walkway widened in the front, on the sides in the back, and at the stern, for areas where people could sit on chairs that were presently folded up.

I went up to the Texas deck, which had only a few cabins and was mainly a large open deck. It had a row of windows that opened into the central corridor of the boiler deck for light and ventilation on each side of the deck.

The deck's slight curvature made it difficult to walk on, especially if the roof was wet or the boat was rocking. However, the curvature gave the deck the strength it needed to allow people to stand or sleep on it. If it got hot at night, people looking for a breeze might decide to sleep up there.

Once on the Texas deck, I located a person wearing the boat's uniform. He pointed me to the stairs that led to the captain's pilothouse. There, I met Captain Harris.

"Good morning, Captain, my name is Johan Volker. The man at the gangplank asked me to introduce myself to you," I said as I opened the door to the pilothouse.

The pilothouse was full of smoke from the captain's pipe. Even with the windows open, the smoke just hung in the stagnant air. The captain, who had been leaning halfway out the window, with a pipe hanging out of this mouth, shouting orders to his crew to make sure they were working quickly, turned and put a smile on his otherwise stern face.

"Mr. Volker, nice to meet you. Your coordinator gave me a letter when we made port. He was very informative as to your needs."

I tried hard, not to act surprised. "Good, is he still here?"

"No, he left right after handing me the note, and paying for the shipping and getting your cabin assignment. I understand you are accompanying a load containing barrels of whiskey, headed for a celebration in Minnesota. I was surprised, and perhaps pleased, that you are honoring the soldiers heading home, by providing fifteen kegs of whiskey for their trip home. Paying for this, and at the same time, reimbursing the boat for the money we would lose in selling them whiskey, is quite thoughtful. I figured I wanted to meet the man responsible."

I blinked my eyes. "Thank you. Please do not let the passengers or crew know that I paid for it," I answered. "There are others on the boat who might be upset for not getting the same treatment." I was adding up the numbers in my head. Somehow, Lewis Patterson's numbers came up five kegs short of what I delivered. I wondered what they had been used for.

"My pleasure," the captain answered. "Your quarters are okay I presume? I was surprised when your coordinator left instructions that you were to have a regular cabin, and not one of the two larger ones up on the Texas deck."

Bayfield's Secret Notebook

"Hmm, yes, I did not want to stand out from the other passengers," I replied, learning to be quick on my feet. "Are we stopping in Louisville tomorrow?"

"Yes, we have close to one hundred passengers to pick up there before we head down river. Once we make that stop, the only other trip to shore before hitting the Mississippi River, other than wooding, should be Paducah. We have package freight to pick up there."

I put a small grin on my face. That was what I was hoping the captain would say; just one quick stop before making the turn up-river.

The captain thanked me again for my generosity, and excused himself from the conversation. He reminded me that there was only óne hour before the boat would leave the levee. He had to make sure the boiler was up to full heat, the wood was fully loaded, and the passengers were all accounted for.

I headed back to the front promenade section of the boiler deck. I found a chair in the shade and relaxed, while I watched the final preparations of the boat. Sitting there, I wondered who my cabin-mate might be.

As I watched people carrying their carpetbags on board, I wondered if any of them might be the mysterious person Lewis Patterson had suggested would be onboard. Perhaps it would be Lewis Patterson himself.

At 10:45 am, the captain blew the whistle. It was the notice to anyone on shore that if they were not onboard, the boat was leaving without them.

The lower deck was filled to the rafters with wood and cargo. Most of the wood was stacked towards the front half of the boat. The deck extended out past the hull. By extending the deck, they increased the deck capacity. Also, the projection of the deck was used to protect the side paddlewheels from collisions with other boats or objects in the water.

There were many people standing along the railing of the boiler deck waiting for the boat to leave shore. As I looked at all of them, I wondered where they were going to put the extra 100 people the captain mentioned we would be picking up in Louisville.

People on shore seemed to be picking up their steps a little quicker to get onboard. There were five people that just made the gangplank, as the captain blew the signal for the crew to hoist the plank and release the lines. The boat was leaving.

There were people on shore watching and waving as the boat's huge bell started ringing and the whistle blew. It was a salute to the town, as well as notice to other boats, that the captain was letting them know the river was his, for the next ten minutes. As the huge paddlewheels started churning the brown water, they backed up and swung the huge boat around in the middle of the river. It was quite the sight. The black smoke and steam was pouring out of the stacks, as the captain used some of the power of the boilers, to churn one paddlewheel in one direction, while turning the other wheel in the opposite direction. The boat turned, as if it was on a turntable in the middle of the river. Then, the big wheels slowed down, and they started to turn in the same direction, as the boat started moving downstream.

It seemed like just a minute or two, but soon I realized we were over a mile downriver. The boilers had been eased down to a lower pressure as the captain let the current do half the work, while the boat maintained its proper cruising speed, downstream. By evening, the boat would be in Louisville.

My mind seemed to drift and I started to think about seeing Louisville for the last time. It would be hard to say good-bye.

Bayfield's Secret Notebook

It was a hot sunny day. I sat on the deck for a few hours before I decided to investigate all the parts of the boat. First call was the latrine. I found they were located on the sides, over the stern of the boat. Sort of an open-air outhouse. As one sat on the latrine, one could feel the cool air, from the mist from the paddlewheels, blowing in the air coming from below, and out the cracks in the door. Thank goodness for rivers. They need to move more than passengers downstream. There were three latrines on each side of the stern. One was marked "Women." So far, I had only seen five women onboard. None were part of the crew.

Water for the boat came from the paddlewheels. In a unique system, the water that was carried up the backside of the paddlewheel was captured and piped into a large settling tank. It reduced the sediment that was in the river. From there, the water was moved by pumps, driven by the steam engine, and made its way to the locations available for the passengers. I think that other than using the water for washing, I will stick to alcohol for drinking.

Speaking of that, there were many people in the saloon already. They were getting something to wet their whistles, along with playing cards, at some of the tables.

About 4:00 pm, they cleared out the saloon to set up tables for dinner. They wanted to clear dinner, before they made Louisville.

Five bells, dinner was served. People quickly filled the long tables and the crew brought out dishes of food. I sat at a long table and was able to talk to about six other passengers. We sat elbow to elbow. It was nice to meet some of the people that were heading down the Ohio. Most of the people that sat near me were destined for St. Louis. There was land that had opened up to the west, and they figured it was their turn to get lucky. They were looking for a fresh start.

Many of the soldiers who were returning from the war sat together near the end of the other long table. I looked over trying to guess which one was my cabin-mate. There were about fifteen soldiers.

We were served pork, potatoes, beans, and bread. For some of the passengers, this was their first food that did not come from a tin kettle, in over a year. Table manners were left behind.

After dinner, I returned to my cabin to see if my roommate had returned. Apparently, he had the same idea. I introduced myself. "Hello, you must be my travel companion," I told him. "My name is Johan Volker."

"Well, Johan Volker, I'm glad to meet you. My name is Sergeant Fry. I hear we will be good friends by the time we hit Minnesota," he said.

I apologized. "I hope you do not mind, I put my things on the top bunk. I figured that since you had boarded the boat first and had not claimed a bunk, you were letting me choose."

"You figured right. Actually, if the weather is good, I thought I might sleep out on the top deck, some of the nights. I'm not sure if this hunk of wood will cool down, or stay hotter than a brick in the sunlight, with that boiler heated up on the first deck and those big tin cans radiating heat, with all the smoke pouring from them."

I could see he had a sense of humor. He was a short man, about five foot five inches, balding head, and walked with a noticeable limp. He noticed my glance at his leg as he walked into the room.

"Logging accident. Stack shifted when I was counting logs and I was not fast enough to get out of the way. Broke it in two places," he told me. "Kept me out of the infantry. I was a supply sergeant during the war. They gave me my papers last week, and I am heading home."

"Where might that be?" I asked him.

Bayfield's Secret Notebook

"Winona, Minnesota. First big town you hit in Minnesota heading up river," Fry answered. How about you? What brings you to the frontier?"

I paused at that last comment. "My brother has been asking me to join him in Still Water. He is a brewmaster there and says it is just like Germany."

"You mean Stillwater," he corrected me. "It is just one word. Know the town well. I did some lumbering up there before the war."

"Good! Maybe you can tell me more about Stillwater, while we are on the boat. I really do not know very much about it."

We talked for a couple minutes, and then went out on the deck by the railing, found a comfortable chair, and waited for the boat to reach Louisville. He seemed like a nice man. He told me that he was made sergeant just a couple months ago when the supply sergeant they had, reached the end of his three-year enlistment.

I told him I had worked in distilleries in Germany before coming to the United States. I worked for Boone County Distillery for many years and started a new distillery in Louisville, with some partners, a few years ago. Now, I was going to help my brother in Minnesota.

*****

Vivian and Barbara sat there most of the afternoon listening to the tale that Stan developed by putting together a combination of the lines in the notebook and the information he found on the internet, about the same period. Stan wondered how they would react when he shifted the story from journal entries to a story about Johan Volker.

"You are quite the writer," Vivian interrupted. "I'm impressed with the story you have made it into. I do have a question for you. Why did they take the riverboat home instead of the train? It was probably a three or four week trip by boat. Couldn't they get home in just a few days by train?"

"Well, you are probably thinking of the present-day, instead of 1865," Stan answered. "I thought the same thing. Then, I saw an account from a group of soldiers who were traveling from Memphis to Louisville. They had been commenting on how the tracks, especially in the south, were in terrible shape. There had been no money or labor for maintenance for years. They said it was no better than a pair of old rusted rails that rarely ran parallel.

"The account I read, said the soldiers had ridden inside and on top the boxcars. The trains travelled at about 15 miles per hour. When a car went off the tracks, some of the people usually got thrown off the cars. If that happened, they would push the derailed car over, out of the way, and reconnect the cars that were still on the tracks. If anyone was injured, they would help them back on the train. Most of the time, the train was packed with people before the accident. If there was no room, with one or more cars abandoned, someone had to walk.

"Apparently, it happened more often than one would expect. Washouts from the creeks rising would wash the dirt from under the railroad ties. When the heavy engine came over the washout, the tracks would bend. After a few cars traveled over it, the tracks bent far enough to derail one of the cars.

"I guess they must have figured it was just as safe by riverboat, and at least they had food and a bed to sleep on. In addition, those railroad cars would be totally packed with soldiers. It might get a little strong inside in the middle of the summer."

Barbara was impressed. "You did a lot of checking to fill in all the blanks of the story. I still want to know what happened to the gold. Also, how much was Volker paid to deliverer it?"

"Good question," Stan answered. "There are some hints, but the actual amount is not in the journal. You will just have to wait until the story gets to Minnesota to find out what happened to the gold."

Bayfield's Secret Notebook

"I think it is time for supper," Barbara told them. "We can finish the story after we have taken a break."

Stan chuckled. He knew the story would take a lot longer to finish than the time left in the evening. He was glad to see that both of them were still interested, and listening to everything he said.

He was hoping it might make a good book when he was finished.

Chapter 15

Ships a Comin'

Stan resumed his story.

*****

July 14, 1865. About 7:15 pm, Sergeant Fry and I almost jumped out of our chairs along the railing, and into the river. We had been startled by the ship blowing the boat's whistle, announcing to Louisville that a riverboat was a comin'.

You could barely make out the town downriver. However, the captain knew that the whistle would carry miles down stream, and it gave the roustabouts time to prepare for the landing of the boat.

"Damn, I'm not sitting in front of that confounded thing when we are expected in a town, again," Sergeant Fry told me. "That's as bad as sitting next to a cannon. If it does not scare you to death, it will definitely keep you from hearing for the next hour. I almost swallowed my chew."

I looked at Fry, and nodded. There was no sense trying to hold a conversation for the next few minutes. I have noticed that Sergeant Fry tended to smoke a pipe occasionally, but seemed to prefer his chew. He

Bayfield's Secret Notebook

has told me that it will keep from smoking up the cabin during the trip. I was grateful for that.

When we approached the town, I was looking to see where the boat was going to pull in at the levee. There were four large paddlewheelers at the levee and three smaller stern-wheelers. We saw an opening between the larger boats, and the captain was planning to slip her in-between them. Captain Harris gave the signal to the crew and the people on shore, the whistle sounded - one long, two shorts, one long, and two shorts.

The pilot did a great job of turning the vessel around and gently bringing it up-river, in-between the two boats. The crew threw the lines to shore, and another set to the boats along side. The ropes they attached to the other steamboats would keep the current from carrying the back end of the War Eagle into the other boats, as she sat against the shoreline. I was surprised at the strength needed to handle the ropes. These were three inches in diameter and as they got wet, they were heavy.

As I looked on shore, I wondered if Lewis Patterson had his man on the boat already, or if it was one of the people who stood on the levee, waiting for the opportunity to come onboard. So far, no one had stood out as though they were on the boat to watch me. Except for dinner, no one had introduced himself, or looked interested. Maybe it was Sergeant Fry.

I looked to see if I could see anyone I knew from Louisville. So far, everyone I saw on the levee appeared to be traveling through town to catch the boat.

Some of the passengers boarded that evening, the rest would board just before we left in the morning.

I was hoping to talk to Sergeant Fry that night in the cabin, but he partied late into the night with the other soldiers, who found the saloon a welcome relief from army life. By the time he retired, I had fallen asleep.

July 15, 1865. By morning, the boat was loaded to capacity. I'm not sure what was keeping her afloat. People were hanging all over the top decks. The lower deck was either stacks of wood or cargo, eight feet high from the nose to behind the side paddlewheels. There was only a small aisle left open for the crew to carry wood to the boilers.

We woke up to the sound of the firebox door slamming, as the crew was stoking up the boilers for a good hot head of steam. Well, maybe I should say I woke up. I'm not sure if Sergeant Fry was fully awake, or just walking in his sleep. The night before was definitely dragging on his enthusiasm. He looked like a dog with his tail between his legs. We had just started to talk when the captain let out a long burst of the whistle. It was almost directly above our cabin. That rattled the cobwebs out of Fry's head. He looked totally dazed.

The whistle indicated that we had only 15-minutes until we left the levee.

Sergeant Fry and I cleaned up, and strolled out onto the deck to see the boat leave Louisville. I looked to see if I could find any of my old friends on shore. Except for my partners, no one knew I was on the boat. I was hoping that Josh and Horace were hard at work. I did not see them, as I watched the roustabouts rushing to make sure the last of the wood was piled high on the front deck.

Sergeant Fry turned to me and asked, "You know why they put all that wood on the nose of the boat?"

I must have looked puzzled, I really had not thought about it. "No, why?"

"As we head down river, the wood stacked on the bow will be the first wood they will use. It will leave the nose slightly lighter than the rest of the boat so it will rise slightly. As we pick up speed, the waves will not splash over the front, and if there is something in the water, with any luck, we will glance off of it, rather than splitting the boat in two."

What an awesome thought. "Does that happen very often?" I asked Sergeant Fry.

"More often than the boat captain would like you to know," he answered. "Before the war, when I was in Minnesota, I used to work with the riverboats, moving logs down river. Now, the Mississippi is shallower than the Ohio in a number of spots. But, when storms come and drop an 80-foot tree along the banks and into the river, you never know where down river you might run into it. The boats always carried a few extra planks, just in case they hit something and had to put her up on a sand bar for repairs. My guess is that the Ohio has the same problem. We would usually let someone know about problems, when we made the next stop, and have someone haul the obstacles out of the main river channel with a team of horses. However, for the first boats out in the spring, or when it was flood time and things were rushing down river; we had to keep a sharp watch for every swirl in the water, assuming something large might be just under the surface. That's why the boats don't run at night. It takes a foolish captain to risk the boat and cargo at night, just to make up some extra time."

"So, what did you do, did you run the boats?" I asked.

"No, just like in the war, I was in charge of supplies. I worked for a mill. It was my job to keep track of the logs we received, who we shipped the lumber to, pay the workers, pay for repairs, and pay the boats that floated the logs. Every once in awhile, I needed to head up to Stillwater to talk to the loggers, or head down to La Crosse to purchase supplies.

"I would usually ride in the pilothouse with the captains of the boats, since they all knew me and knew I was the one that paid them. It was a great working relationship and I really loved being on the river. If it was not for my job, I would probably have been a boat captain. I guess that is why the army put me in charge of supplies, when I enlisted last year. They needed replacements for the volunteers that signed up in '61.' My friend and I had seen all the stories in the paper about the local war hero's, and foolishly, we both agreed to sign up. The war had put a huge dent in the logging business with all the big boats being used to supply the war effort."

Just then, the whistle sounded and the ship's bell started clanging. The boat was pulling out and starting its long journey down the Ohio.

I was relieved, and yet disappointed. It appeared that Sergeant Fry had a great excuse for not being my watchdog. Lewis Patterson was good, but not that good. It would have been a hard reach to find someone in Minnesota, and to have them join the army, just to be discharged to follow me north. No, Fry was not the man. Someone else on the boat must be the person. That is "if" there is someone else.

Sunday, July 16, 1865. In the morning, I was surprised to see that we were not in any hurry to leave the shoreline. We were still tied-up to the same tree, and the crew did not seem to be working to get the boat out in the river.

When I woke Sergeant Fry, he told me, "Do not to worry, it is Sunday."

"So, you mean the boat does not run on Sundays?" I asked.

"That's right. Most of the river pilots are either highly superstitious or religious. Either way, they do not want to tempt fate by running the river on a Sunday."

"Sergeant Fry, why?"

"Well, if you really knew how dangerous the river is, as far as missing all the sandbars and snags, you would know that the pilots do not want to tempt God, by running on Sundays. I am not sure that God would hit the boat with a lightning bolt, if they did. However, these men

Bayfield's Secret Notebook

push their luck everyday and realize that if the boat goes down, they might lose their job. They are a very religious group."

"Should we be worried, as we travel up river?"

"No, I do not think so. Captain Harris is a very respected captain. I am sure the pair of pilots he has, are experts on river travel as well. I have been on his boats before. Unless he is racing another boat on the river, he is very conservative. If he is racing another riverboat, that's another situation. Keep near the front railing just in case the boiler blows. That way you can jump into the river."

"Sergeant Fry, have you ever been on a boat that blew a boiler?"

"No! However, I have seen a couple that blew. Relax, we'll make Minnesota."

The two of us took our time getting up that morning and found that the crew was planning a short service on shore later in the morning.

In the afternoon, the crew did a quick cleaning of the boilers to remove the sediment. During that time, they had dropped the stacks and cleaned the ship's symbols as the owners had instructed. Sergeant Fry informed me that most captains will not allow any work on the boat on Sunday. Captain Harris is not as strict on that account. He figures staying off the river is enough.

I spent the rest of the afternoon updating my journal, while sitting along the banks of the Mississippi River, in the shade of an old cottonwood tree. Many of the other passengers used the time wisely, by going for a walk on dry land, or swimming in the river.

July 17, 1865. Monday morning brought river travel as usual. I woke to the sound of firebox doors slamming, and the captain shouting to crewmembers on shore to release the lines. If that had not awaken me, the clanging of the ship's bell and whistle, would have finished my dreams. We were back on the river at sunrise. Except for the occasional boat heading the other way, the river was becoming rather monotonous.

I looked up at the stacks later in the morning, when we were underway. Once again, the green stripes were visible and the black smoke was streaming across the river, leaving us with clean air.

We headed in for some breakfast – biscuits, grits and gravy. When we opened the door, the room was packed with people. It was obvious that the extra 100 or so people they picked up in Louisville had filled the boat. The food was no longer served on the long tables. Now, the passengers would pick up their food, and wait for a spot at the tables to open up. People ate quickly and were quite courteous about not staying at the table longer than necessary.

After our last stop, there were many more soldiers on the boat than non-soldiers. I am not sure where everyone is sleeping. However, everyone was happy about heading home, especially the injured men. Spirits are high.

As the day wore on, things started to settle down on the boat. The scenery just kept passin' by. Every four hours or so, we would stop by a spot on shore where people had stacked up huge piles of logs. The message would come from a crewmember to "log-up," and in three shakes of a jiffy, we would watch a number of men carrying four-foot long logs onto the deck, for the firebox. It did not take them long, less than an hour to stack up ten cords of wood, and we would be back in the middle of the current watching the trees and water go by again.

Every once in awhile, we would see another boat heading upstream. As soon as we saw one, we knew that that whistle would be a blowing a greeting to the other boat, letting it know that two boats were going to have to find a spot in the current at the same time. It was time to cover the ears or remove ourselves from the front deck. The river was wide enough that meeting a boat in this area did not appear to be a real problem. As the boats passed, they would give each other another salute on the whistle.

I was enjoying the company of Sergeant Fry. He told me earlier that the War Eagle was designed for running in shallow water. He said that boats made like this one, drafted only 18 to 20 inches of water, empty, and maybe 24 to 26 inches loaded. Something about the lack of a solid deep keel that an ocean going boat has, makes them extremely light for shallow water travel. Instead, they used a hog chain. It was a set of rods and chains passing over struts above the boat, from bow to stern, which prevented the sagging of the hull. It acted like a suspension bridge.

I noticed that when we hit areas with more current, or where the river was wider, one of the crewmembers would stand on one or the other side of the front deck, and throw a leaded pipe into the river. It is attached to a rope tied with big knots and pieces of cloth woven into the line at designated depths. Most of the time, I would hear him call out "mark twain," meaning 12-feet. Sometimes, when it got shallower, I heard him call out to the captain, "mark one." That meant the river went from 12-feet deep to only 6-feet deep, and the captain had to worry about trees or snags as they called the depths. Still, I could not see bottom. When they put into shore, the call would be "half," or "quarter," meaning three-feet or eighteen inches. Darn if I know why they just didn't shout the real depth. It was very rare that the sounder called out "no bottom." That meant the depth was over 24-feet deep.

The bottom of the pipe was open for the first two inches. It allowed sand, mud or rock to become stuck in it. If it was shallow and a rocky bottom, the boat had to use extreme caution heading toward shore.

There were a few card games on the deck and in the saloon. Although gambling was prohibited, it did not seem to slow them down much. The games on the deck needed protection from the wind and usually were dice or some other game, when we had a breeze.

In the afternoon, the breeze was coming from behind the boat, at about the same speed we were traveling. It was almost unbearable onboard. The afternoon sun was extremely hot and the moisture was cooking everyone. The black smoke from the stacks tended to keep the boat in a cloud of soot. We kept watching for a bend in the river to change directions, and get a breeze across the boat. With the vibrations coming from engines, heat from boilers, sun baking on the roof, and the stacks radiating heat, as one passenger called it, this was – "hell afloat."

As we stopped for wood, I noticed the "wooders" were less energetic than they had been this morning.

Fry told me the easterly wind direction meant rain. I was looking at the green stripes on the stacks. With the lack of crosswinds, they are getting closer to black. If we get some rain overnight, I will have to look to see, if it washes off or not.

The next morning brought a change in the skies; the air was crisp with a northerly breeze. Overnight, thunderstorms had lit up the night's sky, as we lay tied to the shoreline. The air in our cabin changed from hot and muggy to a wonderfully sweet cool breeze, as the storm passed.

Thursday, July 20, 1865. I spent most of the past two days talking with many of the soldiers returning from their war duties. It was interesting to see the difference between the soldiers who had been in the war since the beginning, and those who were recruited in the later stages as replacements.

I noticed what seemed to be a couple soldiers on the first deck of the boat, one on each side. They seemed to be there for a couple hours and then someone else would take their place. I was hoping they were

Bayfield's Secret Notebook

the ones protecting my barrels. With the cargo stacked on top the hold, I did not think it needed very much protection.

There were only a couple soldiers onboard who had been part of the 1st Minnesota, which were in the Battle of Gettysburg. Unlike the soldiers who had been in just a few battles, these men did not like talking about the war. They had seen enough killing and wanted to eliminate it from their memories. Unfortunately, they would wake up in the middle of the night with such horrible dreams, that they would have to walk the decks for a while before they could lay back down and try to sleep. One man told me that sleeping near the boilers, with the constant noises, was easier than trying to sleep in a quiet room.

I wondered what could have driven the men to such a state. Later, I learned what the 1st Minnesota went through at Gettysburg. It was a wonder that any of the men had re-enlisted. As they put it, they had been so traumatized they could not fit in with family life, until all the ghosts were driven out of their dreams.

Sergeant Fry introduced me to a number of soldiers. It helped me start up a conversation with some of them.

I spoke with a Sergeant Stoltzman. He was from an area close to Wabasha. He told me that he was a private when the 1st Minnesota was sent up on a ridge in Gettysburg, called cemetery ridge. We were to be a last line of defense for the other troops in the battle.

"We were supporting a battery, when two brigades of Rebel troops attacked. When they started breaking through the Union lines, and all hell was breaking out, we were shooting from the ridge. As the battle kept waging, we were down to a couple rounds each. It looked as though the Union might lose the hill.

"Then Major General Hancock instructed Colonel Colville to have the 1st fix our bayonets, we were going to charge the Rebels. He hoped that one solid charge would surprise them into thinking we had more troops in reserve. It was beyond description.

David Fabio

"We had to cross 200-yards of open field. Men were falling to my left and to my right. The flag fell to the ground five times, but we picked it up and kept advancing. 262 men faced the enemy. 215 were left in the bloody fields. Of the 47 men that survived, no one deserted. All of our officers including Colonel Colville were killed or wounded in the charge."

Sergeant Stoltzman told me he was shot in the arm and in the leg, as they made their charge into the Rebel lines. Somehow, by the grace of God, they pushed them back enough to get a foothold. After looking back for his fellow soldiers, he realized that there were just a few of them who survived.

They fell back and maintained their positions until reinforcements arrived. The charge worked. The lines held. After three days of some of the hardest fighting of the war, they lost 80% of the Minnesota Volunteers.

I could see in his eyes that the scars from the battle were still as fresh as though they had happened the day before. No wonder these men did not want to talk about the war.

He also told me that he had rode on the War Eagle once before. When the Minnesota 1st was called up and left Fort Snelling, at the start of the war, they had been put on the War Eagle and sent down river to La Crosse, Wisconsin. From there, they were loaded on a train for the long trip to Washington.

Bayfield's Secret Notebook

War Eagle – Loading soldiers at Red Wing at start of war.
From the collection of the Murphy Library, University of Wisconsin – La Crosse

So far, Sergeant Fry has helped me understand a number of things that happened during the war, which I did not understand. I am glad we were assigned the same cabin.

Just before dinner, there was a scuffle in the saloon. Apparently, one of the men was caught cheating at cards. With all the soldiers, you would think the scuffle would end quickly. It lasted about ten minutes as chairs were being thrown, and many people were gathered watching the fight. Then, three crewmembers showed up with clubs.

I watched, as it was determined that one passenger was indeed shuffling cards from the bottom of the deck. The three crewmembers hauled him over to the stern railing. Captain Harris had been alerted, and brought the War Eagle closer to the shoreline. Without saying a word, they lifted the man and threw him into the churning water behind the boat.

A loud cheer arose from the people on the decks.

I watched as he feebly swam to the shore. I do not know if they asked him if he could swim or not.

I asked those around me, "What will they do with his baggage?" About five minutes later, I saw a carpetbag floating behind the boat. I think it was his.

At dinner, many of the people sitting around me were talking about the event. They said he had been cheating ever since he got on the boat. He might have been a gambler who hoped to prey on soldiers heading home with their last payment. They were surprised one of the soldiers did not get him earlier. He was lucky to get off alive.

Once again, I am very happy to be in the companionship of Sergeant Fry. He seems to know others and they protect each other on the boat.

We pulled up to shore, just as the last whispers of sunlight were lighting up the high clouds in the sky. The river valley had lost its sunlight almost an hour earlier. The Captain pulled the boat up to a sandbar and hog-tied several large trees along the riverbank. The boat sounded like a hissing dinosaur as the boiler pressure was eased down slowly. The men were still hauling wood and throwing it in the fireboxes, which still needed stoking to keep the boat alive.

There is a cool breeze tonight. It will be a good night for sleeping.

Chapter 16

Cruisin' on the River

Friday, July 21, 1865. As the morning sun started to peer over the river valley, Sergeant Fry and I could hear the crew waking up the gentle giant. I could hear the steam hissing from the relief valves.

The firemen were stoking up the boilers, and the shoremen were releasing the lines from the huge trees. With a couple blasts of the whistle, the men jumped on the gangplank, just before they hoisted it into the air. We were backing away from the shore, and traveling toward Paducah. With any luck, we should be there tomorrow.

After eating breakfast, Sergeant Fry and I retired to the stern deck and started to keep count of all the boats we saw along the water. It was one way to prevent boredom.

We watched a few people playing dice on the deck. There always seems to be a game going on somewhere on the ship.

When the boat stopped for wood this morning, one of the wooders slipped and sprained his ankle. They left him on shore. The boat schedule would not wait for anyone. If he could not work, he was not getting a free ride. Life on the river is not easy, and there are no guarantees. I found out that they only charged the man $2 for the trip to St. Louis, since he was a wooder. It was $6 for deck passage, and $15 for cabin rates for that distance. He did not get very much for his $2.

The hot sunlight of the mid-afternoon started to take its toll. Most of the passengers were either sitting along the decks on the shady side of the boat, or inside the saloon. The hot sunlight and the alcohol can take a toll on one's disposition.

It seems like every day, there is a scuffle on the boat. They would usually be broken up, and people escorted to areas to cool off. I found it was a good time for me to catch up in my journal. I picked up a beer from the saloon and found a cool place to write. I was surprised how many soldiers kept a journal of their travel. I guess it was a good way to keep one's self busy during down time.

Later, I took a break to visit the latrine. The beer had finally worked its way through my system. As I approached the stern, I noticed three of the ladies, who had the larger cabins on the back side of the boiler deck, had come over to use the latrine. I had only seen them briefly, as they tended to stick together with the two other women, and stayed in their cabins most of the time, with the exception of meals and occasional trips to the latrine.

As I wandered between the deck chairs toward the latrine, I heard one woman shouting at one of the men who had just come from the saloon. It sounded as if he had been drinking and decided that these fine tarts, as he called them, should keep the men company instead of staying in their cabins. The women were not very agreeable to the situation.

Instead of backing off, the man tried to grab the woman's arm, to lead her back to the saloon. The other women were telling him to take his hands off her. He was just ignoring them; telling the other women that he would be back for them, shortly.

Bayfield's Secret Notebook

The woman was trying to fight him off, but she could not escape his grasp.

I did not see any of the crewmen coming to help, so I told the man, "Let her go."

"Mind your own business," he snorted.

He was a well-built man, about 40 years old, five-foot eight, and maybe 170 pounds. He looked like he had been one of the soldiers.

I repeated my request, "I insist, let her go." At which time, he took a swing at me with his left hand, striking me lightly on the side of my jaw. It caught me by surprise. As I turned, he had let go of the woman, and was about to throw a right hook at my jaw, again.

This time, I was quicker. I caught his fist with my left hand, and bent his wrist back as hard as I could. He dropped to his knees trying to use his other hand to break my grasp.

I could see in his eyes that he was realizing, this was one kraut that he should not have picked on. All my years of picking up kegs and moving them has given me a lot of strength in my hands and arms.

I continued putting pressure on his wrist. I was not sure if I should break it, or what I should do.

Within minutes, one of the firemen came to assist me. The ladies had told the crew what was happening, and Thor came running up to end the problem.

He was dressed in a pair of pants that I think were colored. However, they were so dirty I could not tell. They had holes all over them from sparks. His shirt was almost as bad. A sleeveless shirt that was covered with soot and sweat.

Thor took one look at me, and asked me to step aside.

I watched as he picked up the man with one arm, spun him over to the railing, and clearing the lower deck, deposited him into the river.

This was one man I was not about to arm wrestle with. Thor was so used to shoving four-foot logs into the firebox, that the man harassing the women was no more of an obstacle than one more log to throw.

"Thank you for the assistance," I told him.

"Captain told everyone not to harass the women. Guess he didn't get the word," Thor grunted as he headed back to his job.

When I looked back, I did not see the man in the river.

The woman who had been fighting with the man, came up to me.

"Thank you for coming to my assistance," she said. "I hope he did not hurt you when he hit you."

"I'm okay," I told her. "Too much German blood in me to let him try and take you with him."

"Well, thank you anyway. My name is Miss Kathryn Bell. I could not believe that man would grab me, with the other two ladies accompanying me. The captain told us not to be alone on the boat, and to always have someone with us."

"He had too much to drink. I only hope he could swim. My name is Johan Volker. I wish I could have stopped him earlier."

"Well, thank you again Mr. Volker. I only wish I could repay you for the assistance. Maybe you could allow me to buy you a drink this evening when we tie up and it is not as hot."

"Thank you, I would appreciate that," I told her. We agreed to meet at the back of the boiler deck – near the ladies salon later that evening. She asked if it would be okay if one of the other ladies accompanied her. Under the circumstances of the past few minutes, I told her that would be just fine.

I kept thinking of Thor. If any of the ladies screamed out for any reason, could I be the next person on the bottom of the Ohio?

Bayfield's Secret Notebook

Now that the action was over, the three women headed back to their cabins. I found an open latrine and waited until I was inside, before I rubbed the soreness out of my jaw. Seeing the moving water under the latrine made me wonder; did the drunken fool actually know how to swim?

I hoped the river was shallow in that area.

When I got back to my chair on the boiler deck, Fry was ready to jump me.

"Hey, I heard about your fight back there. Was she worth it? I heard you put the guy down on the deck, with one hand. Hell, I knew you looked like you were in good shape, but he was a soldier. You rammed his right fist almost into his elbow. Where did you get the strength?

"I told you I worked in a distillery. Kegs that are loaded with whiskey and beer are heavy. All that work and my arms get strong. Still, I am no match for that fireman, Thor. Now, that man impressed me. He could probably lift a full barrel of whiskey, maybe in one arm. I do not want to arm wrestle him."

"Yeah, I saw what he did to the guy. Picked him up in one arm and tossed him into the river like a matchstick."

"Did you see if the guy came back up?" I asked.

"Nope! Hit the river like a rock. Told you that some people might not make the Mississippi. Well, he might in a few weeks if someone does not fish him out first. I guarantee you a couple things: no one is going to harass those women for a few days."

"What's the other thing?" I asked.

"Even the meanest soldier is going to stay clear of that fireman. Everyone I talked to just shook their heads, when he picked the guy up. That is one mean man and he has the name to match his strength."

We sat and watched the trees go by, and pointed out the herons feeding along the edges of the river, as we chugged downstream.

David Fabio

At supper, everyone at the table was talking about me, the drunk, and the super strongman who picked him up and threw him into the river, with one arm. It broke up the boredom of the day's river travel.

Later that evening, after we had tied off to shore, I met Miss Kathryn Bell in the back of the boiler deck. She introduced me to two other ladies, a Mrs. Josephine Kane, and a Mrs. Geraldine Lyons. It gave me a chance to get a better look at Miss Kathryn Bell.

In the rush of the earlier moment, I barely had time to see if she had been a blonde or brunette. Now that my jaw was back to normal and my head was not spinning, I could see that she was an attractive slender lady, appeared to be about 30 years old, brown hair and eyes, and about five-foot three. She was wearing a blue dress.

The other ladies, Mrs. Josephine Kane and Mrs. Geraldine Lyons, were related. They were both attractive blondes that appeared to be in their late 30's or early 40's. Their husbands had gone ahead of them and were establishing farmsteads in the new territories of Missouri. The women had agreed they would join their husbands as soon as it was safe to travel. Apparently, between the war and concerns about Indians in the area, they had delayed their journey almost two years. Now their husbands had written to them, letting them know that the farms had been planted and cabins built, it was time for them to join them. They were traveling as far as St. Louis on the War Eagle. Then, they would take another boat up the Missouri River.

I wished them good luck with the trip. It sounded like a long journey for the two women.

Miss Kathryn Bell offered me a beer for all the help I had been earlier. I thanked her. We found a few chairs in the corner of the deck, sat, and talked, along with her friends.

Bayfield's Secret Notebook

She told me that her two friends had one cabin, there were two sisters heading to Illinois in another cabin. Miss Bell was traveling by herself to Minnesota. She was a baker, and had a contract to do the baking for a lumber mill in Minnesota. They were paying for her boat fare.

"Where is it located?" I asked.

"My uncle owns a mill in Stillwater," she replied. "He requested that I join him. "He told me that feeding the men is a requirement in keeping the good workers on the logging booms. The war has caused too many problems in Indiana, so I decided to join him. He told me that the men outnumber the women ten to one. I told him that is good, it takes 50 of them to find one good one."

I laughed. "I guess that man this afternoon wasn't one of your choices."

"I feel sorry for him, now. At the time, I was glad they threw him overboard. He had no manners," she answered.

"I think a lot of people on this boat are carrying a lot of problems with them. Alcohol is probably their way of forgetting them. I hope you still feel safe?"

She showed me a small derringer she carried. "Oh, I think I can take care of myself. I am thankful for your assistance, but if you had not come along, he might have been missing a few toes."

"You need to aim a little higher. If you shot him in the foot, he could have broke your jaw with his backhand. He was quite strong."

"I noticed you didn't have a problem with him. And that crewman, he just picked him up like a rag-doll and threw him over the rail."

"Just a suggestion, if you plan on shooting, make sure you hit someone, so that they will not get back up," I told her.

I was wondering how many others on the boat had guns. Passengers were supposed to turn them into the crew for holding, when they boarded. Just as Kathryn Bell had kept a gun, my roommate had one in his grip as well.

We sat and talked for almost an hour before heading back to our cabins. I enjoyed talking to someone other than soldiers. She seemed like a very nice lady.

Sergeant Fry was back in the cabin early tonight. He gave me a hard time when I returned. Told me he had five dollars on the bet that the crew would toss me off the boat for harassing the ladies. He said he even offered Thor two of those dollars, to get the job done.

I told him he was just jealous, no one was buying him a beer.

*****

Vivian commented to Stan, "You make it sound like river-life was rather brutal and perhaps unfair. If you cheat at cards, they put you off in shallow water, to make sure you do not drown. However, if you get aggressive with the women, your life does not matter. That is a little different from the present day. Too bad that standard did not last. Maybe some men would be a little more considerate of women."

Barbara gave her a stare. She knew that Vivian's comment was addressed to people like Barbara's first husband. However, she was right; the respect for life on the river seemed a little short, especially for a soldier returning from war with a little too much liquor in him. They could have at least put him off on shore.

"You have to remember, the captain's rules are the only rules on a riverboat. Once the example was set, the whole boat knew what to expect. Right or wrong, it sent the message. It was no different from what they expected from their military commanders," Stan answered.

Bayfield's Secret Notebook

Chapter 17

Paducah

Saturday, July 22, 1865. About 10:30 the next morning, we heard the whistle. It was blowing the "I'm a comin'" salute to the shore workers. We must be approaching Paducah.

The Kentucky River meets the mighty Ohio just before Paducah. As a result, the river is wide. We pulled into the levee along side a number of riverboats. I asked the crewman, "How long are we stopping?" He replied, "We'll be leaving at 1:00 pm." That meant that I had time to get off the boat, stretch my legs, and buy some clothes, before it left.

Earlier this morning, before we got to Paducah, I wrote a letter to my partners back in Louisville.

Dear Josh and Horace,
In the past couple of weeks, I have thought about joining my brother in Minnesota, and starting a new distillery. On the trip down river, I thought it over and decided to join him.

David Fabio

I want to thank you for all the help you have been in establishing our distillery.

As such, I am enclosing a notarized title to the distillery in which I am selling my share evenly to the two of you. I will keep the final payment for the delivery of the whiskey in my possession, as my payment for the business. I have already paid for the barrels and whiskey, so you will not be receiving any bills for the cargo.

Please show this letter to our banker. He will transfer the balance of the business account into your names.

I would like to thank you for all the help you have given me, and for your friendship.

If de go'd Lord's willing and de crick don't rise, we'll meet ag'in when we're all successful.

May God protect you and may you prosper.
Sincerely,
Johan Volker

When I got off the boat, the crewman reminded me, "Be back in time. We leave exactly at one bell." I knew what he meant. Be back, or wave the boat good-bye.

I found the post office, asked them to notarize my letter, and dropped it off for delivery. That was the main reason for leaving the boat. I hoped that the letter would make it to Louisville, quickly, and not get lost.

Then, I walked over to a mercantile store and purchased another set of clothes, including a new pair of shoes. As I left the store, the clerk told me, "Y'all come back now."

Bayfield's Secret Notebook

I stopped and realized that it would not be long before I reached new territories where they did not talk like southerners.

When I got back to the boat, I was relieved that I had accomplished one of my most important tasks. I needed to close the book on my days in Kentucky. Now, I could relax, until I reach Minnesota.

Fry saw me coming aboard the boat. He called down to me. "Damn, I thought I had the cabin all to myself for the rest of the trip."

I laughed at him. "You must have been smoking that pipe too long, again," I shouted back. "What did you put in it this time?"

When I got up to the deck, I gave Sergeant Fry some licorice I had picked up in town. He looked at it and told me, "Thanks, I have not tasted licorice since I left Minnesota."

I saw a tear in his eye, as the memories of his life in Minnesota came back to him, while we were sitting, enjoying the treat. I wondered what kind of life he had left behind to be part of that horrible war.

At 12:45 pm, the captain let out a blast from the whistle. Those that went ashore to stretch their legs, or make purchases, rushed back onto the boat. As the ships bell rang one bell, he blew the whistle again, to raise the gangplank. All those still ashore, stayed ashore.

The boat pulled out from the levee, heading for the big bend at Cairo, Illinois, and the junction with the Mississippi River.

By evening, we should be on the Mississippi.

The boat was fully loaded with wood when we left the levee. With the swift current of the lower Ohio, we watched as the shoreline moved at a quicker rate. There was a lot of action on the river. Boats were traveling both ways, bringing goods downriver towards Memphis and New Orleans, as well as boats that were heading up-river to St. Louis, and points beyond.

While we were floating down the river, I asked one of the assistant captains about the story of a hole in the stack, which Fry and I had heard the day before.

He told me, "You know river travel is not that boring all the time. At the battle at Shiloh, in 1862, we were carrying troops and stopped for woodin. We caught some gunfire. Next thing you know, someone had shot a small cannonball right through one of the stacks. It looked as though someone had shot at the stack for some contest, and hit it squarely. The Rebels were hiding in the trees, on the banks of the river. We had a small cannon on board and had to use it to defend the boat. We patched all the holes in the wood. Captain left the stack for a while, as a reminder to the crew that we have to be on guard for people who don't like a Yankee boat traveling through their waters, until we were in a safe port and had a chance to weld in some patches."

"Is that the only time you were fired upon?" I asked.

"No, we have been in the middle of conflicts a couple of times. Fortunately, we have not seen anything too serious."

"Well, with all the soldiers on board, I don't think anyone will try that again," I told him.

He laughed. "Here's hoping for an uneventful trip," he said as he headed up to the pilothouse.

I turned and asked Fry if he knew how to fire a cannon.

He said he did not need one; he would just aim that damn whistle at the shoreline and break all their eardrums. If they were smart, they would just give up.

We reached Cairo, Illinois at dinnertime. Since we did not have to drop off or pick up cargo, the captain did not put in at the levee. He

Bayfield's Secret Notebook

knew he could pickup wood up-river, after they made the bend into the Mississippi.

When we made the bend, we could feel the difference in the boat. Heading up-river, the boilers were fired-up to buck the swifter current. It felt as though the boat slowed to a crawl, as we met the five mile per hour current, with lots of waves in the main channel. The huge paddlewheels were churning up the dark river water, and the whole boat seemed to vibrate as we headed north.

About two hours later, we stopped to wood-up. I heard the crew talking about stacking it up to the rafters, so that they could make Cape Girardeau, Missouri in two days.

I wondered where all the wood was coming from. There were huge stacks of wood every once in awhile along the river. Sometimes it was stacked in rafts that could be towed along and then released after they had been emptied. The people on shore would pick up the raft and re-load it. Occasionally, the crew would leave food in exchange for the wood. Other times, they must have paid for the wood. I was not sure how the payments were made.

We found a sheltered area to shore-up for the night. The captain knew of a spot where a small stream came in. It had a small island protecting the area, which sheltered the boat from the current. We headed in, and tied-off for the night.

I saw Miss Kathryn Bell and the other women heading back to the latrine. I decided to wait by the side of the ship to talk to her when they headed back to their cabin areas.

When she came around the corner, she put a smile on her face when she saw me standing near the deck chairs. "Mr. Volker, I hope you had an enjoyable day."

"Yes, it was very pleasant. Did you get a good breeze all day," I asked her.

"Yes, it is very pleasant near the back deck today. Would you like to join us on the deck?"

I joined the ladies as they found an area on the back side of the Boiler deck to sit and enjoy the cool evening breeze. After while, the other ladies retired and left the two of us to talk. Apparently, Kathryn Bell felt safe on her corner of the deck, talking with a man. With the other women's cabins near by, she knew she could call out for help, if needed.

We spent the next hour talking. I told her all about my traveling from Germany to the United States. I explained how my brewmaster had received a letter from the United States, asking for recommendations for a candidate for a brewmaster job in Petersburg. I guess I was just young enough and foolish enough to leave Germany, and come to the States without even meeting the person I would be working for. I was lucky. The job was as good as I could have expected.

She told me she had never even seen an ocean. She could not imagine spending days without seeing land. "Why did you leave Petersburg?" she asked.

"The war changed things. My boss sold the business, and I realized I needed to make a change as well. Now, I am hoping that Minnesota will be a great place to restart my career."

She wished me well.

Later, I saw her to her cabin, and thanked her for spending the time talking. Then, I headed on over to the saloon to get a drink before heading off to my cabin.

Apparently, many others had the same idea. The saloon was packed.

Chapter 18

Up the Mississippi

Sunday, July 23, 1865. Sergeant Fry and I went down to breakfast; biscuits and gravy again. I had been wondering what it would be like as we headed north, up the Mississippi River. Would the menu change? It was hard to believe that we had been on the river for a week.

We spent the day tied to a tree along the riverbank.

It was a nice cool morning. The crew was talking about the next stop. Tomorrow, we would be in Cape Girardeau, Missouri. There, we would be restocking our food and fuel supplies. The crew told me that they stopped at that city because they had coal available. Since it had twice the heat per cubic-foot of storage space on deck, they would fill the two large storage bins with coal. It would allow them to travel further up-stream before having to find wood on shore. With the high water this summer, the current is stronger than normal heading up river. Several of the bigger towns, served by the railroads, were starting to stockpile coal for the trains and riverboats.

It was a cloudy day, which kept the heat of the afternoon sun, at bay. I spent the afternoon talking to soldiers. Most of them were more willing to talk about their hometowns and their travels, than about the battles. Some of the men from Minnesota, talked about a wilderness, with lots of trees, lakes, and fields that were just waiting for someone to turn the prairie sod. They also told me that many of the Minnesota soldiers who were not part of the Civil War, were now fighting Indians.

My brother has not told me about this. I spent as much time as possible trying to find out what Minnesota was really like. I was worried about stories I had read in books, that Indians would be hiding around every tree, and I would have to carry my gun to protect myself. I was quite relieved to hear that the Indian problems were out in the Dakota Territory, and the Indians that lived in Minnesota were not like the ones I read and heard about, in stories about the Wild West.

Monday, July 24, 1865. We pulled into Cape Girardeau, about 3:00 pm. The Captain told us we would be here until 4:30 pm. Anyone who wants to leave the boat has to be back onboard before the boarding whistle. A number of people appear to want to get their shore legs back under them. The longer you stay on the boat, your body tends to leave you with the feeling that you are swaying on the waves.

The people who were getting on and off the boat tended to slow down the off-loading of cargo and loading of the supplies, for the next leg of the journey. However, the captain expects that whenever the boat stops for more than one hour in any location, some people will need to get off and stretch their legs.

The boat took almost a full two hours to get the people, cargo and fuel taken care of. The most important items; food supplies, were stocked up for the next four days – until we reached St. Louis. That meant lots of salted pork, potatoes, and flour for breads. The menu had not changed.

At five bells, the boats whistle finally sounded, and the gangplank was hoisted high. Within minutes, the ropes were guided loose as the boat backed out, without touching either boat on each side. So far, the pilots have done a spectacular job of handling the big riverboat along the levees. It must have come from many years of practice. I wondered what would happen if one of the boats got out of control, while the others were tied up. With the current, it could make quite a mess trying to straighten the boats.

I watched to see if anyone came running along the levee in a vain attempt to get the boat to come back to shore and pick them up. I did not see anyone. I knew, if anyone had missed the boat, they were on their own.
If they were lucky, they might catch a train to St. Louis, and re-catch the boat there. If not, they would be looking for another ride.

*****

Chapter 19

Preparations

(Continuation from Chapter 1)

It had been over a week since Captain Travis and his men, ex-Confederate soldiers, had gotten the message to sink the War Eagle. During that time, his first team of men had worked their way into jobs at the loading area of the levee, at St. Louis, Missouri.

Sergeant Pettit and his two other companions found that jobs were plentiful. With all the riverboats heading up and down river, and now with the railroad trying to compete for hauling cargo, there was real need for strong men who were willing to work hard. They had spent the past few days hauling cargo from the boats to the rail lines. On the return, they would haul wagonloads of coal to the levee.

On Monday, they got the word; the War Eagle would arrive late on Wednesday or early Thursday, looking for a load of coal and wood. Some cargo, which was picked up in Paducah, was to be delivered to the railroad, after she docked. The cargo would be unloaded first. Then, the new cargo and fuel would be loaded onboard, before they were to haul the goods to the railroad.

Their shore-boss was very specific as to how each boat was to be attended. Since they had been seeing as many as twenty boats each day, they needed to be efficient to get the boats in and out on schedule. He kept a close eye on the new men. If they worked hard the first week, they kept their jobs. If not, well, as soon as someone strong came along, they were gone.

He had the levee organized, so that fuel and cargo for each expected boat was set out in the area where they wanted the boat to dock, hours before it came in. The captains appreciated the organization, and made this the required stocking point along the river.

On Wednesday morning. Sergeant Pettit had several coal bombs ready for the War Eagle long before she made port. He made sure that his people were on the group of men assigned to loading the War Eagle.

The gunpowder was loaded into small steel cylinders and inserted into the bored out holes of large chunks of coal. As the cylinder saw the heat of the firebox, any explosion would puncture the steam tubes that passed through the firebox. The sudden flow of water into the firebox would cause the entire boiler to explode.

He and his men had the charges hidden in an old supply box near the coal supply. As they loaded the ship, they could hide them in the middle of the number one storage bin. If they ran on the coal, which would be the easiest to load for the firemen, the boat would see the bottom of the river, a few hours after leaving St. Louis.

*****

Barbara stated, "I was wondering when they would show up in the story again. You had mentioned them earlier, and I had almost forgotten about them. Did they really blow up ships and riverboats during the war using coal bombs?"

"Yes, it was interesting to see how resourceful the South had become. They had definitely been at a disadvantage against the North in firepower. But, they devised interesting ways to keep the Union forces at bay. Remember, it was the Confederates that were the first to use a submarine to blow up a ship. They found the submarine, which had sunk, only a few years ago. Someone had shot a hole in the viewing port, before the Union ship blew up. As a result, the submarine sank in the Charleston harbor. It was amazing what they accomplished without a lot of engineering," Stan reminded her.

"What if the crews were switched at the last minute, and the coal bombs were loaded on the wrong boat," Vivian asked.

"Well, that's why they had people up-river to finish off the boat. I suspect they would have just let the other boat blow up too. They couldn't let people know what they were doing, or they would have been shot on the spot," Stan replied.

"Remember, all these people cared about was revenge. If others were involved, it did not matter."

*****

Bayfield's Secret Notebook

Chapter 20

St. Louis

David Fabio

Wednesday, July 26, 1865. As the boat pulled into the levee in St. Louis late in the morning, it was as if we had passed into another generation. There were boats all over the river. Some were smaller and others even larger than the War Eagle. There must have been 20 boats, at or near the levee.

Close by, we could see the trains that were ready to haul people and cargo to their destinations. It was so busy that it made Cincinnati seem quiet.

Most of the soldiers were heading on to Minnesota. A few of the passengers were getting off here in St. Louis. Many of them were going from one boat to another. With the confluence of the Missouri River and the Mississippi River nearby, those that were heading for the western frontiers would end up taking another boat up the Missouri River.

The three ladies who had been staying near the back of the boiler deck, left the boat to travel up the Missouri. About half of our cargo was unloaded at this stop as well.

St. Louis is an interesting city. It is very robust with many people still using it as a gateway to the west. Because of this, it has become a central point for steamboat, railroad and stagecoach travel.

The War Eagle will spend a little more time at this stop as it transfers its cargo.

There was a lot of talk about those who were heading out west on the Missouri River. It was still a very dangerous voyage along that river valley. The shallow, muddy waters were treacherous to riverboats. The river depth varied and the sandbars migrated with the current. This year, the current was high because of all the rain along the Missouri River watershed. On top of worrying about the river, the territories were still wild. Territorial fights often found their way, all the way to the

Bayfield's Secret Notebook

river. There were even stories of boats being forced to shore. Earlier this year, a large paddlewheeler hit something and sunk on the Missouri.

For those who were getting off to head west, they needed to be the strong adventurous type to survive. This was one of the reasons the three women, who were transferring to other boats, had waited a year until their husbands had established farmsteads before joining them.

*****

Sergeant Pettit and one of his men were working as roustabouts on the shoreline, waiting to assist with the lines, when the War Eagle pulled into the levee. His other man was called over, to help finish another boat that was late leaving.

As the boat pulled in, Pettit and his man tied off the main line to the piling on shore as well as the safety line. The crewmembers ran lines to the boats on each side of the ship to secure it from the current, and prevent the War Eagle from bumping the other boats, while tied up.

When the gangplank was lowered, and the captain gave the order that all was secure, Pettit's men waited patiently as people started leaving the boat. Sergeant Pettit watched and observed each soldier heading off the boat. Most of them could be easily identified by the army-issued pants they still wore. He kept a close eye on them to make sure that his team was not being observed by any of them.

As the last person left the boat, Sergeant Pettit and four other men started removing cargo from the middle, side cargo-area. The captain had made sure the cargo for St. Louis had been loaded near the front.

Sergeant Pettit was almost ready to start loading the coal and logs onto the vessel, when he heard a loud, shrill whistle coming from the boat next to the War Eagle. It was his other man. He was trying real hard not to be very noticeable as he made every effort he could, to get Pettit's attention.

As Sergeant Pettit looked over at him in disgust, worrying that he was starting to draw attention, he saw the man was pointing upward. He was pointing to the stacks.

Sergeant Pettit looked up, concerned that his man had recognized someone on the crew and it was time to jump ship before he was recognized. That was when he saw it; there were two green stripes on the stacks. What had happened? Did someone fail to send the message? Was it a mistake? Did someone paint the stacks by accident? Now, he needed to make a decision fast.

The stripes on the stack had been a signal worked out long ago, that the boat had safe passage. Now, he had to get rid of the coal bombs before someone loaded them on the War Eagle. If it was a mistake, they could still sink the boat further up river.

Sergeant Pettit waved to his man and ran down the gangplank. Before anyone knew what was going on, he quickly pulled the old box out of the area, and placed it where cargo from the boat was to be hauled to the railroad.

He knew it would be safe there for the next hour or two without being spotted.

*****

As we were getting closer to departure time, I noticed that the boat was not as heavily loaded as it was on the trip to St. Louis. I asked one of the crewmen about it, wondering if there was less cargo heading north.

"We could load the boat from the deck to the ceiling, if we wished," the man answered. "With all the people onboard, we have to cut the load slightly on the upper river. The Missouri River is high this year. The Upper Mississippi has been running low. We don't want to become a permanent fixture on one of the sandbars, waiting for the river to rise and let us free," he told me. "It is either that or unload the people and cargo, out in the middle of the river, to try to get her free."

I understood the problem. It was better to run a little light rather than have major problems. Looking at the vast river with all the current, it was hard to imagine that the channel would be very shallow anywhere near St. Louis.

At three bells, the boat's whistle sounded, and the gangplank hoisted high. The boat untied, and we started the next leg of our journey, up the Mississippi River.

*****

Sergeant Pettit and his men had to stash the coal box and finish hauling the freight the two blocks to the rail line, before they could get away and find out what was going on. If they did not, someone might suspect that they were up to something.

He sent one of his men to the meeting place across the Missouri River with Colonel Travis, to tell him what they found. Travis could send a telegraph message to his man and find out if the order was changed, or if someone had accidentally painted the stacks.

In the meanwhile, Pettit and his other man would grab the bombs, ferry across the Missouri, and ride north by horseback. They would try to meet-up with the other groups, before they blew the War Eagle out of the water. This event was not supposed to happen. All the planning they had made left no contingency for a question on the plan.

The shore-boss was surprised when he realized three of his hardest workers were gone. They had not even asked for their pay.

It took a couple of hours before the messenger got to Colonel Travis, and informed him about the change in plans. The War Eagle was already steaming north of town.

Travis wasted no time in getting to the telegraph office in St. Joseph. A coded message was sent to Louden. "Green stripes. Plan on or off?"

He waited impatiently at the office. His only hope was that Louden was at his office, and would get the message immediately. It felt like it took forever to get a reply.

Finally, a message came back from Louden. "**Remove cargo – now.**"

Something must have happened. Why did they wait until the boat left St. Louis, before someone let them know? Now, where was the War Eagle? How could he get the message to his men before the boat got to them? All he could do was to ride out by horseback, and try to get to Private McCoy's band, way up river, before the boat reached them.

There was no time for him to get to Private Scruggs's men. His only hope was that Sergeant Pettit would get to him in time.

Colonel Travis along with Sergeant Pettit's man rode north out of town. Colonel Travis would stay on the Missouri side of the river. Sergeant Pettit's man would cross the river and head up the Illinois side.

The plan had been too perfect. As a result of splitting Private McCoy's men to both sides of the channel, they would have to find both groups of the hidden marauders.

Travis figured that Sergeant Pettit was probably ten miles up-river from them by now. There was no way to get a signal to him informing him, for certain, the mission was off. He had always trained his men to make the critical decision, when the leadership was not there.

As a result, he hoped Pettit would do the right thing. So far, he had at least kept the coal bombs off the boat.

*****

Bayfield's Secret Notebook

The War Eagle was making good time chugging north of St. Louis.

Chapter 21

Shallow Waters

As the boat passed the junction of the Missouri and Mississippi Rivers, there was a line in the water. It marked the merger of the muddy Missouri with the "less muddy" Mississippi River. I looked out at the two mighty rivers and could see the line in the water extending for almost a half a mile downstream.

I wondered how they decided on the names for the rivers. With all the big rivers dumping into the Mississippi River, how could the early explorers tell which was the main river? Surely, the Ohio was huge. It had almost the same amount of water flow as the Mississippi. Now, the rain swollen Missouri River looked like it should have been the major river, not the Mississippi.

I was thinking, *"What would have changed, if the names of the Mississippi and Missouri Rivers had been switched when the maps were made. The Missouri would have made it a much longer river."*

Later in the day, it became more obvious that we had lost the flow of the Missouri. The Mississippi River was not at a high water stage. This was due to the fact that the rains had obviously fallen far to the west, and had only found their way into the Missouri.

Bayfield's Secret Notebook

The Mississippi had become a river with vast backwaters and minor channels. During flood season, when the snow-packs from up north melted, the water rose into one large and wide river. As the waters dried up in the heat of the summer, many marshes were left in the areas where the feeder channels once fed.

Now, the depth sounder was busy, not only on the bends of the river, but in the areas where the water was wide. The channel was moving from side to side. There was a constant watch for sandbars and snags in the river. When we stayed in the main current, the water depth call was usually mark one – 6 feet. This would have been a hard area to negotiate at night.

As we traveled well above the confluence of the Mississippi and the Missouri rivers, the deep channels disappeared, especially when the river was wide. Twice, we found the pilot slowing to a crawl as they tried to find the river's three and one-half foot deep channel. It seemed to wiggle its way across the river at will. The low water level was definitely slowing down our travel.

Sergeant Fry and I were sitting at our favorite spot near the front railing. It had the luxury of picking up the breeze from the front of the boat as well as the shade of the overhanging deck.

We were enjoying the wildlife that we found along the Mississippi River. There is a constant supply of ducks and other waterfowl along the edges of the backwaters.

We were thinking, with such a supply, it was too bad that we could not make use of some of the sharpshooters from the Minnesota Volunteers, and have a little more variety at the dinner table. The problem, as I see it, the captain would not allow the pilots to slow down long enough to pick up the game, if they could shoot it.

David Fabio

At dinner, we were surprised with wild turkey instead of pork. Someone had sold turkey to the boat when we wooded up this afternoon. It must have been planned. It was greatly appreciated. We guessed that they served the salted pork most of the time, because it did not spoil in the heat.

After dinner, we had a few drinks and sat on the deck, watching the sun slowly set over the river valley. The boat was heading northwest as the river curved back and forth. The setting sunlight was drawing its long shadows down the river towards the boat, as we headed into the blinding sun.

One would have had a hard time painting a more lovely setting. The War Eagle fit perfectly into the elegance of the scene. It would have been a perfect evening to sit on the shoreline and watch the bright red sun setting over the trees.

*****

Chapter 22

Fire in the Hole

Sergeant Pettit was still trying to catch up to the War Eagle. He knew that he was running out of time.

As the sun was setting, somewhere up ahead Private Scruggs and his men would be setting up on a bend of the river waiting for the War Eagle to make its presence. Since they did not hear a loud explosion, they knew it was now their turn to sink the boat.

The trails that followed the river were narrow and overgrown by trees. They were not meant to be ridden hard on horseback. Because of the constant flooding of the river, the main route was almost a half of a mile away from the river on higher ground. The trails curved with the river, and were constantly crossed by creek beds, which were fed from the surrounding hills.

As Sergeant Pettit and his assistant reached a long straight section of the river, they could hear the noise of a riverboat in the distance. His only thought, *"I hope it is the right boat."* It was probably six miles ahead of them.

David Fabio

They checked the sunlight. There was about an hour's worth of running-light that the boat could use. After that, it would slow to a crawl until it found a good spot on the shoreline to overnight. That did not give them the time they needed to catch the boat and get ahead of it. Even if they did, they still had to find their men.

Sergeant Scruggs and his men were already listening to the clatter of the approaching paddlewheeler. If their calculations were correct, it should be the War Eagle.

They had found a good spot along a curve in the channel, and patiently waited for the boat. One of the men waded out into the water, close to the end of the hook in the river, so the boat would not see him until they were already in the bend.

He found a few branches that he could drape next to his body, dangling into the river, making it look as though he was a snag that got held up in the current. It concealed the grappling hook and coil of rope he carried. An old sack over his head, with eyeholes, would make it hard for the pilot to see he was not a stump as he approached in the low light.

The spot was perfect. The channel was narrow and he could wade out and still touch bottom, close to the area the boat would travel. Now, he waited. He could hear the riverboat getting closer. The last of the shadows from the sunlight was disappearing from the banks of the river. He made sure that his knapsack and matches were just out of the water.

The War Eagle was entering the long bend of the river.

*****

Aboard the War Eagle, Captain Harris and his pilot were straining to watch the river for snags and sandbars. Heading into the bright sunlight had affected their vision, and they were just starting to adjust to the low-light conditions.

Bayfield's Secret Notebook

Captain Harris spotted the snag at the end of the bend and instructed his pilot to steer over toward the opposite side, slightly, so as to miss the snag with the side-wheel as the boat was swinging in the turn.

*****

Sergeant Pettit knew there was only one hope for stopping his men from sinking the War Eagle. He had to get their attention. Moreover, he had to do it now.

Since he was still behind the War Eagle on the river, he had decided that he would use the coal bombs to try to send a signal. If he could light them, he would either arouse the attention of the boat, or perhaps, his men. Either way, it was his only hope.

They got off their horses along the edge of the river, and while Sergeant Pettit got the bombs out of his bag, his partner gathered some kindling wood. As quickly as possible, they started three small fires along the river. Each contained two coal bombs. It would not take a lot of heat to set them off.

They lit the fires and rode away as fast as their horses could run.

*****

The War Eagle was almost half-way into the bend. Sergeant Fry and I were just talking about heading back for one more drink, when we heard it, a series of explosions.

In the river valley, it sounded like someone had set off a cannon salute. It echoed back and forth between the banks of the river. I thought perhaps the boiler blew.

Even the crew looked to see where it was coming from. They could see some flashes and smoke coming from the shoreline about a mile and a half behind the boat.

The pilot quickly turned back to navigate the bend. Meanwhile, Captain Harris was trying to determine what was going on.

David Fabio

*****

Private Scruggs and his men were caught by surprise, also. As Private Scruggs tried to peer from behind a set of trees to see what was happening down river, his man was getting set to throw a hook over the railing, and pull himself alongside the boat.

From his spot out in the channel of the river, the man could see the explosions along the shoreline. He also saw that everyone on the boat was looking to see what was happening.

So far, the people on the boat were looking downriver. It was going to be more difficult to carry out his task without someone hearing or seeing something.

As the boat came by, the man threw the hook catching the railing near the front deck of the paddlewheeler. The load of wood had protected the hook from being seen from the boat. The wooders were near the stern, behind the side-wheel, and the noise of the side-wheeler had hidden the sound of the hook hitting the wooden rail. So far, things were working as planned.

He had a short rope. Only 25-feet. It was just long enough to catch the boat, yet keep him from being dragged into the side paddlewheel. He felt the instant tug of the rope as he was pulled along and toward the boat. Now, he needed to grab the rail and pull himself up without anyone seeing him. He could see the doors to the boilers were wide open as the crew had been stoking the firebox. It would be easy to throw a stick of dynamite in and sink the boat.

He reached up and grabbed the railing. The deck was only about 20-inches above the waterline. As he slid his leg up and over the edge of the deck, he slithered through the railing.

Just as he was about to stand up, Thor came out of the boiler room to get some logs. Scrugg's man was a sitting duck. Both men looked at each other.

Bayfield's Secret Notebook

Thor took one look at the rope still attached to the soaking wet man's waste, and figured that he was trying to get a free ride. The man never saw it coming. Thor gave him a quick kick to the side of the face, and he slid back, unconscious into the water. He just dragged there like a fish on a rope, until the boat stopped to tie-off about a half-hour later.

It was only then that the captain was informed of the attempt by the man to steal a free ride. When they found the rope, which was still caught on the front rail, they found a man still attached to the other end of the line, floating in the water – face down. Later, when they looked into his backpack, they found the sticks of dynamite.

Sergeant Pettit and his partner finally caught up with Private Scruggs. Scruggs had figured that the explosion might have been a signal. However, it was too late to do anything about it. All he could do was watch as it took place. If the fireman had not come out and spotted his man, he was already considering shooting a warning shot into the side of the boat's door, to tell his man to abort, and jump back into the river before anyone spotted him. Unfortunately, it was too late.
Scruggs asked Pettit, why they had to abort the action. Unfortunately, he did not have an answer for him. He just told him, "Green stacks."

Now, the question was how to find the other team. It was dark. The next team would be up-river at a spot the War Eagle would hit by about 9:00 am. There were several spots along the river they might pick, to give them the heavily wooded protection they needed to attack the boat. But where? Which one?

The problem was, the woods also would make it hard for the first two teams to find them, and they were running out of time.

Chapter 23

The Shot

Sergeant Pettit's and Private Scruggs's men had little sleep that night. They had to find their other group before the boat headed up river, and was attacked by men on both sides of the channel. The only problem, all of the men were tired and exhausted from the experiences earlier in the day.

Now, they needed to move slowly in the darkness of trees along the river and attempt to find two groups of men who were doing their best to stay hidden. The horses were just as exhausted as the men. Long rides at full speed were not in the cards.

Private McCoy's men should be ten or so miles up river. They needed to watch for a narrow area in the main current with lots of tree cover. This was exactly the set of circumstances that was going to make it hard to find them.

If there was a lot of cover, there would probably not be a trail close to the water. Also, they had not met up with Colonel Travis and Sergeant Pettit's man. With any luck, they were somewhere in the hills looking for Private McCoy's ambush point as well.

Bayfield's Secret Notebook

As they started to move out, they realized that it would take all night just to get close to where the men should be. They decided to split up. Sergeant Pettit's men would cover the Illinois side of the river, while Private Scruggs's men would head up the Missouri side. Since the ambush was supposed to come from the Missouri side first, the odds were that Private Scruggs's men would find them first.

Either way, they figured they only had until about 9:00 am to find them. After that, the boat would be steaming past the men, or at least steaming.

So far, this adventure was becoming almost as difficult as some of the battle planning for the war. Crossing the Mississippi River in the middle of the night was a recipe for disaster. If a horse hit an unexpected drop-off, or hit its leg on a snag submerged underwater, it might get spooked and throw its rider into the current. This was another reason Sergeant Pettit and his men were selected to cross the river – they could swim.

It took a half hour to find what looked like a good spot to safely cross, where the river was not a half-mile wide, and another thirty minutes to get to the other shore. Time was not working on their side. There were no wide trails along the edge of the river. They would have to go slowly and break a trail close enough to the river that they could see or hear the water. They thought about going along the shoreline. However, the old dead trees that had fallen into the river created a problem. If they had to climb the bank every time they reached a dead tree, they would not make three miles by morning.

Private Scruggs's men were not having any more luck covering the territory. They did not have to swim the river, but the shoreline at night was proving to be a strong enemy. After getting whacked in the head a dozen times by tree limbs, they were down to walking their horses. At that rate, they would not make the ten or more miles by morning. They needed another solution.

They split the group in two. One man would continue up the river near shore on foot, leading his horse when necessary. The other three would go inland, looking for a good riding path.

If they found a wide trail, they would ride about eight miles north, and then head back toward the river. When they reached the water, they would leave one man to build a fire on the riverbank. The other two would start up-river leading their horses, until they found Private McCoy.

The fire would give them a reference point as well as try to attract attention. The men walking up river would know that they reached the spot at which the other men started. This would give them a location at which they could stop and get some sleep.

The fire would tell the men on the other side of the river where they were, and with any luck, get the attention of Private McCoy's men.

They had one fear though; Private McCoy might see the fire and head to another location further north, so that spectators did not see them attacking the riverboat.

By dawn – 6:00 am, as the sunlight was starting to let the men see where they were walking, they were still a long way from their hoped for destinations.

The man walking along the Missouri side had only made five miles. He could see the smoke of a fire along the banks up-river. It was too far ahead to see the flames.

Sergeant Pettit's men were having the same problem. Because of having to cross the river, they were actually a mile south of the others. When they saw the smoke hanging over the valley, they were relieved. They thought it might be McCoy. Then they realized McCoy would not have left a smoky haze over the river announcing to the boat that he was there. It was someone else.

Bayfield's Secret Notebook

Private Scruggs and his other man were about three miles north of the fire signal. There was still no sign of McCoy. In another two or three hours, the War Eagle would be puffing its way past the area. They needed to find them, and soon.

*****

Thursday, July 27, 1865. This morning, the boat left as usual. What the passengers did not see, was that four people had been sitting on the deck all night with rifles, two on each side, watching the railings of the ship. Captain Harris was not taking any chances that there might be others that were trying to sabotage his boat. Only the wooders saw the men sitting with their rifles.

The passengers on the War Eagle never knew what had almost happened. Word spread on the boat that someone had stepped on a rope and fallen overboard. Unfortunately, the rope had caught on his leg and he drowned. The man's body was dragged ashore and buried last night.

*****

At 7:00 am, Sergeant Pettit was across the river from the fire. He decided it was time to see who was on the other side. He walked down to the riverbank and fired off his rifle two times, hoping it was Scruggs and McCoy on the other side. A minute later, he saw one of Scruggs's men standing on the opposite shoreline waving. It was only one man.

He fired three times into the air to see if the others were close. The man on the other shoreline did likewise.

Scruggs heard the signal from up-river. It was not what he had hoped to hear either. He fired his rifle three times also, hoping to let his men know where he was, and hoping that McCoy would hear the shots and start looking for intruders. There were no shots heard from further up-river. McCoy was hiding very well.

Sergeant McCoy and his men were in position, waiting for the War Eagle. They picked an area with lots of trees and cover. When they heard the gunshots from down-river, they were on alert. Hunters? It was too far away for them to know if it was on one side of the river or both. The gunshot sounds echoed along the banks of the river.

They could see a haze down-river. It might be a fire or might be a riverboat belching out smoke. Either way, they needed to be ready. Perhaps the War Eagle had overnighted down around the next bend, and decided to shoot some game before untying. It might even be another boat.

The men made sure they were well hidden in the trees.

*****

The War Eagle was running at her normal cruise speed. The cooks were preparing breakfast, as some of the early risers were starting to move around on the decks of the paddlewheeler. With all the noise the boat made, the faint sounds of gunfire well ahead of them were never even heard.

As we went down to breakfast, everything appeared to be as normal as the day before. Oh, there was the chatter about some poor devil slipping on the rope the night before, and being dragged by the boat.

Some of the men were joking it was probably some poor guy who got drunk and assaulted one of the ladies. Maybe Thor tied the knots. That got a good laugh.

We were almost done with breakfast when I heard one of the crewmen talking to the spare pilot, "Smoke up-river, Captain wants you up on deck - Pronto."

I turned to Sergeant Fry, "Wonder what that means. Do you want to go take a look?"

Bayfield's Secret Notebook

"Probably nothing," he answered. "Sure, I've had enough grits for a while. Let's see if it is a boat or a campfire."

The Captain had a spyglass trained on the area of the shoreline where the smoke was coming from.

When we looked up at the bridge, I could see him motion for his crew to grab some rifles, they had stored on the bridge. I figured that he had seen enough action in the war that he was still a little gun-shy about unexpected people. However, this person was not hiding. The fire gave his position away. I wondered why the Captain was so worried?

As we got closer, I could see a man standing on the shoreline. He had a rifle in his hands. Probably a hunter. We were hugging the eastern shoreline giving him a wide berth. Up ahead, the river snaked around yet another bend. We slowly moved back into the middle of the channel before we approached the bend.

*****

Sergeant McCoy's men could hear the puffing of the steam pistons turning the paddlewheels. It would only be another ten or fifteen minutes before the War Eagle made the bend in the river. Everything was in place. Sergeant McCoy gave a wave to his men on the other shore, letting them know, this is it. It was the right boat.

Sergeant Pettit and Private Scruggs had watched in vain, as the War Eagle passed their positions heading up-river. There was nothing else they could do. It looked as though the boat was about to become history.

*****

On the boat, the Captain had just given instructions to his pilot about staying in the center of the channel around the bend, and told his men that right after the bend they could stow their rifles, when he heard the left side window of the pilothouse shatter. A second later, a bullet hit the bell outside the window.

Quickly, the Pilot turned the boat and headed for the other side of the channel, while three other crewmen sprayed rifle bullets into the trees along the river.

Captain Harris turned immediately and told the Pilot to stay in the middle. "Don't get trapped into running aground."

When the gunfire broke out, the military men scrambled. Shooting was one thing they understood. In less than two minutes, there were at least two dozen men lying on the deck, wielding pistols. I was hiding behind a wall.

Sergeant Fry looked at me and shouted, "That thin piece of wood is not going to stop a bullet. Get the heck out of there, and behind the bar."

I dove for the floor behind the bar for safety. Everyone was ducking for cover and wondering what was going on.

We were only a hundred yards from the bend. The Captain shouted to the boiler room to lay the coal. I saw the black smoke as they also threw in some pitch and fat, to get the fire up as fast as possible. Unfortunately, it takes a little while to build up the steam.

We were almost half-way into the bend when we saw it. Someone had lit a fire on the shoreline, and was about to shoot a flaming arrow at the boat. I heard one of the soldiers shout, "Open fire." Then, it sounded like the start of Gettysburg.

All the men on the left side of the riverboat started shooting at the area near the fire, trying to hit anyone that might shoot at the boat. With rifles in their trained hands, it would have been an easy shot. However, with the accuracy of a pistol at that range, it was like shooting a duck with birdshot. They hoped that one of the bullets hit something.

Bayfield's Secret Notebook

Everyone on the boat gasped as one flaming arrow did hit the side of the boat. It was quickly put out before it could cause any damage. It was the only arrow that came from the shoreline. The volley of gunshots into the trees and brush seemed to end the attack as quickly as it started.

I heard the Captain shout, "Other side, other side." From his high perch, he had seen men on the other shore, and realized it was a trap to get the boat closer to the other side of the river. His men on the bridge started firing their rifles at the men in the brush. Soon, I heard pistol fire coming from the deck of the boat, on that side as well. It seemed that others had found weapons also. The men in the brush did not stand a chance with all the firepower coming from the boat.

After a few minutes, we rounded the bend in the river and hit the open water again. By that time, the boilers were at maximum pressure and we were quickly steaming away from the danger.

*****

The three men in the brush did not have a chance. Before they could even consider shooting or throwing a stick of dynamite, the bullets from the boat tore them to shreds.

Even the other two, on the opposite shore, were badly wounded. They had only gotten off one arrow. Unfortunately, it missed the areas of the boat that might have caught fire quickly. With the crew and passengers on alert, the chances of success had been greatly diminished.

About an hour later, Pettit and Scruggs met up with them and attempted to patch up their wounds. The men had been pretty shot up from the spray of gunfire. After they bandaged up the wounds, they looked for their other men.

When they forged the river to the small island to check on the others, they found Colonel Travis. He had reached the men from the other side, after the shootout. Travis and their other man were burying the dead in a shallow grave, which they covered with river rock found on the island.

"I hope like hell, whatever reason Louden had for not finishing off the boat was worth the price," Colonel Travis told his men. "This one really hurts." Travis told his men that he had received a telegraph to abort the mission. "Something, or someone, valuable must have been onboard.

Our signal was the only thing I could think of, to keep the War Eagle from looking like match-sticks, since we could not get to everyone and stop them. The only option was to shoot out the captain's window with my long rifle."

Travis, and what was left of his men, crossed the river and packed up their gear, before heading back to the woods near St. Joseph, Missouri. It would take a long time for them to regroup after the attempt on the War Eagle. They had lost many of their men and were in no shape to tackle a group of soldiers in the near future.

*****

"Wow, I'm glad I was not on that boat," Barbara said. "I'll bet people were running all over the place looking for their guns."

"It is a good thing they had some close by," Vivian said. "Stan, you definitely got my attention with that story. Was all of that in the notebook?"

"Yes, at least the information from the perspective of the boat. The rest I had to put together from information I found elsewhere. The coal bombs were a definite possibility, and Robert Louden was a suspect in the sinking of the Sultana. I just tried to put the pieces into the puzzle."

Bayfield's Secret Notebook

"You did a good job. Now I want to hear the rest of the story," Vivian told him.

Just as she said it, the smoke alarm went off in the kitchen. For a second, they all looked at each other wondering what the sound was. Then, as though everyone's mind was running at the same speed, in unison they shouted "smoke detector."

"Did you leave something on the stove?" Barbara asked.

Vivian jumped out of her chair. "I forgot I had a stew simmering on the stove. I guess your story was better than I thought."

When Vivian got to the kitchen, she could see that her stew had been left on the stove with a higher heat setting than she had planned. In her rush to get something on the stove that would be ready for supper, somehow she had forgotten to turn the burner down to a low simmer.

As Barbara and Stan opened a window to clear the air, Vivian turned to them, "Anyone interested in a pizza for supper? I think this meal might be a little on the dry side. I'll get a pizza out of the freezer."

Chapter 24

Calming the Nerves

The Captain checked out the boat.

I was glad to see that we were extremely lucky, and came through it. Excluding the broken window, no one was hurt, with the exception of my bruised knee from hitting the floor behind the bar.

The arrow had lodged into the side of the first deck, near the boiler room door, and had only caused a smudge in the paint before someone had grabbed it and threw it over-board.

Captain Harris considered himself lucky. As an offering to the passengers who had help defend the boat, with some form of weapons, which were not supposed to be in their hands, he offered them free drinks from his private stock of Kentucky whiskey. One drink now to calm the nerves, and another later this evening, after we shored-up.

He did not want to give us too much. He needed to make sure our hands were not shaking from too many drinks, in case they were needed again. He told everyone that he was keeping the boiler stoked to the max, to put as much distance as possible behind us. After a couple hours, we should be in very safe territory.

Bayfield's Secret Notebook

You could feel the relief spreading amongst the passengers.

I had a feeling that I had just uncovered the missing five kegs of whiskey from my list. Lewis Patterson had definitely covered all the bases. I had almost forgotten about him. Hopefully, one of the bullets did not go through the hull and hit any of the cargo.

I was starting to relax, when I looked around and realized that Sergeant Fry was no-where to be seen. It was not like him to miss a free round of liquor. Finally, I spotted him coming down the steps from the Texas deck.

"I suppose you were up there asking permission to check on the ladies," I told him.

"Well, you did not do it, so I figured it was my turn," he replied. "No, the Captain asked for my opinion on something, and wanted me to join him at the pilot-house. It appears that just before we had our little fight, someone shot-out the window. He wanted my judgment on the shot."

"Oh, I suppose your days as a clerk made you an expert? Or, did he want you to make him a new piece of glass?"

"Well, sort of. He showed me the window, and then showed me the bullet that hit the wall on the other side. It did not penetrate very far."

"Pistol?" I asked.

"Well, he doubted that, but that's what he wanted to know. No, it was a rifle slug. One hit the bell, too. Put a slight nick in it."

"Lucky shot? Too bad they didn't get the prize."

"That was what the Captain was wondering about, also. A rifle slug that barely breaks a window? And another that just dings the bell? I agreed with the Captain. His men, who were shooting at the shore, were probably scaring every squirrel in the woods. No, whoever shot those bullets was a long ways away, probably up in the hills."

"Good thing they missed," I quipped.

"Or, did they?" he replied. "I think it was a hell of a shot; a moving boat, probably a quarter mile away, with people all over the boat and no one hit. Not even the four people in the pilot-house. Heck, it is hard enough to try and throw a stone through there, without hitting someone. Besides, the shot did not come from the man on the shoreline. It hit the bell. It came from slightly ahead of the boat.

"The Captain called me up to ask what kind of gun could hit the target from that range. I looked at the bullet and thought about the range. One of our very best sharpshooters could have made the shot, but the bullet was wrong. No, my guess was a Tennessee long rifle. Some of those boys from the hills were damn good marksmen. That was my guess. I told him that if he found someone with a Tennessee long rifle, he probably found his shooter.

"We both wondered if someone had shot out the window to warn us of the danger ahead. If everyone had not gotten their guns out of hiding, we might have been on the bottom of the river – looking up. Lieutenant Palm was up in the pilot-house also. He agreed."

"That makes a heck of a story for my journal," I told him.

Later that afternoon, I was putting the story in my journal, when I saw Miss Kathryn Bell and another lady, head to the back of the boat, toward the latrines.

I waited until they came back around the corner before greeting her.

"Miss Bell, I'm glad to see you and the ladies made it through the battle this morning. Everything okay?" I asked.

"Well, Mr. Volker! Yes, thank you. Didn't even have to take a shot. Good thing all those soldiers were between them and us," she told me, "Otherwise, all of us ladies would have had to show them how good of shooters we are."

It was not quite the answer I expected. She did get a smile out of me, with that answer.

She waved and proceeded up to her cabin area.

When the boat stopped to wood-up, you would think we were the entire Minnesota 1st Battalion. The Captain had warned everyone before we headed to shore, "Please don't shoot any poor farmers that might be coming down for a drink of water." Good thing he said it. If the soldiers did not have a gun in their hand, they had it hidden on them. This boat was never safer.

By evening, when we shored-up for night, everyone had another drink, compliments of the Captain. We were starting to feel like the pressure was off. The morning activities had taken a toll on some of the soldiers. Even though they had not fired a gun at the enemy in months, it brought back the memories.

We were almost 100-miles up-river from our ambush, and starting to feel safe from whomever it was that was shooting at the boat. It had taken most of that distance, just to finally relax from the morning activities.

Tomorrow would be Sunday, and the crew and passengers could relax before continuing their journey.

Sunday morning. This morning's religious service on shore was well attended. After this week's activities, there was much to be thankful for.

The day of resting from our travels helped everyone relax before we headed for the set of rapids.

Chapter 25

Rapids

In the few days it took to travel from St. Louis to Keokuk, Iowa, we found ourselves on sandbars twice. The first mate told me that this was the lowest he had seen the river in several years. The threat to the boat had shifted from worrying about Rebels, now that we were further north, to watching the main channel.

The crew was very experienced and knew how to get the big boat off the sandbars and back into the wandering channel. So far, except for some paint, no damage had been done to the boat. The occasional gentle sand bar was far better than running into rocks or tree stumps.

We were told that there had been some talk about maintaining a four and one-half foot channel all the way up the river. Maybe now that the war was over, the government would attempt to maintain it. For now, the boats had to be extremely careful when the water level was low.

I wondered how much lower the river could go and still be open to travel by the large steamboats. You could see on the banks where the level was normally at least two feet higher.

Bayfield's Secret Notebook

Tuesday, August 1, 1865. The morning before we approached Keokuk, the Captain informed everyone at breakfast that we were approaching the Des Moines River rapids. "This area of the river is normally rather treacherous and shallow. Because of the low water, for the safety of the passengers and for the boat, I am going to make use of some of the smaller ferry boats to transfer most of the people and some of the cargo around the rapids."

He said that we would have to do the same thing in another two days at the Rock Island rapids. In the rapids, the average water depth was normally less than four-feet. To make it through the rocks safely, they needed to lighten the boat as much as they could.

Around 1:00 pm, we saw the boats lined up along shore near the mouth of the Des Moines River. The sand that was carried downstream from the farmland had made the area very shallow, and most of the boats were much smaller and had stern-wheels on them. Obviously, their captains knew there was business moving people and cargo over the rapids for the larger vessels. They had been lined up waiting for business at the levee.

Most of the people were transferred along shoreline to the smaller vessels. There were four boats that carried the 150 passengers up-river. Another boat carried some of the cargo up stream. Barrels of nails, plows, and other cargo made the boat too heavy. Only my barrels, stashed below deck were left on board. I watched very carefully to see if they would take the whiskey off the boat or not. The captain had allowed his wood stock to be decreased to about a fourth of what it was normally, and did not wood-up, while tied to the levee.

The small boats navigated the rapids without problems. They had been running this stretch of the river all summer, and knew exactly where the deeper current was.

I was nervous about the rapids. I did not know what to expect. Were there large rocks and huge waves? Would we be bumping bottom along the rapids? What if the engine broke? Would we be dumped into the Mississippi River?

As I got into the small paddlewheeler, I noticed that Miss Kathryn Bell was on the same boat. I tried not to let her see that I was nervous, as I climbed onboard.

"Mr. Johan Volker, we meet again," she greeted me. "Ready to splash the rapids?"

Those were not the words I was hoping to hear. "Yes, thank you. How has the trip been for you so far?"

"I think I will be glad to see Stillwater," she answered. "I don't mind a day or two on a boat, but I will be glad to be able to get off and walk. How about you?"

"Well, the scenery is getting better. I hope Minnesota is like this. This reminds me of Germany. We have rivers just like this that run through the country. However, when we arrive, I think I will stay on land for the next month," I told her.

As the boat started to travel up the rapids, I was glad to see that it did not have any problems.

The Captain watched the small boats. He knew that they would show him whether or not the current had shifted and where the sandbars were. When everyone was up-river, we could see the black smoke rising from the War Eagle. They had dumped some fat into the fire, to give it more heat and steam, prior to getting a run at the rapids.

Captain Harris had both pilots on the bridge with him, as he made the run. He wanted all the experienced eyes on the river.

With the black smoke billowing out of the stacks, and the steam rising out of the pipes from the pistons for the side-wheels, the War

Bayfield's Secret Notebook

Eagle came up the rapids, as though it was just another cruise up the lazy river.

When it cleared the rapids, Captain Harris gave a long blast of the whistle, letting everyone know that it was time to head back on board, for the next leg of the journey.

Within an hour, everyone was back on board along with our cargo. As we were watching the loading, from the front promenade area, Sergeant Fry told me that this was an area of the river that many passengers, and sometimes part of the cargo, parted ways with their boats. If passengers did not pay attention and strayed while on shore, occasionally someone was left behind.

If the boat had a renegade captain at the helm, once the passenger had paid for the passage, if the customer or cargo was not in the right place onboard when it was time to leave, they could be left on-shore to deal with things on their own. Fortunately, Captain Harris was not known for leaving people behind.

The travel up-river went back to a normal cruise the rest of the day, keeping a close eye out for switching channels and sandbars.

Sergeant Fry and I sat in our chairs on the front of the boiler deck watching the scenery go by. Often, we wondered how the captain and pilots knew which way the channel was coming from. There would be splits in the river, and both directions looked like it might be the main channel. If they took the wrong channel, it might end up as a dead end, or just a shallow small branch of the river.

The amount of wildlife was amazing. All along the river, we saw ducks of every type, great blue herons, snowy white egrets, hawks, and every type songbird you might imagine. I was glad that Sergeant Fry likes to talk. His experiences from Minnesota, has taught me a lot about the river. I did not know all the details about river life, until this trip. I am starting to get anxious about seeing Minnesota.

The next evening, we tied-up ten miles before the rapids at Rock Island.

August 2, 1865. The next morning, when the Captain came down to breakfast, we all knew the procedure to get around the rapids long before he gave his speech. "At Rock Island, there is a strong set of rapids, which are very shallow. We will go around an island in the river, where the Rock Island Arsenal is located. Once again, all passengers are to be ferried around the rapids in smaller vessels, and the War Eagle will battle the current and shallow water on its own."

The Captain also told us about the Arsenal that we would be traveling around on the island. "The island has been used for munitions manufacturing since 1816. In 1809, Congress declared the island a military reservation.

"In 1816, Fort Armstrong was built as part of a system of forts in the Upper Mississippi Valley, following the demise of Fort Madison just down river. Lead from Galena, Illinois was shipped here to be made into bullets. The fort had an important role in keeping the peace during settlement of the area. It also served as military headquarters during the Black Hawk War of 1832. The name of this boat came from that war. The War Eagle 1 played an important part in supplying troops for the war. When the original boat was abandoned, and the new boat was built, the name was carried on.

"The fort was abandoned in 1836, but remained an ordnance depot until 1845.

"The Rock Island Arsenal was established in 1862, and is located on the island in the river between Illinois and Iowa. The official location is Rock Island County, Illinois. During the Civil War, it was used as a prisoner of war camp."

The Captain continued, "In 1856, the railroad bridge company completed the first railroad bridge across the Mississippi River. They built a wooden bridge with five spans, and a swing span at mid-channel.

"After only fifteen days of operation, the steamboat Effie Afton, struck the bridge. The Effie Afton was destroyed. Part of the bridge was burned in the collision. This incident led to a famous court case that pitted steamboat interests against railroad interests.

"Abraham Lincoln, was a lawyer in Springfield at the time. He defended the railroad. The trial ended in a hung jury. The US Supreme Court eventually decided the case, in a subsequent suit, in December 1862, and the bridge remained operational. However, it still blocks normal river traffic.

"Just wanted to let you know that when you see us up in the pilothouse, occasionally we read things too."

That got an arousing cheer from the crowd. Now, I finally had a reason for the name of the boat. It was not named after the Civil War battles after all.

The Rock Island rapids were indeed shallow and rocky. Less than four feet of water. Just like we did at the Des Moines River rapids, the passengers and cargo were off-loaded and put in smaller boats prior to the War Eagle running the rapids.

Again, I was glad to see that neither the small boats or the War Eagle had any problems making it through the rapids. Once on the other side, the Captain gave a sigh of relief, and we reloaded the boat. The Captain told us that this would be the last time we had to get off the boat before Minnesota, unless we found a sandbar.

We were all very happy to hear that.

Chapter 26

Celebrations

August 4, 1865. Friday morning. We were tied up about 40 miles south of the Galena River, which leads into Galena, Illinois. At breakfast, the Captain came in and made an announcement.

"Good morning, everyone. I have a short announcement that I am sure everyone will want to know about. Sometime after eleven bells, we expect to enter the Galena River delta, where the Galena River empties into the Mississippi River.

"I am told that we are expected this morning. With all the soldiers onboard who are returning from duty, I expect some kind of reception from the town. So, to return the favor, I would ask that as many of you as possible put on your good clothes and be out on the deck, as we proceed up-river, in the back channel, to the levee at Galena."

The first mate told me that many of the cities were caught unprepared last year when many of the soldiers who had signed up for three year terms returned home. The hometown heroes arrived without the fan-fare and large celebrations. They realized very soon that those returning from battle deserved recognition. Otherwise, when the next call came for volunteers, people might not be willing to drop everything for their country or state.

Since that time, the cities had been doing a better job of welcoming the troops back. Even the cities where the boat did not stop would have people come down to the levee and wave. They knew a boat with returning soldiers was heading back home.

He told us that only ten years earlier, they would have travelled up the Galena River, all the way to Galena. It used to be 150-feet wide and 15-feet deep. Unfortunately, over harvesting of timber and erosion of farmland had silted in the river, and left the water impassable for large boats like the War Eagle. Only the smaller boats can make it up to town to haul cargo.

When we arrived at the mouth of the Galina River, we saw a large number of people lined up along the levee waving at the soldiers and a band playing as the boat slowed to a crawl and tied up at the levee. If any of the soldiers did not feel proud about returning from the war, this would definitely help their egos.

While I was waving, I thought about the Confederate troops who were returning home from the war. How were they received? They fought for their communities. Unfortunately, they were returning broken and defeated. Such a difference it was for them.

We only made a short stop at the levee before heading up the back-channel and into the main channel of the Mississippi River. We topped off the logs after exiting the shallow back channel, before continuing up-river.

You could feel the difference in spirit on the boat, after the stop. Men were much more talkative and smiling a lot more. I had a feeling that Captain Harris made the stop for the troops, rather than needing the stop for cargo. He seems to be a very good captain. I can see why Sergeant Fry had a lot of respect for him.

I had a chance to speak with Sergeant Stoltzman. I asked him about all the generals who came from Galena, Illinois. I was wondering if he knew any of them.

He told me that he had met three of them. "General Grant was the one that I thought was the best of them. He had a reputation for drinking too much, and the other generals did not want him to be in charge at the start of the war. After the Union started losing the battles, it was his strategy that helped turn the war."

"Is that why the South hated him so much?" I asked.

"Well, if you mean that between him and Sherman, they finished off the Confederacy. Actually, Grant was probably the most compassionate of the generals I met. Did you know that he ordered his troops not to attack homes or burn them as long as there were not Confederate troops inside them shooting at the army? He wanted to cut the support for the war, not kill-off all the people. He told me that you had to remember that after the war, these people might be your neighbors."

"I did not realize that," I told him. I did not tell him that I had met several of the generals, when I was arranging prisoner of war exchanges.

We talked for a few minutes, before he left to get a drink to help forget the war.

As we chugged up-stream, we were aware of more and more signs of logging on the river. Several times, we needed to pull off into a channel to let a mile long raft of logs go downstream. They would push the logs with a large riverboat and have a small paddlewheeler tied sideways to the front of the raft to move it right or left in the river channel. Since they had little control and they usually took up the whole river channel, we had to just sit there and wait as it passed by.

Bayfield's Secret Notebook

The other thing I noticed was a large number of cut trees that were along the shoreline, or stuck on sandbars. These were probably leftovers from other rafts that had gone down river, and could become a problem when the river rose and they began moving freely downstream.

Now I could see why Fry had told me about hitting a log in the middle of the river, and how it could easily sink a boat.

We saw lumber mill after lumber mill along the river. When we reached La Crosse, Wisconsin, it looked as though lumber mills or logjams took up every inch of the shoreline. I am not sure how many there were, but I lost count after about fifteen mills.

Where in the world was all the wood coming from? It looked as though they had cut half the trees in the world for lumber. According to Fry, the lumber business was just a fraction of what it was before the war. He said they used to run log-rafts a mile long down the river all the way to St. Louis. Now, railroads and barges were taking much of the cut wood down river.

Sergeant Fry was getting very anxious. The next stop on the river was Winona, his hometown. He was excited to get back home, and hoped that his job would still be waiting for him.

Saturday, August 5, 1865. We pulled into the La Crosse levee to unload some cargo and a few passengers. There were about fifty people at the levee to greet the soldiers.

Sergeant Fry went back to the cabin to make sure all his possessions were in his carpetbag. He also left me a note with his address on it.

While he was gone, I heard a discussion up on the top deck. One of the shore crew was talking to the captain, asking him why they had painted the stacks with a green stripe. The Captain explained that he had gotten a letter from the home office telling him that all of their boats were to have green stripes visible from the shoreline. The shore worker pointed to a couple other boats on the levee. "Do you see stripes on any of our other boats?"

Captain Harris was at a loss. He thought the idea was silly when he first read the note. Now, the question was, who sent it, and why?

It took about an hour to unload and get ready for the next leg of the journey. Soon, the bell was ringing and the whistle sounding as the boat was pulling out from the La Crosse levee.

All the people on shore waved as we left La Crosse.

Chapter 27

Minnesota Bound

Saturday, August 5, 1865. The river valley is broad and deep. It looks like the Rhine River valley. As the War Eagle pulled out of La Crosse and headed for Winona, Sergeant Fry pointed out every bluff and bend in the river, to me. This was his home country and he knew it well.

There had been a small welcoming group in La Crosse. Now, everyone waited to see what type of welcome the boat would get in a Minnesota city, greeting all the soldiers onboard.

When the boat made the bend, heading into Winona, it gave a long blast on its whistle. It seemed as though everyone in town showed up that day at the levee to greet the soldiers.

Sergeant Fry and I said good-bye to one another just prior to the last bend of the river. We told each other we would write when things slowed down.

I watched as he stood by the railing with his carpet bag and strained to see friends standing by the levee.

There were twelve soldiers getting off the boat at Winona. The city had shut down the lumber mills so everyone could be at the landing.

David Fabio

There was so much cheering that you could hardly hear the boats bell or whistle, as it approached the levee.

The Captain made sure we stopped long enough so that all the soldiers would feel that the city and state was there to welcome them back.

I gave a wave to Fry as he headed down the gangplank, and was greeted by some of his friends and family. Then, I lost him in the crowd of well-wishers.

I would have a cabin to myself now for the rest of the trip. Unfortunately, I had also lost my good traveling companion of the past few weeks.

We pulled out of Winona and headed up-river toward Wabasha. It was like a replay of Winona. Everyone in town showed up for the boat and ten more soldiers got off, including Sergeant Stoltzman.

I had a quick chance to say good-luck to him before we reached the landing.

I was waving to the soldiers as they left the vessel, when I noticed Miss Kathryn Bell standing near the back of the boat, by herself, waving at them also.

I walked back and started a conversation with her. I told her that Sergeant Fry had gotten off in Winona. The boat seemed a little empty, since he left. She told me that it was that way for her, ever since the other women got off in St. Louis.

We found chairs along the back deck, and sat and talked for the next hour. You could tell from our conversations, both of us were anxious to get to Stillwater. We were getting close, and with every stop, the anticipation was increasing.

Tomorrow was Sunday, and the boat was planning on tying-off for the night just above the landing. As a result, they had not been in the normal hurry to pull out. They took their time loading wood, and then pushed off right at dinnertime. I asked Miss Bell if she would like to join me for dinner. She said she would enjoy the company.

We went into the dining area, and found a quiet table near the back of the boat to eat. It was nice having company and I am sure Kathryn Bell felt the same way. I am not sure whom she had been eating with, since we left St. Louis. I am convinced that she was cautious with all the homesick soldiers on the boat.

Dinner was better than usual. I am not positive if it was the food we loaded in Wabasha, or the company. Probably my dining companion.

After unloading several passengers at La Crosse, Winona, and Wabasha, there were actually empty tables for eating. The result was a nice quiet conversation at dinner – just the two of us.

Miss Bell told me that she spent a lot of the trip in her cabin reading. She had brought two books, and picked up a few more in the boat's library. Occasionally, she would take a walk round the deck for some exercise, but since her companions had left in St. Louis, she had restricted her walking to a couple trips around the boat at meal times. She was really looking forward to getting to Stillwater, and being able to get exercise every day. Her uncle had told her a number of things about the town, and she was quite excited to be getting close.

"My brother has written me about Stillwater, also," I told her. "He says it is a wild town with lots of lumbermen."

"Well, I guess with all those men that cut trees all winter, the town probably gets a little wild when they come out of the forests. I'm sure I can handle things, okay," she answered.

We heard the boat's whistle and decided to watch as they tied-off to a tree, in a sheltered area.

David Fabio

After the boat was secured, I suggested that we take a walk along the riverbank and get some exercise. The shoreline looked sandy and reasonably flat near the river. It felt good to get off the boat and walk along the shallow edges. We walked until the War Eagle was almost out of sight and back. While we were walking, we saw a bald eagle fly out of a tall tree and catch a fish in the middle of the river. Kathryn said she had never seen an eagle before.

When we got back onboard, I said goodnight to her. She thanked me for escorting her on the walk. She said she really enjoyed the chance to get off the boat without worrying about other people.

As I headed back to my private cabin, all I could think about were two things; the walk with Miss Bell, and the fact that soon I would be seeing my brother.

I laid awake half the night thinking about both thoughts.

Since the boat would be tied off tomorrow, it gave me a chance to stop and reflect on my long journey, and think about what I had ahead of me.

Chapter 28

St. Croix River

Monday, August 7, 1865. In the morning, we were on the river again, or should I say on the lake. The river was partially dammed-up at the junction where the Chippewa River met the Mississippi. All the sand that washed down the Chippewa River formed a huge lake up-stream in the Mississippi. It was probably three to four miles wide by about twenty miles long. I could see why the boat tied-off before entering the lake. If a storm came up, there was no shelter from the wind or waves for many miles.

The river was as wide as it had been when all the rivers were together, back where the Ohio joined the combination of the Mississippi and the Missouri Rivers. The only difference, there was no current. The lake was wide and deep. The visible current had disappeared.

By late morning, we were once again back in the narrow river channel, pulling into the town of Red Wing, with another crowd of people greeting the boat. It seemed that each city was trying to out-do the other one in the size of its greeting. This time, the band looked like they had been practicing the music for the occasion.

About twenty of the soldiers left the boat and were instantly surrounded by the people cheering on shore.

I looked and saw Miss Bell standing by the railing near the back of the boat, and walked down to talk to her. As I did, I noticed three men, with carpetbags, board the boat. They were obviously heading up-river with the rest of us.

Miss Bell saw me coming and greeted me with a big smile. "Getting close," she told me.
"Yes, I heard one of the pilots tell a crewman that they were planning on one stop for wood, and then turn into the St. Croix River. We would be in Hudson, Wisconsin, by afternoon. My brother had told me, in a letter, that Hudson was only twelve miles from Stillwater. We are getting very close."
We found two chairs and sat and talked for the next couple hours, watching as the river got smaller and smaller. Soon, we stopped to wood-up. We could see the split in the river up ahead. Just like where the Missouri and Mississippi Rivers came together, there was a line in the river showing the merging of the St. Croix with the Mississippi River. This time, it was the Mississippi that looked dirty.

It seemed like it took only minutes to wood-up. We were back on the river and making the bend into the St. Croix. Both Kathryn and I felt as though our journey was almost over. We could almost smell Stillwater.

Miss Kathryn Bell and I sat in the back of the War Eagle, and watched as the boat traveled up the St. Croix. The St. Croix River seemed like a lake compared to the Mississippi. It was wider and deeper. There was hardly any current either. That meant the War Eagle could make good time without fighting the three to five mile-per-hour current of the Mississippi River.

We slowed for a couple shallow areas. One was called "Catfish Bar." Right in the middle of the long lake-like river, was a bend with a long sandbar that ran all the way across. The boat had to slow to a crawl to find the narrow opening through the bar to proceed. The water was so clear, with the sun shining into the water, we could see fish swimming in the water over the sandbar.

Once we passed the bar, it was clear sailing to Hudson.

As Hudson appeared in the distance, I walked up front to find out what time we would be getting to Stillwater. I found one of the crew, and was told we would be making Stillwater about 5:30 pm. As I was walking back to meet Miss Bell, I saw the three men who had gotten on the boat in Red Wing.

I greeted them and asked them where they were heading. The one man told me he was meeting with a group of men, who were working on putting the train through Hudson, on the way to Chicago. They had a meeting to discuss the right-of-way.

I told him that I was going to take the train in a few days as well. I was heading for Bayfield.

The men just stared at me. I asked, "Why? What is wrong?"

"The train does not go that way," the one man said. "They have not built that track yet."

"Are you sure?" I asked. "I was told about the train from Hudson to Bayfield, on Lake Superior."

He said he was sure. They had worked with the railroads for several years. The track to the north has been delayed by the war and so far, it leads to no-where.

I was quite perplexed as I walked back to Miss Bell. When she saw me, she asked, "What is wrong? You look like you lost your smile."

David Fabio

I told her that I was planning to take the train to visit a friend in a few weeks. I was just told the train tracks did not make it out of town in the direction I wanted to go. It was delayed by the war. My friend had told me the train would be running by the time I got here.

We sat in the stern promenade area, and Miss Bell tried to cheer me up. She told me that I could always travel by road. I did not tell her the real reason for needing the train. In fact, I was not sure they had a road that went from Stillwater to Bayfield. When I had looked at a map, it did not show many towns between the two towns.

When we pulled into the landing for Hudson, I decided to get off and talk to someone on shore, to see if the train ran north. I knew it had to be a quick stop, so I hurried off and found the shore supervisor. He told me that the train had indeed been delayed for a couple years.

I thanked him, and quickly got back on the boat.

As the boat pulled away from the levee, it passed another sandbar before reaching another wide reach of the river. Miss Bell found me, and asked if I had found anything different on shore. She had hoped I could find a sign that the railroads were operational.

I told her no, it looked like the train ran into some muddy ground in Congress. The men she saw me talking to earlier were trying to build a train that traveled from St. Paul to Chicago. So far, they did not even have a bridge.

I wondered if my brother knew about it, or was too busy working to know what was happening twelve miles down river. In another hour, I will have my answer. The question is going to be, what to do with the barrels.

Maybe Lewis Patterson will have a letter waiting for me at the landing with some detailed instructions as to what to do next.

Bayfield's Secret Notebook

I never did see anyone on the boat who looked like he might be Patterson's man. If someone was watching me, that person was an expert at staying hidden.

*****

"Oh my, can you imagine coming all that way to find out that the train does not exist?" Barbara stated. "That would be rather depressing."

"Better yet, think what must have been going through his mind as he realized that the quick end to his journey was not even in sight. He had to figure out another way to get the barrels to Bayfield," Vivian told her.

"Makes you wonder if Johan would have taken on the journey if he knew all the obstacles he was going to run into. What started out as a cruise up river just became a lot more difficult," Barbara told her mother. "Stan, how did they get the barrels to Bayfield, if the trains did not exist?"

"Just hold on, the story is not over yet," he answered.

Chapter 29

Stillwater

August 7, 1865. As the War Eagle paddled down the lake toward Stillwater, I said good-bye to Miss Kathryn Bell and hoped that she would find a wonderful job baking for the lumbermen. Then, I went to my room for the last time to gather up everything into my carpetbag, before we reached the landing.

I looked about the room, but did not see any notes from Lewis Patterson.

I grabbed my carpetbag, and went out on the front deck to watch for my brother as we approached the levee. I could see several boats tied up on shore. Lumber mills were billowing smoke from both ends of town. Stillwater looked like a booming town.

Stillwater was located at the beginning of Lake St. Croix, where the St. Croix River widened out. The water formed a deep valley as it cut its groove in the limestone hills on each side of the river.

The widening of the river slowed down the current and made a great place to locate several lumber mills. The logs that were floated down the St. Croix could easily be stored in the water, and sorted upstream of the mills. Then, they could either cut them up for lumber in

Bayfield's Secret Notebook

Stillwater, or send them down by log raft to other cities, including all the way to St. Louis.

As a result of the deep river valley, the town was built along the hillside with many of the houses perched high to get a great view and to be seen in the prestigious setting of the town.

When we got closer to town, I could see what appeared to be a hundred people gathered on shore to greet the boat and the soldiers. What a reception. They even had a small band. I searched as hard as I could, but could not pick out Wilhelm in the crowd.

The first mate came up to me and told me, after all the people had departed; they would off-load my barrels to the shoremen. They would stack them up and wait for my orders as to how I was going to move them.

That was a real concern. What if my brother was not at the boat to meet me? What would I do with the twenty barrels of whiskey?

The boat pulled in-between two other large paddlewheelers. I watched as about thirty people, including myself, got ready to exit the boat. Those that were staying onboard would be heading back down the St. Croix to the Mississippi River. The next stop would be up-river at St. Paul.

I saw Miss Kathryn Bell waving to someone on shore. I figured it was her uncle, who had come to meet her at the boat.

They let the soldiers off first. It was a fitting reward for their service to the Nation. As they left the boat, they carried two caskets with them. The other soldiers onboard saluted the caskets as they were carried off the gangplank to a waiting cart.

After a few minutes, the rest of us got off the boat.

David Fabio

Chapter 30

Family Greetings

Stillwater is a bustling town. It reminds me of La Crosse, Wisconsin. There are a number of lumber mills along the river in the heart of the town.

I got off the boat and looked in utter hope for my brother. Without his help, I would have to start making drastic decisions very soon. There was a large group of people at the levee to greet their hometown soldiers back from the war, along with giving a heart filled cheer for those still on the boat.

I was about to give up and start looking for options, when I felt a stern hand on the back of my shoulder.

"Johan, you made it to Minnesota."

I recognized the voice as I turned to greet my brother. He threw his arms around me in a strong embrace. I was so pleased to see him that I forgot to get a good breath before he almost collapsed my lungs with his strong arms.

When I finally took a deep breath, I told him, "Wilhelm, business must be good; your arms are stronger than ever. Thank you for meeting the boat."

Bayfield's Secret Notebook

"It is good to see you," he told me. "Welcome to Stillwater. I have so much to tell you. Do you have all your things?"

"No, I am waiting for my cargo to be unloaded. Did you make any arrangements to haul the barrels?"

"Oh, yes! We take care of that. First I take you to my place where we can sit and have some food."

Wilhelm had no idea what was in the barrels other than whiskey. He had arranged for a couple men to haul them up to a warehouse for me. I informed him that I really needed to be present when they were hauled from the levee. Since the whiskey was for the ten-year statehood celebration ceremony, which was still three years away, I had to guarantee the quality, including the storage conditions.

"With all that whiskey, it is going to be one big party someplace," he told me.

The twenty barrels made quite a noticeable stack on the levee shipping area. I was concerned that someone walking by might pay too much attention to the barrels. The one good thing, many items arrived in barrels and kegs; including nails, and goods for the mills. I hoped that the curious person that saw the stack would think they had been for the mills.

I watched as two men in a wagon hauled my precious cargo up the road a mile. It had taken four of us to load four barrels at a time onto the wagon. It took five trips of the wagon to get all twenty barrels to the cave. Since they weighed over 550 pounds each, four barrels were all the horses could handle at a time.

They stored them in the back of a storage building, which was a cave dug into the limestone hill. It was a cave that Wilhelm was using for storage of beer and whiskey supplies. He did not have a storage rack for the barrels, so they were left upright until we got one made.

I stayed with the barrels at the levee, until the last load was hauled down the road.

When they had been safely locked in the back of the storage area, I took Wilhelm up on the food he'd offered. By that time, it was dark and I was starved.

Wilhelm had a house in the German part of Stillwater called Dutchtown. The small white house with two bedrooms on the upper floor was located on the far north end of town, near the storage cave and brewery.

"You can stay with me, until you get your feet on the ground," Wilhelm informed me.

"Thank you, I appreciate that, Wilhelm. It will be like old times at the Boone County Distillery. I have missed the times we used to get together and talk." I was trying to figure out how I was going to tell him about the content of the barrels, however, I was too tired tonight. It would have to wait for another day.

We went to his house and had some food and talk, before I finally told him I needed to get some sleep. We could talk again in the morning.

I must have been very tired; I slept all night. It was either the sense of relief that I was finally in Stillwater, or the lack of hearing the firebox doors slamming all night on the War Eagle. Either way, I woke to the sound of a work whistle at the lumber mill. When I heard it, it took me a second or two to realize I was not back on the boat.

I got dressed and went downstairs. Wilhelm was waiting for me. He had gotten up early and bought fresh bread and rolls from the bakery in town. The smell of the fresh bread was a treat for my senses, as was the coffee Wilhelm had cooking on the stove.

"What time do you need to be at the brewery?" I asked.

"I will go later in the morning. For now, tell me about your trip. Did you have any problems getting here?"

"Oh, we had a little excitement on the way. First, tell me about your job. You said you sold your share of the brewery and now you are brewmaster at two places?"

"Yes, things change quickly in a young lumber town like Stillwater. Let me try and explain things to you."

Wilhelm proceeded to tell me how he met a German man on the boat from St. Louis to Stillwater. After getting acquainted with the man, they agreed to go into the brewery business together. Since Wilhelm knew how to make liquor, he would handle the distilling; his partner would handle the selling.

When they arrived in Stillwater, they used most of their money to build a saloon. It would take some time to build a distillery and order in the proper equipment for distilling the alcohol. By the time they had a building completed, Wilhelm's partner had run up a big debt gambling and borrowed heavily on the saloon. They were almost out of money.

"I just was not sure what to do at that point," Wilhelm told me. "I thought he could be trusted. I decided that we needed to get out of the business before I lost everything."

He told me how they sold the saloon for almost no gain after the loans were paid off. Wilhelm ended up with his partner's house as part of his payment of the initial investment. His partner took a boat to St. Paul and the last Wilhelm heard, he was heading to a town further up-river, Minneapolis.

"So, what do you do?" I asked him.

"Well, I have been working for two breweries. Another German, Gerhardt Knips, approached me. He was starting a brewery and heard that my partner and I were having problems. Knips asked me to help him make beer. Since he had the money to buy the equipment, I agreed to work for him. He bought the building and lives in the upper floors above the brewery."

"Your letter said you were working for a distillery in St. Paul also," I mentioned.

"I tried it. However, it took too long by boat or by road to go back and forth. Besides, I found another distillery in Stillwater that needed my help. The Knips Brewery did not take all of my time. I found that after I taught him what he needed to know the first year, between us, we could split the time needed to brew the mash. The town has good water for brewing. There are several springs coming out of the limestone hills. One man in town makes a living hauling spring water to people. One of the springs is behind the brewery.

"The other distillery on the south end of town, the former Kimmick Brewery, which is now the Aiple Brewery, is where I use my whiskey knowledge. Kimmick was making whiskey in his kitchen and selling it to the saloons. The year after I got here, he died. His wife tried to run the business until she married Aiple in 1860. Unfortunately, their whiskey did not taste like Kentucky Whiskey.

"One day, Mr. Aiple saw me in town and asked if I would consider working part time for him, making whiskey. Since they did not compete with the beer Knips was making, I agreed. I made some big improvements in the taste of his corn whiskey.

"So, I gave up my dream of having my own distillery, and now I work for two places. Since I own my own house, I really do not have very many expenses. I probably make as much money as I would have originally without the worry about losing the business."

Wilhelm told me he had almost enough money to pay me back for the stake I had given him when he left Petersburg. He had paid back all his loans and had money safely stashed in the bank.

"So, whose warehouse cave did we put the barrels in?" I asked.

"That's Knips's warehouse. We have been digging out a couple shallow caves in the back of his place for storing supplies. The caves work out great for wintertime. Temperature stays between 50 and 60 degrees all year around in the cave, as long as we don't leave the door open."

"Is it safe there?" I asked.

"Yes, we are using the other cave for the kegs, bottles, and other supplies. We just dug the new one this summer. For some reason, Knips does not believe in storing the finished product in caves. We are hoping to increase production this winter. I told him that I would be storing some barrels in there for a while. So, tell me the story of your trip. What are you doing with 20 barrels?"

I told him the long story about my trip, the excitement when a man was thrown off the boat, and when people tried to attack the boat.

When I was all done with the story, Wilhelm told me about his boat trip to Minnesota. He said the captain had left five people on a sandbar when their boat got stuck, and needed people to push them off the bar. He learned quickly that he had to watch after himself first.

"So, what about the barrels?" Wilhelm asked.

I was a little apprehensive about telling him the whole story. However, I figured he needed to know. I would need his help trying to get the gold to Bayfield, from which it could make it to Canada. So, I started from the beginning…

"… and as you can see, I got the barrels to Stillwater. Now, the problem is how to get them to Bayfield. Do you know how far that is?" I asked Wilhelm.

"Too far! There is just a wagon-rut trail that heads that way, as far as I know. I'm not sure I would even trust a rider and horse along that trail. You would need an oxen train of wagons to make that journey. On top of that, you might go for a few days without seeing any white folks. Maybe a half-breed or two, but that is it. If you were lucky, you might see some fur traders.

"What are you going to do?" he asked.

"That is my problem. I am not sure. I may have to wait until they finish the train.

"One thing I forgot to tell you, this Lewis Patterson knows all about you. I mean, even before I mentioned I had a brother, he knew you were my brother and that you lived in Minnesota. He knows that I am staying with you. Therefore, he may be watching both of us, until the gold is in Bayfield.

"Please do not tell anyone about the barrels, until I have a plan."

Chapter 31

Waiting

Tuesday, August 8, 1865. After breakfast, Wilhelm took me for a walking tour of Stillwater.

He told me that Dutch town, where he was living, was the oldest part of town. "It was originally called Dakota, and was part of the Wisconsin territory. They had big plans on how it was going to be one of the biggest cities on the river.

"When the government got done carving up the states, they used the St. Croix River as the dividing line between Wisconsin, and the new territory of Minnesota, in 1849. So, when I got here, the town was now part of Stillwater, Minnesota.

"After Minnesota became a state in 1858, those first couple years were interesting. They tried to make Stillwater the capital of Minnesota, but finally settled on having the state prison in town."

We walked by the limestone walls and buildings of the prison.

"The prison was built in a hollow where a famous Indian fight between the Chippewa and Sioux had taken place years earlier, in 1839, below the north hills of Stillwater. It was the last fight between the tribes." Wilhelm told me. He said there was an interesting story in just about every place you went in Stillwater.

"You would not believe the way they built that place. It is where the state's worst prisoners are sent. I heard that the first few years after it was built, if you were in prison you could just walk away at night. The guards were only paid to be there in the daytime. They shaved half of the inmate's heads to let people know they were prisoners. I guess the cell walls were made using the soft limestone of the hills that surround it. Anyone that wanted to get out, simply carved a way out"

"Did they catch them if they escaped?" I asked.

"Some! Most took off for the woods, and shaved off the other half of their hair. By the time anyone came looking for them, they had an even crop of hair on top. Finally, by 1860, they made the inmates wear striped clothes, and replaced the warden with someone that might keep the prisoners inside. He even put them to work.

"Minnesota does something strange, they lease out their prisoners to the factories. They make shingles there. I wondered who had the lumber contract. Then, when the Steven's shingle mill burned in 1861, they started making flour barrels instead. I guess that answered my question. Now, I guess William Webster has the contract and uses the prison as cheap labor for his business. Since I came to town, the number of inmates has increased from four to forty-five. I guess they are doing a better job keeping them inside the walls."

We walked by a couple big lumber mills. It was impressive to watch how they would haul the big logs out of the river, and saw them up into lumber. The downtown streets were covered with sawdust. Wilhelm told me that a mile up-river there was a spot where they had a cable strung across the river, called the boom site. They would hold and sort miles of logs in the river during the spring thaw. When the spring floods filled the river at the boom site with logs, the loggers would slowly direct them to the mills.

Finally, we reached the levee and downtown of Stillwater. There were several saloons, a large hotel, and a number of stores along the main streets. We walked all the way to the Aiple Brewery on the south hill of town.

"How often do you walk all the way down here?" I asked my brother.

"Usually four days a week. It keeps me in shape just in case I need to walk up the hill to meet someone. It is not too bad. Sometimes I get a ride on a wagon heading in or out of town."

We stopped at the brewery, which was located directly behind the large stone house of the owner. Wilhelm introduced me to Mr. Aiple. He wanted to check the condition of the mash.

Before heading back after all that walking, Wilhelm offered me a taste of the corn whiskey. I thanked him. I needed something to wet my whistle.

It did not have the full flavor of Kentucky Whiskey. However, I did not mention that until we were heading back to Wilhelm's house. Then, we discussed the ingredients that were available for the brewery.

"What do you think of Stillwater?" he asked me.

"Reminds me of tales of Germany or England a hundred years ago," I answered, "sort of a combination between the Black Forest in Germany and Sherwood Forest in England. Wonder how many years it will take before this 'frontier' catches up to the rest of the world?"

"It has changed a lot since I came to town," Wilhelm said. "It is starting to look like a town instead of a large logging camp. I'm told it is one of the most active towns in Minnesota."

Bayfield's Secret Notebook

As we were walking past one of the saloons, a huge burly man walked out. I took one look at him and stopped in my tracks. Wilhelm noticed my staring at the man.

"I told you this is an interesting town," Wilhelm quipped. "That's Sandy McDougal. One of the more famous lumberjacks in town."

I stood there motionless. The man put Thor to shame. In fact, if there were to be a fight, I would want both him and Thor on my side. They could protect me from any army.

"You say he is a lumberjack?" I asked.

David Fabio

Alexander "Sandy" McDougal
John Runk collection – Stillwater Library.

"Yes, everyone in town has a tale to tell about Sandy. Every lumberjack in Stillwater simply says 'yes sir' to him. Actually, I have only heard of him getting in a fight and causing a problem a few times compared to the rest of the lot. Probably because of his size, no one wants to be on the other end of his strong arms. I have heard stories of men getting drunk at the bar and trying to tease Sandy until he got mad at them. Last time I heard a story about him, they said he threw five men out the door of the saloon.

"They joke that he can cut down three trees with one swing and carry a pine log under each arm. Amazing what a few drinks and a good storyteller can do for a man's reputation.

"He is one of the boss-men for a crew up-river. Only comes to town a few times a month, to check with his boss, on where they are going to cut next. From what everyone says, Sandy is the best of the lumberjacks to work for. Someone took a picture of him last winter on top of a log skid, with 35 logs being dragged down to the river on an iced trail. That's one lumberjack."

I told my brother that someday they will probably make legends out of people like Sandy McDougal, and the big fireman on the War Eagle, Thor.

Chapter 32

Directions

Wilhelm and I headed back and stopped at the brewery. He wanted to check his brew, and I wanted to figure out how we were going to properly store the whiskey barrels in the cave.

Wilhelm introduced me to the owner – Mr. Knips. We did not mention the barrels. Wilhelm had told me that the owner never went in that cave, and Wilhelm had told him that he was going to put a few barrels in there that I brought up from Kentucky. I do not think the owner realized how many barrels we had put in the cave.

I was shown the beer making process. With Wilhelm's help, they were making a quality beer. They delivered it to the local saloons and even sent some as far as Hudson, Wisconsin and Red Wing, Minnesota downriver. After sampling a few of the processing steps, we continued on to Wilhelm's house.

Once inside, I decided that we needed to sit down and figure out how we were going to handle the barrels. Eventually, someone had to start asking questions.

Bayfield's Secret Notebook

We sat down at the kitchen table, to have a piece of bread and discuss our situation. The aroma of the freshly baked bread was wafting thru the room, when I noticed a note on the table. It was addressed – Mr. Johan Volker.

Wilhelm noticed the letter, also. "How did that get here?"

"Well, if I am correct, it is probably from the owner of the barrels. He seems to be able to do things that amaze me."

I opened the letter. It was from Lewis Patterson, although he did not sign it. The directions were simple – "Wait for the train."

I showed it to Wilhelm. Any idea how long it will be before they build the railroad?

"I think we are looking at years rather than days," he answered. "Once they get the right-of-way, they have to build bridges across rivers and swamps, and then lay the tracks. You better plan on at least five to ten years. Those railroad boys are fast, however, this is not the race across the nation. This is through Wisconsin. Money will come in stages."

"I think you are right. We need to come up with a plan to protect the barrels until that time comes."

The rest of the day, we bounced several ideas off each other. By evening, Wilhelm and I had reached an agreement – we needed to separate the whiskey from the gold. If anyone ever attempted to steal a barrel, they might discover what lay hidden in the remaining barrels and come back to investigate.

The first part of the plan was simple. Find a safe place to hide eighty bars of gold. Unfortunately, it was going to take more than one day to execute the plan.

The way the barrels had been made, the wide staves that held together the bottom of the barrel could be removed, and the false bottom would slide off. Once that was completed, the barrel would look like a standard barrel. Not many people would realize it was only a 50-gallon barrel, instead of a 53-gallon barrel.

We went to sleep that night thinking about the problem. There had to be a safe place we could hide the gold without having to worry about it everyday for who knows how many years.

Thursday, August 10, 1865. After two days, Wilhelm came back from work early, all excited. "I think I have the answer," he shouted at me.

"I was down at Knips Brewery and one of the prison guards had come in – a Mr. Victor Lawson. He had asked Knips to ask, if I would come down to the prison and give him some advice on storage caves. Apparently, they use a root cellar for food storage at the prison. They wanted to make a food cave, and were wondering how we kept ours from caving in.

"Well, when I went over to the prison, they showed me one very small root cellar. They said they had heard about our storage caves and with the limestone cliffs around the prison, they figured that they could make a couple caves into the cliffs to store food and supplies. When I was over there it occurred to me, where is the safest place to hide the gold? How about a fully guarded prison? "Who's going to break into it to steal something? Better yet, who is going to go there looking for something?"

"Whoa! Wilhelm, that's good thinking, but have you forgotten something? There are eighty heavy bricks that someone has to get into the prison. That's without anyone knowing about it. If we succeed, we have to have it hidden for years. Then, if all those miracles happen, we have to figure out a way to get it out without the guards seeing us."

"You got them to Minnesota without anyone knowing," Wilhelm told me. "This may not be as difficult as you think. How many shots of whiskey are in one of those 50-gallon, Kentucky Whiskey barrels?"

Bayfield's Secret Notebook

Wilhelm had an idea. With the right person inside the prison working with us, it might work. We sat down and laid out a plan; one that would keep the gold hidden, and at the same time, we could expect to get it back out.

Wilhelm felt that Victor Lawson was someone that he could work with. He had known the guard for a couple years, and knew that they were not paid a high salary. If he approached him in the right way, he felt that he could convince the guard to allow us to store the gold in the floor of the food cave.

If the caves were built under Wilhelm's specifications, he could direct the construction in such a means that they would be oversized. That way, additional construction in the caves would not be needed for many years.

To keep the food dry and prevent movement of sand into the food, a raised floor would be needed. It would allow carts to be rolled in and out of the cave with supplies. They would also need a strong door that would be locked except for when supplies were needed.

By the time Wilhelm was finished designing the cave, it was almost as secure as a bank safe, only better guarded.

Chapter 33

Supervision

Wilhelm worked the plan to perfection. Over the next few weeks, he was involved with the planning stages of the storage caves. He was so involved that the guards at the prison would see him coming and just ask if he was having another meeting on the construction of the caves. Then, they would just let him through the gate, into the offices.

Monday, September 11, 1865. After only four weeks, the plan was approved by the warden. They would use prisoners for the manual labor. Then, when the cave was the appropriate size, outside labor would be used to construct the floor and secure the lockable door and gate at the entrance of the caves. The location for two caves were marked on the limestone cliff. They would be about 50-feet apart to insure safety from cave-ins.

The biggest concern appeared to be about the possibility of hitting a hidden spring. If they did, they would try another location. They would make the caves four feet above the bottom of the cliff.

I asked Wilhelm if he had approached the guard with the concept of storing things in the cave. He said that he was working on it. He wanted to make sure that he could trust the man first.

Bayfield's Secret Notebook

While he was working on the cave issue, I built some racks for the Knips's cave, so that the barrels could be stored on their sides. This allowed them to be rotated each month.

Monday, September 18, 1865. When the cave digging was about half finished, Wilhelm came home with a smile on his face. He had spent the afternoon with Victor Lawson. It had been Victor's day off.

Wilhelm had brought over a sample of the whiskey from Aiple's Brewery and they had spent part of the afternoon checking out the quality of the brew. After a couple hours, Wilhelm and Victor had a discussion about the wages at the prison. Even though Victor had worked his way up the ranks, the wages were still less than the average lumberjack was paid. Even Warden Proctor was paid only $750.00 a year.

Wilhelm felt that it was a good time to bring up the subject of storing some objects for his brother in a safe place.

It took a great deal of talking, and Wilhelm was rather elusive regarding what Johan had that needed hiding. However, Victor agreed they could hide it in the floor of the cave. He would do it provided that Wilhelm guaranteed that no-one would find out. If they did, and Victor lost his job, Wilhelm would have to pay him for the loss of his wages. Even before Victor knew the exact item they were going to hide, the deal was struck. For $5 a week and two bottles of whiskey a month, Victor would make sure the prison would protect Johan's goods. That sum of money would almost double Victor Lawson's income.

I could hardly believe it. I gave Wilhelm a big embrace and asked him when he thought we could move the gold.

"Well, Victor had a little whiskey in him when he agreed. I think we should let him think on it for a day before we let him know what we are really doing. If he agrees, probably in a couple weeks we can move it to the prison."

At the end of the prison shift the next day, Wilhelm met Victor Lawson on his way back home.

"Wilhelm, I am glad to see you. The item we were discussing yesterday. You forgot to tell me how long we would have this agreement. Also, what is it that your brother has with him?"

"Victor, I am not sure how long we will need your help. But, let's put it this way, by the time we need it, if you put the money in the bank, you will have enough money to pay for the house up on the hill with a view that your wife has been asking for, and have a shot of whiskey each day to get you going."

"Sounds better every time you say it," he replied. "So, what are we hiding?"

"Johan's bankroll. The money he got from selling his distillery in Kentucky. He does not trust banks, and wanted me to find a safe place."

"Why don't you just bury it in a can behind your house?" he asked. "Fire will not destroy money underground."

"He got his payment in gold bars. That's why he wanted a safe place to put it until he builds a new distillery in Wisconsin." I stretched the truth a little, but figured it made more sense than trying to tell him the real story.

"It will be safer than in the church," Victor replied. "No one other than us will know anything about it."

"Good, we can discuss how to do it as soon as the caves are finished and the floor is about to be laid."

They parted company. Both men were pleased at the decision as they headed back home.

Bayfield's Secret Notebook

Thursday, September 28, 1865. As the caves were completed, the concern for water seepage was visible, just as they anticipated. The cave in back appeared to be the driest. The one in front definitely had a small flow that came out of one of the layers of rock. To make sure that the caves were usable, they dug a small trench around the inside and sloped it so that any water that came through the limestone would be funneled back into a weep hole, dug in the lowest back corner of the cave. With the porous rock layers, any of the water that was collected should follow the natural slope of the rock structure, which sloped away from the cave.

It worked so well that both caves were designed the same way.

The rear cave was completed first, so that food could be stored in the cave without concerns for temperature changes. They constructed a solid door, with a shutter that could be opened to control humidity if necessary, and an iron gate on the outside to control entry. It had a raised floor that kept the contents dry. Wilhelm reminded them that humidity was their best friend as well as an enemy. Maintaining the natural humidity would prevent the stone from drying out, which might cause a cave-in.

The cave towards the front needed an extra layer of flooring to make sure the contents stayed dry. The design called for the double floor, with a space between, to reduce the effects of the increased humidity. Since thick boards were plentiful at the mill, the top floor was to be made of 2" by 12" cedar – 12-foot long boards. They would be lag-screwed down to the framework such that any inspection or replacement could be made at a later date. Wilhelm's drawings were followed to the letter.

When the first layer was completed and the four-inch braces laid on top, the final wagon load of lumber was delivered to the prison. When the guards inspected it, it was loaded with 2" by 12" planks and some smaller boards to be used as spacers. Wilhelm, Victor, and I unloaded the wagon in front of the cave. The eighty gold bricks, painted brown by Lewis Patterson, were laid in the center walkway of the cave and covered with the 2" by 12" plank, which had been drilled and counter-sunk before it was screwed in place. If anyone was watching, it would have appeared that we had reinforced the centerline of the cave where all the carts would travel when moving supplies in or out. Later, with the aid of the other workers, the remaining floor was finished in just a couple hours.

Now, it was up to Victor Lawson to control what was stored in the cave, and to make sure the access was limited to only people he could trust.

When Wilhelm and I got back to his house, we had a drink to toast a job well done. Wilhelm had even gotten permission from the warden to inspect the caves each month to make sure that the conditions were correct to keep them stable.

"Johan, what are you going to do for the next few years, while you wait for your train?" Wilhelm asked.

"That has been bothering me also," I answered. "I can't just sit around all day. Besides, I have to pay Victor and give him two bottles a month. I need to find something that will keep me busy and allow me to watch for the railroads. What do you suggest?"

"There are lots of jobs here. With your German university education and talents, it would be a waste to see you work in the mills. The breweries in St. Paul could use your talent. However, you would probably want to stay here to watch your gold. I do have an idea."

Wilhelm proceeded to lay out a job that would use Johan's expertise and allow him the freedom to talk to the railroads. He suggested that Johan become the distributor for the local breweries to the saloons. He could market the product to the towns nearby. That way, he would make use of his talents, make contacts with the shipping people, and know about any future plans for the railroads.

"You think they would pay me for that?" he asked. "What would I use for a warehouse?"

"You would get part of the profit for anything shipped out of town. You would not ship from a warehouse. You would use their stock to fill the orders. I'm sure Aiple and Knips would love to get better distribution. I have another idea that we could use to pay for Victor Lawson. How much of that Kentucky Whiskey is committed to the governor?"

"I do not know that any formal letter was ever sent to him," I replied. "The only way he may know about it, is if someone on the War Eagle told someone in St. Paul. Wilhelm, what do you have in mind?"

"Well, that corn squeezing we have up here is okay for the lumberjacks, but I'm thinking about the rich people. We could get some small casks and tap a few gallons to sell for special occasions, say Thanksgiving, Christmas, or perhaps New Years. I know you would like to age that whiskey at least three years, but even at nine months, it is a whole lot better than anything they have here. I met a few people in St. Paul that would pay a fortune for a cask of it. If we siphoned off five or six casks, we could pay for Victor Lawson's cost for a year," he told me.

"Wilhelm, you know, I was worried about your coming to Minnesota by yourself. Especially, when you told me that your distillery plan failed. It looks to me that you got educated during this time. You would have made the good distributor. You have a sharp sense of how to make money.

"I think three barrels would make a great gift to the governor. Just in case someone told him about the gift. We can notify him that we are storing it for the State of Minnesota, and that will allow me to make some connections with the government. That leaves seventeen that we can use for income when we need it.

"Tomorrow, you can help me convince your owners that distribution outside of Stillwater will make money for them."

The next morning, September, 29, 1865, Wilhelm brought me to see Mr. Knips. We explained the need for him to increase his distribution outside of Stillwater. He was receptive to the idea, especially since his local customers were not part of the agreement. I would get paid from new business only.

Mr. Aiple was just as easy to convince. It appeared that both of them preferred to stay in town watching their operation, rather than try to find business in the other saloons in the area. Both agreed to provide me samples that I could take to the other towns close by on both sides of the river.

As we left Aiple's Brewery, Wilhelm had that smile on his face again. "What now? I asked.

"I think you just got your two bottles of whiskey you promised Victor Lawson. When you talk to the other saloons, just save a bottle or two here and there."

"Wilhelm, if you were a horse trader, you probably would have been shot by now. You are quite the businessman. Let's just make sure that everyone gets something out of the deal."

During the next couple of weeks, I took the stage from Stillwater to Bayport, Afton, Marine, Taylors Falls, Center City, Lindstrom, and Chisago City. It was easy to convince the saloons that they should have more than one brand on the shelf. I came back with orders from each city. It gave me a chance to see who the competition was, and compare their quality – or lack there of. I even got the Marine Brewery to sign on with the distribution. I discovered I needed to slow down my travel. Soon, I would run the breweries out of supply. Shipping by wagon is slow. It will be much easier to ship product when trains come to our area.

Wednesday, October 18, 1865. I went to the hotel to have lunch today. It is a very large place. I chuckle every time I go by it. The big white building in the middle of town has a huge sign on top, "Minesota House." You would think someone in town would tell them to spell Minnesota correctly.

While I was there, Kathryn Bell walked in with another woman. I was surprised to see her. She did not look like someone who had just come in from cooking at a logging camp. Her clothes were too fine. I gave a slight wave to her when she looked my way. She smiled back.

I waited until after I was done eating before walking over to her table to greet her.

"Miss Bell, it is nice to see you. Have you recovered from the long boat ride?" I asked.

"Johan, it is nice to see you again. Let me introduce you to a friend of mine, Mrs. Arlene Olson. Arlene and I are starting a new business."

Arlene gave me a pleasant smile.

"Pleased to meet you," I told her.

Kathryn told me, "The job at the logging camp was a little too demanding for me, and I met Arlene one morning at church. I had told her that my uncle asked me to help cook for the loggers. I did not realize it was for all the loggers in town, who worked the boom site and the mills, and that I was going to be the only female there. I thought it would have been a small logging camp with maybe a dozen or so loggers. Maybe you have seen the huge dining hall they have. They can feed over a hundred men at a time.

"After hearing my story, Arlene suggested that this town really needs a store that sells material for clothing, and someone to do sewing and alterations. So, we are going to open a shop next week, on Second Street."

"Are you still staying with your brother?" Kathryn asked.

"Yes, temporarily. I started a distribution business here in town. I am helping several breweries distribute their liquor to saloons in other towns in the area. Wilhelm is working for two breweries, maintaining their quality during production. Eventually, I plan to start up my own brewery again when I finish my research and find a good location. I do not want to interrupt your dinner. Hopefully, we can run into each other again some time and have a chance to talk."

"Yes, thank you. I would like that also. If you have time, maybe next week you can stop by our new shop, 'Olson's Sewing,' and see how it looks."

"I will plan on doing that." I nodded to Mrs. Olson and excused myself from the room.

I was wondering how long Miss Bell would last at a lumber camp. It was long hours, with lots of smelly men who spent months in the woods, or all day on the river sorting logs. I was just surprised that she had given it up this quickly after coming all this way to do the cooking. I would have thought that she might have picked up a new job cooking at one of the cafés, the bakery, or the hotel.

I had been in Stillwater almost two months. After this short time, I had started a job and was making more money than our friend, the guard, at the prison. Somehow, it did not seem equitable. If I was working as a brewmaster and being paid more money, I could understand this based on my education. I made sure that the breweries were selling enough extra product to warrant my payments.

I visited Kathryn Bell's new store after it opened. It was a small shop that catered to the women in town for making clothes, and they did mending for both women and men.

Bayfield's Secret Notebook

She was pleased to see that I was interested enough to visit the shop. We chatted for a few moments until two customers came in with some clothes that had torn along the seams. When they left, we had a chance to talk for a few minutes. I asked her if she would like to meet for dinner later in the week, perhaps Friday.

"I would love to," she answered. "However, I may be real busy this first week, I need to talk to Arlene to make sure she can handle closing the shop."

She checked with Mrs. Olson and came back. "Arlene said she could handle the after hours chores Friday. How about 6 pm?"

"Six o'clock it is. Where are you staying? I'll meet you there."

"Thank you. I'm staying at Polly's boarding house, just down the street."

I left the shop to go check with the mayor. There were rumors that the train was planning on running tracks into Stillwater. I was hoping he had the time plan that was proposed.

When I got to the mayor's office, he told me that the rumors were true. However, the timetable for the train reaching Stillwater was still undecided. They needed to purchase right-of-ways, and they were hoping to link up with the track proposed to cross the river at Hudson, when the Chicago to St. Paul line was built.

I told him that I was representing several breweries along the river and I was hoping to be able to ship product by rail to reduce breakage.

He said he would keep me up to date. He thought the line to Stillwater might be completed before the bridge was built in Hudson. They would need the tracks in the area to build the bridge. So far, it looked like it would be three to five years before the line to Stillwater was built.

David Fabio

I left the office with mixed feelings. Progress was coming; it just was not coming at the rate I was hoping for. Victor Lawson was going to have his extra income job for a number of years.

Later in the day, when Wilhelm came home, I told him what I had found out. The railroad would be a boom for Stillwater businesses. It would allow easy shipping to St. Paul and beyond. Currently, everything has to go by horse drawn wagon or by steamboat.

Friday, October 28, 1865, I met Kathryn Bell at Polly's boarding house. We walked down to Main Street and found a table at the café. It was an unusually warm day this late in the fall. We spent most of the time talking about what each of us had done since arriving in Stillwater. The noise of the crowded café made it difficult to have any real conversation.

The food was good. I had a hot roast beef sandwich with mashed potatoes; Miss Bell ordered baked chicken.

As I walked Miss Bell back to the boarding house, I told her I really enjoyed the evening.

"Thank you, I enjoyed it as well. It was nice to have someone to converse with other than talking about the shop."

"I know how you feel. Most of my conversations are with my brother or saloonkeepers. After a while, you feel like you need a diversion."

Miss Bell asked, "Are you interested in having a picnic lunch on Sunday, when the store is closed? I can pick up some meat and cheese at the store, and we can eat down by the river."

"That sounds wonderful. Let's see if we can find a nice quiet area where we can talk, and not be rushed as we were at the café. I'll bring something to drink."

Bayfield's Secret Notebook

I told her I would pick her up at the boarding house she was staying at, just before noon, and we would walk the two blocks to the riverbank.

When I got back to Wilhelm's that night, he gave me a hard time.

"I can't leave you alone for an evening without some woman throwing a chain around your neck. Were did she come from? I have not heard her name around town before."

I reminded Wilhelm about how I met Miss Bell on the boat, and how she had come to Stillwater to cook for the lumberjacks. "If anything gets more serious, I'll make sure that you meet her. Right now, she is just a little lonely."

On Sunday, I went to church in the morning. Afterwards, I met Kathryn Bell and we walked down to the levee. The leaves were off the trees and signs of fall were definitely giving everyone signals that winter was coming soon. So far, the warm weather was holding. We found an empty loading cart, and sat on the back end, away from the sawdust on the ground. It was peaceful near the river. The boats were not running and the noise of the busy town was gone. We dined on sausage, cheese, and bread that Kathryn had purchased. It tasted good, along with the bottle of wine I bought for the picnic.

We had a delightful afternoon. It was nice to stop everything for several hours and just sit and talk.

She told me all about her experiences at the lumberjack dining hall. The day started at 4:00 am with baking rolls and biscuits, and ended about 9:30 pm when the food was finally put away and things were organized for the next morning. It was not quite what her uncle had promised in his letters. She had the feeling that the male cooks were just dumping their schedules on her – the new person.

David Fabio

After a week, she decided that it was not what she wanted to do for the next year. Apparently, there is a fair turnover of the crew, so they were not too upset that she quit.

Kathryn's new job was much more peaceful. She and Mrs. Olson would switch off between doing the sewing, alterations, and sales, until the shop becomes too busy for a couple of people to handle. They had hired another woman to work in the alterations area full time, starting later in the month.

Now, they were waiting to see if their business sense would pay off. It was one thing to set up a business. It was another to make it successful.

Late in the afternoon, a few merchants brought crates of goods down to the levee for the first boats in the morning. The intrusion into the quiet atmosphere, which had been our private lunch area, created an excuse to take a walk along the river's edge. We talked about the steamboat ride and the interesting things we saw on the trip. Then, about 4:30 pm, I walked Miss Bell back to her boarding house.

We had both enjoyed the afternoon. I asked her if she would like to go out for supper the next week. She told me to check with her come Wednesday. She needed to see how busy her business was going to be.

I headed back to Wilhelm's and enjoyed a beer with him. Most of the evening I kept thinking about the afternoon with Kathryn Bell. I wished that I had spent a little more time with her, while on the steamboat.

Chapter 34

Seasons

Monday, November 13, 1865. A couple weeks have gone by quickly. Wilhelm made his monthly inspection of the humidity conditions at the prison caves, Victor Lawson collected his money and two bottles of whiskey, and between talking to saloons about liquor, I continued to see Kathryn Bell for dinner several times.

I saw my first snowflakes of the season today. The snow did not last long, but it was a reminder that winter is about to come to the northern states. To the lumberjacks, it is a welcomed sign. As soon as the snow comes and the temperature drops below freezing, they can freeze tracks for the big sleds that will haul the trees to the rivers. The colder it is, the better for them.

The mills have large stacks of timber that can be cut during the winter while the river is frozen.

My travel to other saloons in neighboring towns is decreasing due to weather. During the winter, I will try to visit my customers once a month to keep the orders coming. My vendors have lost only a few bottles in shipping over the roads. I am surprised; I thought there would

David Fabio

be more. I try to ship kegs and casks whenever possible to eliminate the problem.

Miss Kathryn Bell has offered to cook a Thanksgiving dinner for my brother, Wilhelm, and I. She will need to cook it at Wilhelm's house since she lives at a boarding house and cannot cook there. She told me that she misses cooking. I was surprised that she did not eat with her uncle. For my brother and me, we are pleased to have some home cooking for the holiday. I offered to pick up a turkey and some wine for the meal.

I had ordered a fresh turkey from the store along with a few other items Kathryn had suggested. I picked them up the afternoon before our feast. In the morning, my brother and I will kill and pluck the turkey for the dinner.

On November 30, 1865, we had a wonderful meal, prepared for us by Miss Kathryn Bell. She spent most of the day preparing the meal. For two old bachelors, it was the best meal we had tasted since we left Germany many years earlier. We had a few drinks during the day, while preparing the meal.

By the time the bird was cooked, and we sat and enjoyed the food, we had finished off a few bottles of the wine I had picked out. After dinner, Wilhelm and I polished off part of a small cask of Kentucky Whiskey that I had filled from one of my barrels. Kathryn had a glass, also. She told me that it was the most liquor she had ever drunk in one day. Apparently, Wilhelm and I were not keeping track of how much we had consumed either. The cask held about a half gallon.

After Miss Bell had cleaned up Wilhelm's kitchen, with a little assistance from us, I told her, "Your cooking is so good that I wish I could marry you and eat that kind of food forever," or something like that. Apparently, Miss Bell was a little light headed as well, and said, "Well, if that's an offer, I accept."

We christened the offer with a short glass of Kentucky Whiskey.

Bayfield's Secret Notebook

The next morning, when I came down for breakfast, Wilhelm asked me when I was getting married.

"Married! Oh, so that was not a dream I had last night."

"No, I think you both agreed to be married long before you walked her home last night, and warmed back up with a couple more shots of whiskey."

I sat there astounded. What had I done? I had never had that much to drink in mixed company. In all my training in Germany, it was a rule that the brewmaster did not drink so much as to deaden his taste buds. In addition, until I got rid of the gold, I was not planning to complicate my life. As I sat and thought about it, I still had no idea when that was going to be. If I was to marry, Miss Bell was as fine a woman as I knew. I decided to meet her as she closed up her shop today, and talk to her.

About 5:00 pm, I wandered into her store. It was her day to mind the counter. When she spotted me, she asked, "How's the head? It took a while for the cobwebs to leave mine and I did not have as much to drink yesterday as you did."

"I am sorry. I think we got carried away with all the good cooking and company. Can we talk over some supper when you close up?" I asked.

She looked as nervous as I was. I did not know if she really wanted to get married, or if she was regretting the decision under the duress of the alcohol.

"Sure, only let's find a quiet place to eat. I do not think my head can take a noisy café."

When the shop closed, we walked down to a small café in one of the smaller hotels and talked over a light meal. Neither of us was very hungry after the huge meal yesterday.

"We probably had a little too much celebrating yesterday. Do you remember what we said after dinner?" I asked her.

"Yes, I do. Since we were both a little light headed, if you want to change your mind, I would understand."

I sat and looked into her eyes. She had not told me that she wanted out of the agreement; she had given me the option. A fine person like her did not come along every day. "No, I was worried that you might. If you did, I would understand."

She smiled and told me that she would love to spend the rest of her life with me. Ever since the day I stopped the soldier from accosting her on the boat, she knew that I was the right person for her.

We sat and talked until they closed up the café. Then, I walked her home.

When I got back to Wilhelm's house, Wilhelm was waiting for me. "You kept me in suspense for many hours. What did she say?"

"We decided to get married just before Christmas," I told him. "That way I can remember our anniversary. I guess I will have to find a place to stay."

"Housing is rather hard to find this time of the year. You can live with me until you find a house," Wilhelm stated.

I told him I would discuss it with Kathryn.

Saturday, December 23, 1865. Kathryn Bell became Kathryn Volker in a small ceremony conducted by the justice of the peace at the city hall. It gave us a Christmas celebration we could remember for years. This time, we were careful how much we drank.

Kathryn said she had always wished for a wedding at a big church, however, Stillwater has very few church buildings. Only my brother and a couple friends of Kathryn's and mine were in attendance. I was surprised that Kathryn's uncle did not come.

Bayfield's Secret Notebook

The dress she wore for the ceremony was made by the women in her sewing shop. While they were making it, several of the women customers commented on the quality of the dress. After seeing Kathryn's dress being made, the shop received several more orders for wedding dresses.

The night after the ceremony, we stayed at the Sawyer House Hotel for a night, before moving in with Wilhelm. With 75 rooms, it is one of the best hotels in Stillwater. We plan to stay with Wilhelm until we can build a house in the spring. Wilhelm was correct; winter was not the time to start construction on a house. With the boom in Stillwater, existing houses that are for sale are very difficult to find. Those that are for sale are usually the houses that were put up in a hurry and were very small. Some of them were built where moisture comes out of the hills in the springtime.

It still concerns me that I have not told Kathryn the story about the gold. I did not want the knowledge of the gold hidden in the prison to affect her decision to marry me.

Now, I am concerned, when I finally tell her, I do not know how she will react to it.

*****

"Stan, I think you have a date wrong in your story," Barbara told him. "Thanksgiving is never on November 30th. You need to look at your calendar."

"You are thinking present day again. It was not until 1863, during the days that Lincoln was President, the Thanksgiving Holiday was officially declared a national holiday. It was set for the last Thursday of November. It remained that way for many years.

"However, Franklin D. Roosevelt changed that. It was changed to the fourth Thursday in November, in an attempt to move it away from Christmas and help the merchants.

"Apparently, money talked back then as much as it talks today. I was surprised to see that a holiday was moved to increase sales of Christmas presents.

"Sometimes we forget that some things were definitely different years ago.

"I thought you were going to comment on their engagement," Stan mentioned.

"Not the most romantic I have heard," Barbara responded. "It looked like they both accepted the best option they had available.

"Just remember, that worked years ago. Don't even consider dropping the romantic part if you know what is good for you."

Stan took the hint.

Vivian just sat there with a smile on her face as she looked at Stan.

*****

Chapter 35

Fire

Monday, January 1, 1866. We looked out the window and saw smoke coming from the roof of a house nearby. When we looked closer, we realized it was coming from the wooden frame upper portion of Knips Brewery. It was where Gerhardt Knips, his wife and son lived. We rushed over to see if there was anything we could do.

By the time they had the fire out, it had burned almost his entire residence. The storage area and most of his stock, which had been in the basement, had been saved with the help of many residents who were worried about losing their favorite brewery. Even though they had enough liquor to last for a month or two, it would take some time to rebuild the building and restart production.

Fires are a problem here in the winter. Too many people are not careful enough with fireplaces and candles. A week ago, twelve buildings burned to the ground in the downtown area before they could put the fires out.

The next day, Wilhelm and I met with Gerhardt Knips. For Wilhelm, it meant that one of his jobs did not need him for the next couple of months. For me, it was an opportunity to use my distribution to keep Gerhardt's saloons stocked until he could start to supply them again when the new brewery was completed. I assured Gerhardt that I would not try to permanently steal any of his current business, for which he was grateful. In fact, I suggested that we use a brewery in St. Paul that made beer close in taste to the Knips Beer, and have them private label it for him, until his production was up and running. Gerhardt was pleased at the suggestion.

I asked Gerhardt why he had not used his caves for storage. He told me that he thought the dampness would change the taste of the beer. For the next couple of months, we will use one of the caves as his storage area, until his business and house is rebuilt. Lumber is not the problem, temperature is. It was minus twenty-five degrees last night.

With the cold temperatures, I have been concerned about Kathryn walking to and from work. Between Wilhelm and me, we try to time our work such that one of us walks with her one way or the other. I am surprised at how stout the people are in Minnesota. Even in a snowstorm, they still walk in town.

Tuesday, February 20, 1866. Kathryn informed me that she was with child. We will have to make some changes in the near future. I am glad that winter is almost over. Kathryn has made a difference in Wilhelm. I think she has changed some of his bachelor manners.

Wilhelm seems restless. Not being at the Knips Brewery, due to the fire, has given him too much spare time. I asked him to check on the prison caves today.

The Stillwater Messenger had an article last week talking about the need for trains in our area. Financing is still the problem. The lumber mills are pushing for a spur that would serve Stillwater and allow them to ship lumber west. For now, they have to ship by boat.

Bayfield's Secret Notebook

I had a long discussion with Wilhelm about Kathryn and my future. We planned on building a house this summer to give Wilhelm his freedom. Especially with a child on the way, we would be a burden to him to continue to stay hat his residence.

Wilhelm, had another thought on the subject. "Are you going to build a house only to sell it when the trains come? How long do you think it will be? They could build it in a year or two if they wanted to."

He was right, I needed to decide what we were going to do when the trains were built. Were we going to stay in Stillwater or move somewhere else? What about Wilhelm? Did he want to move with me?

After talking it over for a couple days, we decided that the best plan was to put an addition on Wilhelm's house. Many of the families in the area had several relatives living under the same roof. Wilhelm said he enjoyed the company. We could easily add on to the house, putting a couple rooms on the backside. This would give both of us our space to live. When the time came and the trains were running, we would still have our options open, whether to stay or move.

I told Kathryn about my decision.

Friday, October 12, 1866. We have a son. His name is Christian. We shall call him Chris. Everyone is happy.

Monday, May 11, 1868. Time has gone by quickly. Family life has kept me busy and I confess I am not as regimented with my writing as I used to be. I now have two journals. One I keep for records at work and one for my family life.

There is a big celebration planned in St. Paul. It has been ten years since Minnesota became a state. Last week, I shipped three barrels of Kentucky Whiskey to the governor for the festivities. He has invited my family and Wilhelm to the celebration.

They are planning a big dinner followed by fireworks in the evening. We will need to stay in St. Paul overnight. Chris will stay in

David Fabio

Stillwater with our neighbor until we return tomorrow. It will be the first time that he has been away from us. Kathryn is concerned.

Wednesday, May 20, 1868. There has been a devastating fire at Aiple's Brewery. It will take months to rebuild, because everything was lost. Wilhelm is talking to another man, Martin Wolf, who is starting up a brewery. Helping him will keep him busy.

Thursday, November 5, 1868. Frank Aiple died from a fall while working on the roof of his new building, which was almost completed after the big fire.

Mrs. Aiple has asked Wilhelm to help her with the business until she can decide what to do. Wilhelm decided that he needed to leave the Wolf brewery to help her. I was glad that he decided to assist Mrs. Aiple.

On Wednesday December 14, 1869, Mrs. Aiple married Hermann Tepass. After spending over a year managing Mrs. Aiple's brewery, Wilhelm is now back to a flexible schedule where he can work several jobs, and not have to worry about the everyday business of selling the liquor. Mr. Tepass is planning on taking over the brewery operation, and will keep Wilhelm on as an advisor for the preparation of the mash and distilling.

Wednesday, October 5, 1870. Wilhelm and I met with Gerhardt Knips. We were discussing an article in the paper that stated that by next summer we would have a train running from Stillwater to St. Paul. It was good news to all of us. A line from St. Paul to Duluth had opened in August, which went through White Bear Lake and Forest Lake. The plan would have a spur run south into Stillwater.

Gerhardt decided that storing beer in caves made more sense than enlarging the basement storage area. He said he was going to open up the number one cave to 40-feet. It will give him a lot more storage space to store up supplies for when the trains start running. He asked me to go to St. Paul and talk to saloons about selling his beer.

I considered using the new train to ship the gold to Duluth, where it could be taken to Bayfield. When I talked to the people in St. Paul, the plan looked too dangerous to consider. Too many people involved and too many transfers of the gold.

Monday, May 16, 1870. The newspaper reported that yesterday, the steamboat War Eagle caught fire and burned in La Crosse, Wisconsin. They had been carrying barrels of oil that were supposed to be non-explosive. Apparently, one of the barrels suffered a leak. When the oil reached a flammable source, it ignited. Attempts to roll the barrel overboard failed and the entire boat burned to the waterline.

I was very saddened to hear the news. It was as if someone was closing a memorable chapter of my history.

Tuesday, December 13, 1870. Stillwater's new newspaper, the Gazette, published an article about Knips's new cave for storing beer. I sent copies to six saloons in St. Paul. This will show them he is serious about being a major brewery.

Chapter 36

Big Events

Saturday, August 12, 1871. It has been a long time since I wrote. My life is busy and I forget to put entries in my journal. Since I am not traveling, my journal tends to be forgotten.

Finally, this summer, we got our first railroad in Stillwater. It was part of the Mississippi & Lake Superior line that entered town from the north coming in from the town of White Bear Lake. This line pleased the owners of the lumber mills. They had been anticipating that they were going to start running out of lumber up-river. With the rail lines, lumber can be shipped down to Stillwater for cutting.

Later, we got our second rail line – the St. Paul, Stillwater & Taylor's Falls line. It came in from the south. Finally, we were connected to the Chicago and Milwaukee Road line that ran through Hastings. Now, lumber and finished products, including barrels, doors and shingles made in the prison, can be shipped to customers in Minnesota, Iowa, Missouri and the Dakota Territory. The only problem was each railroad had its own depot, one on one end of town, the other on the opposite side.

Bayfield's Secret Notebook

The Chicago and Milwaukee line opened a set of tracks from La Crosse to St. Paul.

The North Wisconsin Railway has started building a rail line from North Junction near Hudson to New Richmond, while the West Wisconsin has completed a line from Tomah to Hudson.

It feels as though it is just a short matter of time before a rail line between Hudson and Bayfield will finally get going. The question now, is how many small railroads would build it.

Saturday, October 5, 1872. The West Wisconsin railroad erected a bridge this summer across the St. Croix River. Trains run into St. Paul for the first time connecting New Richmond, and Hudson, Wisconsin with St. Paul and the other railroads in Minnesota.

On nights where we have a south wind, we can hear the train whistles as they approach the bridge in Hudson. The sound echoes up the river valley. Tonight was one of those nights. As I heard the whistle, I wondered why I have heard nothing from Lewis Patterson. It is frustrating to know that I have been taking care of his gold for seven years, and I still do not know when I will get it to Bayfield.

Victor and Wilhelm have done a great job keeping the gold secret in the prison. Wilhelm's inspections have gone like clockwork since the gold was hidden under the floorboards at the prison.

We are still living in Wilhelm's house. Had we known how long we would be here, we would have built our own house. So far, Wilhelm seems to enjoy the company. He seems to enjoy talking to Chris and to Kathryn.

Chris is getting older. Soon, he will be six years old. We have been educating him at home. When he gets to school, he will be ahead of many of his classmates.

Kathryn has been able to take a lot of her work home and work on alterations from home the past few years. As a result, she has been able to work out a schedule with her partner and co-workers so that she has only had to be at the shop two days a week and just a few hours the other days. When she has to be at the store and Wilhelm and I are working, Chris stays with our neighbor.

Thursday, November 12, 1874. Time to catch up on my writing once again.

Watching the railroads is like watching a bunch of kids trying to divide a bag of candy. Last year, there was a purchasing war going on between all the rival rail companies bidding to get all the land grant possessions in Wisconsin. Each company thought they could build from one city to the next, instead of giving one of them the right-of-way over the entire route.

This year, the Wisconsin Legislature finally stepped in and granted the land to two railroads – the North Wisconsin and the Air Line. North Wisconsin has the land to build from New Richmond to Big Marsh, and from North Wisconsin Junction to Bayfield. Air Line will connect the line east to Superior.

My business has been brisk. I feel guilty collecting money for simply directing the orders to the proper brewery. I have a number of saloons in the area that we supply. I have found that I had to limit how many saloons I signed up, due to production limitations. I have been encouraging my suppliers to increase their production facilities.

I had a long discussion with Wilhelm yesterday. I am very frustrated with no communications with Lewis Patterson. It has been years since I have heard from him. Does he have that much faith in me that I will deliver his gold? Even a short note would let me know that he still exists.

Wilhelm told me, "Do not to worry about it. The gold is safe. Our lives are good. When the time comes that the trains are running, it will be time enough to worry about it. Look at it this way, if he does not exist anymore, you may come out ahead."

Bayfield's Secret Notebook

Wilhelm and I have talked about starting up a distillery after we deliver the gold. Between us, we have enough money to start one up; not including the money Lewis Patterson promised me for delivering the gold. At this point, I am not betting on getting the money he promised or even meeting his representative in Bayfield. I will cross that bridge when it finally happens. It has been far too long since I have heard from him. That war has been over for nine years. For all I know, he might be dead or in another country. My next question: I wonder if someone in England knows that I have their gold?

Tuesday, May 9, 1876. Chris and I went down to the celebration for the opening of the first bridge over the St. Croix River from Stillwater to Wisconsin. It seemed like the whole town was there to watch as the bridge was officially opened. There was a lot of celebrating. Now we can cross into Wisconsin without having to use a ferry, or wait until the river freezes over.

Tuesday, July 4, 1876. Stillwater had a large fireworks planned for the centennial of the United States. The celebrating started early. Kids with firecrackers announced the start of the holiday shortly after breakfast. The loud noises announced to the town that the celebrations had officially started. Before long, they had spooked a horse. It was last seen heading south out of town without its rider.

There were people selling foods along the street, including breads and cookies. In the afternoon, we watched a parade and listened to the band playing marches. That was followed by races of all kinds, with prizes given to the winners. Chris won twenty-five cents in the egg-on-spoon race. In the evening, the celebration ended with a wonderful display of fireworks.

Last month, Joseph Wolf purchased the brewery from his brother Martin. Both Wolf's beer and Knips's beer have found a solid place in the celebration. It took a while to pick up the stray bottles after all the partying.

Saturday, November 18, 1876. I just got the news that the notorious bank robbers Cole, Jim and Bob Younger pleaded guilty to their crimes and were being sent to Stillwater Prison. They were all part of the Jessie James gang that had robbed the bank in Northfield, Minnesota. The rumors I heard were that this gang could smell gold two towns away.

I decided that I needed to talk to Victor Lawson and see how the prison had planned to keep this gang in their cells.

After talking to Victor, he agreed that he would keep a close eye out for the gang and try to find any information he could about them. He would let me know when he heard anything.

On Wednesday November 22, 1876, the Younger brothers arrived at the prison. I saw the black, hard-sided wagon with bars on the windows pull through town. It was escorted by several heavily armed officers on horseback.

Victor Lawson was in a few meetings to discuss the prisoners brought in. The prison decided to keep them in their cells for the first few weeks, and then assign the new prisoners to work details.

To make sure they did not have any trouble or escapes, the prison decided to keep them separate from other inmates and not occupying the same cells. Cole was in cell number 64, Bob in 65, and Jim in number 66. They had also been assigned different work details. Victor was surprised when he looked at the prison's history sheet on the brothers. There was a lot more on it than the public had been told, more than just robbing banks.

The next day, he stopped over at Wilhelm's house to tell Wilhelm and me what he had heard and seen. Wilhelm got them each a bottle of Knips Beer and they sat at the kitchen table discussing the latest prisoners.

"I had heard stories about the Jessie James gang, but I did not realize all the things they had done before they botched the Northfield Bank robbery," Victor told them. "I'm surprised that someone didn't send a posse after them years ago.

"The sheet I looked at had the history of all the gang members. Did you know that these guys were bad all the way back to the Civil War? Jessie and Frank were on the Confederate side and apparently committed a number of atrocities against Union soldiers. They used guerrilla tactics and did not care if someone had a gun or not. They were just plain vicious.

"Now the Younger boys were no saints either," Victor continued. "Cole is the oldest. He and Jim rode with Quantrill's Raiders in 1863 when they killed over 200 men and boys, and looted and burned a town. That gang hated the Union forces along the Kansas/Missouri line, and even citizens who supported the Union forces. Jim was caught and was thrown into prison when the Union soldiers killed Quantrill. They let him out after the war. Cole escaped capture. Bob was only eight back then, or he would have ridden with them too.

"Somehow, they all got together with the James gang and started a life of robbing trains and banks. They lasted a long time because of Confederate sympathizers who gave them shelter. I guess their big mistake was to head north, where no one would come to their aid. The authorities shot up Cole and Jim pretty good. I'm surprised they survived. Bob was shot in the elbow during the escape.

"They had a trial in Faribault. The gang pled guilty to keep from the gallows. In my mind, that is where they should have gone.

"Well, now we have them here to take care of. The warden told us he wants them separated. When they spend a little time in their cells getting used to the place, his plan is to split them up. Jim Younger is to be assigned to the barrel factory. Bob Younger assigned to the laundry, and cleaning detail and Cole to the kitchen.

"You can bet that someone is going to be watching them every day to make sure they do not escape. The warden knows it will be his job if the prisoners even see the outside of the walls."

"So you think they can keep them in line?" I asked.

"With the reputation this prison had ten to fifteen years ago, you bet. I doubt the warden wants to hear any stories about prison breaks. The bigger question is how long are they going to survive in prison. The lack of freedom can do strange things to some people."

After Victor left, I told Wilhelm, "Maybe God does have a sense of humor. Who would have thought that someone who hated Union people so badly would be stuck up north, working over and probably protecting more Confederate gold than they stole in all their train and bank robberies? What do you think Cole would say if he found out?"

Just then, Kathryn walked into the room. She had heard my last comment. "What do you mean about protecting gold?" she asked.

This was not the way I planned to tell her the story of my mission. However, the cards were on the table and I was not about to lie to her. Fortunately, Chris was not in the house.

I asked her to sit down at the table with Wilhelm and me.

"Kathryn, there is a story you need to hear…"

"… and you see, that is why we keep an eye on the prison and talk about the trains so much."

Kathryn sat there for a while without saying a word. "I am glad you finally told me. What are you planning on doing with the gold?" she asked.

"When the tracks are finished to Bayfield, the gold will be shipped up there. After that, I do not know who will receive it and take it to Canada."

That night, Kathryn and I talked for several hours about what happened and the possibilities of what might happen in the future.

Thursday, November 30, 1876. Thanksgiving Day. We had a dinner at the house. Kathryn invited another family for the meal that was having problems making ends meet, and we all enjoyed a turkey dinner. As we did, I was thinking about the Younger brothers in prison. My guess is that they were not having a wonderful day.

*****

Barbara was a little uneasy with the story and told Stan, "You mean that Johan was able to keep the gold a secret from her for eleven years, without telling her? Is that the way it is going to be in our marriage? What secrets are you going to keep for years without telling me?"

Stan joked, "Well, we probably won't have that problem. You will catch me talking in my sleep and pry it out of me."

"No, I will record it first, and then I will beat the tar out of you for holding back secrets. I just can't imagine the conversation the two of them must have had that evening."

Stan told her, "Life was different back then. People did not sit around and discuss things as they do now. Women and men stayed out of each other's dealings until something happened to force them to discuss them. However, you are right; I'll bet the conversation was interesting."

Vivian knew that Barbara had just dropped another big hint on Stan's shoulders – hold back secrets when we get married, and she will beat the tar out of him.

David Fabio

Chapter 37

Biding Time

Monday, September 24, 1877. I have not written in the journal this year because everything is running its course. I am still waiting for the railroad to complete its tracks.

My family life is very good. As I look back at all my adventures, perhaps this one thing was the best result of the whole experience. Had I stayed in Kentucky, I would probably still be single, working every day at the distillery. I have also learned patience. I am still in control, but life is leading me in a direction at its own time. I have to wait for the next event.

Staying with my brother has been good for both of us. He is enjoying the company of family life and I think it has mellowed him also. He treats Chris as if he was his son.

In February, the Knips Brewery was sold. It has been leased to a group of men; Fred Maisch, D. Millbrook and J. Honar. They have a background in brewing, and I was concerned that Wilhelm would be out of one of his jobs, or that we might lose the cave we use for the storage of the barrels of whiskey we have left.

Bayfield's Secret Notebook

So far, the new owner has kept Wilhelm on part time for maintaining the consistency of the current business. I have begun looking for purchasers of the barrels of whiskey I have left.

I do not know if we will move when we deliver the gold, or stay in Stillwater. I need to keep my options open. I will probably put some of the whiskey in kegs, in our basement, for use at special occasions, while selling the rest of the whiskey at a good profit, through my distribution.

Cole Younger is still working in the kitchen area of the prison. The food selection allowed by the prison for the inmates does not allow for a lot of variation. The typical inmate's diet consists of boiled meat, potatoes, a vegetable and two slices of bread, served with a cup of water. Coffee, tea, and porridge are served at breakfast. Little does he realize that every time he has to get food out of the storage cave, he is walking on gold. According to Victor, Cole has been a model prisoner. His younger brothers are a little more difficult to handle.

Wilhelm's monthly inspections of the caves have shown no attempts to remove any boards. They store the vegetables, potatoes, and coffee in the caves. Wilhelm told me that he could see that they have to remove the sprouts from the potatoes; there are scraps on the floor each month when he checks the caves.

Friday March 1, 1878. I am becoming concerned about Kathryn. In the past few weeks, I have observed a man down the street. At first, I did not pay attention to him. However, after seeing him several times in the morning, I have become suspicious of him.

It is as though he is watching the house, waiting for Wilhelm and me to leave. I asked my neighbor to watch today to see what he is doing. I do not know if this is Lewis Patterson's man watching the house or just someone I am overly suspicious of.

David Fabio

When I came home from my office, my neighbor told me that the man came to the house about twenty minutes after I left, and stayed for about a half an hour. The neighbor did not see him carrying anything into or out of the house. I thanked her and asked if she would keep an eye open for me.

When Wilhelm came home, I asked him if he had seen the man in the mornings. He told me that he had not paid a lot of attention, but would keep an eye out for anyone that was hanging around.

That evening, as we were heading to bed, I asked Kathryn, "Did anyone come to the house today?"

"No, just a few customers picking up or dropping off clothing that needed alterations."

"Was Chris at school all day?" I asked.

"Yes, he was at school just like every other school day. Why do you ask?" Kathryn replied.

"I have seen a man hanging around the neighborhood lately, and I was concerned. It is spring time and you need to be a little careful with all the lumberjacks around town."

"I'll keep my eyes open," Kathryn told me.

I did not feel like pushing the issue. Between Wilhelm and me, we will watch for anyone hanging around the neighborhood during the next few weeks.

Tuesday March 5, 1878. This morning I spotted the same man about a block from the house. This time, I walked toward town a short way and then cut back along the hills to the backside of our house. As our house came within eyesight, I spotted him going to the front door. He was not carrying any bags or clothes.

I moved into the neighbor's back yard where I might have a better view of the windows of our house. I could just make out two people inside. They appeared to be at the table talking.

Bayfield's Secret Notebook

About forty minutes later, the man left. I watched him from a distance to see where he was going. He headed towards town. There was only one road that goes in front of the prison. That made it harder to follow him. I had to stay way behind him not to be noticed.

I lost sight of him as he turned a corner downtown. I do not know if he went into a shop or a hotel.

Finally, I walked down the street to Knips Brewery so that I could talk to Wilhelm. He had informed me that he would be there most of the morning. I'm not sure what is going on, but I am hoping that Wilhelm might have a suggestion on how to find out.

I caught Wilhelm at the Brewery checking out the grains, and filled him in on what I observed this morning.

"Johan, don't go jumping to rash conclusions," he told me. "There is probably some simple answer for this. Let us just sit back and observe for a couple days. If all they are doing is talking at the table, you don't have too much to worry about."

"And what if it goes further than that?" I asked.

"Let's find out who it is first. Then, we can find out why he is talking to Kathryn."

We set up a plan. Wilhelm would hang out at a shop on the north end of town about the time I lost the man this morning, and he would watch for someone coming down the road. I would watch the house, and if the man repeated his visit again in the next couple of days, I would signal Wilhelm when the man was just past the prison, by waving my hat, so he could spot him and follow him in town. With any luck, Wilhelm might even recognize the man as he walked by.

On the way back, I stopped off at the clothing shop, Olson's Sewing, to see if Mrs. Arlene Olson had seen anything unusual lately. I told her that I was concerned about someone watching our house. She told me that she had not seen anyone strange around the shop, especially on the days Kathryn was working at the shop verses at home. However, she would keep her eyes open.

That evening, Kathryn did not say anything about her visitor and acted as though nothing was going on. Wilhelm asked if anyone had come to the house. He told her he was expecting a package. Kathryn did not say anything odd or different.

Wednesday March 6, 1878. I did not see anyone this morning. When I got to town, Wilhelm met me on the street. He had not seen anyone near the house either. We will keep this up all week if necessary.

Thursday, March 7, 1878. As I left the house and started toward town, I noticed the same man about a half a block from the road, standing by a fence. I continued towards town and then circled back to the house. Wilhelm did not see me heading towards town along Main Street and figured that I might have seen something. So he waited patiently for either my signal or for me to head his way.

When I returned home to the backside of our house, I could see them sitting at the table. Whatever was going on, this time I was going to find out. I waited until he left, and then followed about two blocks behind him as he headed towards downtown. When he was in front of the prison entrance, I waved my hat. I made sure the stranger was not looking back to spot me.

Wilhelm was standing outside the tobacco store and saw me signal him from the end of the street. He also saw the man, who was passing the prison. As the individual got closer, Wilhelm walked into the store and watched from inside as he walked by. Unfortunately, it was not someone he knew.

Wilhelm crossed the street and watched from the other side as the man continued another block, and then turned to head up the hill. The streets heading up hill to the houses on top of the bluff are steep.

Bayfield's Secret Notebook

Wilhelm followed him from a distance until he reached the top of the south hill, and then to a house on Third Street. He went into the house and stayed there.

Wilhelm got the address of the house and headed back down the hill to Main Street. He met me at my office and told me everything he had observed. Whoever that was, it was a long walk from his house to our house for a short conversation. Why was he at the house?

I walked over to the city hall. With all my conversations about the railroads, everyone over there knew me. I told them I was interested in buying a house, and was wondering who owned it. When I gave them the address, I got a name: Arnold Simley.

According to the city records, the owner was married and had three children; ages eighteen, fifteen and thirteen.

When I walked back to the office, my mind was running in circles. Why was Simley visiting my house for short periods of time? Why hadn't Kathryn told me about him? What was I to do to get an explanation about this? Should I confront Kathryn or confront the visitor? I pondered on it all afternoon.

I did a little checking with a few other people I knew in town to see who this Arnold Simley was. After talking to four people, I finally found someone who could put a description to the name. It turned out that Arnold Simley owned several buildings in town and owned a large parcel of land north of town that had been forested for its trees. He had made money on the trees and was currently selling off parcels of the land for farming. According to the person I talked to, he had known that man for fifteen years and found him to be an honest businessman.

The picture was starting to have a face and a few more pieces to the puzzle. It still did not explain why he was visiting with Kathryn and why she had not told me about him.

Wilhelm stopped in to the office on his way back through town. I told him the information I had gathered from the address he had given me. Somehow, something was missing. If Kathryn was seeing someone on the side, they would not sit and talk at the table. What was I missing?

I waited until after dinner that night to take Kathryn aside and find out what was going on. I had started to run out of patience and did not want to let things get worse. Wilhelm offered to take Chris for a walk since it was a warm spring day and the temperature had risen to close to freezing.

While they were gone, I asked her, "Kathryn, I need to know something. What is going on between you and Arnold Simley."

She looked at me with a look of surprise. "What do you know about Arnold Simley?"

"I know that he has come to the house several times after Wilhelm and I have left. I think you owe me an explanation," I told her.

"It is not what you think. He asked me to do him a favor without anyone knowing about it. If I tell you, you have to promise that it will not leave this house."

"You may have to tell Wilhelm as well. We have been watching this guy for several days."

Kathryn proceeded to tell me that Mr. Simley stopped at the store a month ago and asked about a wedding dress. "He was rather vague about it and after some conversation, asked if we could talk in private about it.

"Apparently, he had a daughter before he was married. His wife and family know nothing about it. For the past nineteen years, he has been giving the mother some money each month to help raise the child. Now, she is old enough to get married, and the mother is still unmarried and does not have a lot of money. Mr. Simley stopped in that day to see if I could make a dress for his daughter and only charge them a small amount for it, so they could afford it. I have been working on it at the house.

"The daughter does not know her father. That is part of the problem. Mr. Simley and I have been talking things through for the past few weeks. He does not know what to do. He does not want to tell his family, and the relationship with the mother has not allowed him to meet his daughter.

"I really should have told you about it, but he asked me not to say anything to anyone. I have been honoring his wishes. At first, he wanted to see what they picked out. Since then, we have been talking about his feelings toward his daughter and what it would do to his family if they found out."

I felt relieved and upset with myself. Here I was concerned that Kathryn was up to something behind my back, and I should have realized that she was above that.

"I will not say a thing," I told her. "When Wilhelm gets back, I'll let him know what is going on. If you need time to talk to Arnold Simley, it's okay. Just let me know."

"Thanks, I knew you would understand. I'm sorry I did not say something earlier."

The mystery was over. I was impressed that Arnold Simley was still worried about his daughter after all these years. I could not imagine what it might be like to watch someone grow up and never let them know you are their father.

Thursday, March 28, 1878. Kathryn told me that Arnold Simley's daughter was getting married on Saturday. Simley was coming over to the house this morning to see the finished dress. It would be the only time he gets to see the finished product.

She told me later that he was extremely pleased with her workmanship.

David Fabio

Sunday June 30, 1878. We rented a wagon and took the whole family up to Square Lake for a picnic. It was a wonderful day. Everyone talks about how clear the lake is up there.

Chris was surprised when he ran into the lake. Unlike many other lakes in the area, the water was still very cold. Square Lake is spring fed and stays cool most of the summer.

Tuesday July 9, 1878. The Chicago, Milwaukee and St. Paul railroad has a total of 825 miles of track and 135 locomotives. Compared to the competitors, of which there are many, it is one of the larger railroads. There is talk that they may be interested in purchasing the St. Croix and Lake Superior line from Hudson along with other smaller railroads in the area. If they do, it will speed up development.

Last year, the North Wisconsin built its line from Clayton to Comstock. This year, it looks like they will have the line between Cumberland and Shell Lake completed.

The development is slow. Sometimes, I wish I could pick up a pick and shovel. I think I could open a path quicker than they do. I do not know what the land is like, but they seem to have a lot of problems.

My business is going very good. It is easier to ship by boat than by wagon. This summer I have stopped at a number of towns along the river system in hopes of finding new saloons for my brewers.

Monday, October 20, 1879. The railroad is half way to Bayfield. They have opened a line from Cumberland up to Mud Lake. There will be a major junction close to Mud Lake, at Chandler, where several railroads will meet and allow travel in many directions across Wisconsin.

Bayfield's Secret Notebook

Chapter 38

Trains a Comin'

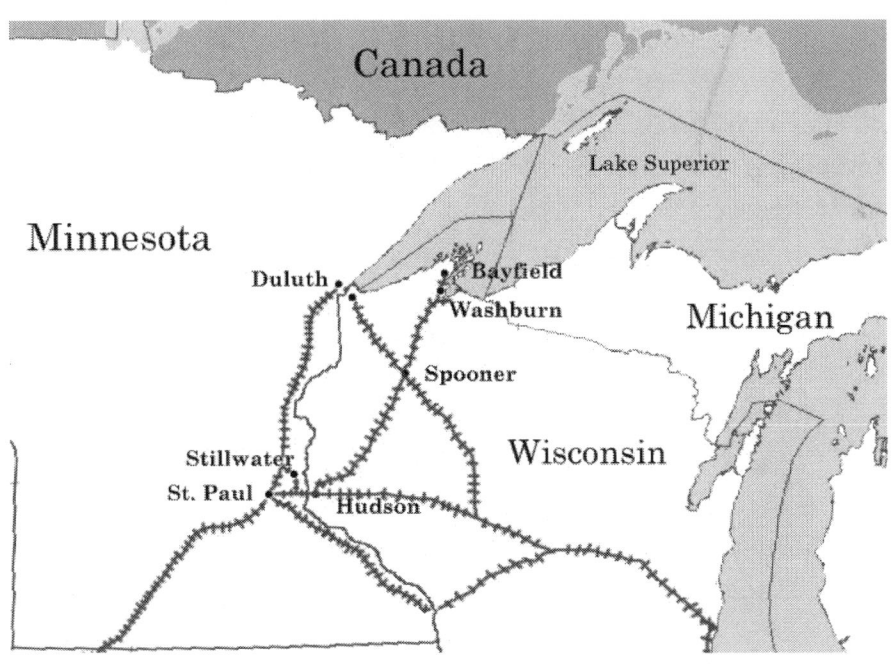

Proposed Rail Lines

David Fabio

Wednesday, May 26, 1880. More train news.

I have spent many hours talking to the railroad officials about the planned routes. My job distributing liquor has allowed me the excuse to talk frankly with them about the routes they expect to open up in the next year or two. It appears that the State of Wisconsin has caused many of their own problems with the trains in the western part of the state. By granting right-of-way options to many individuals and rail lines, it has slowed down development by years compared to other states. At the same time, we are still in the infancy of railroads. The number of miles of tracks laid has jumped each year by a magnitude of two or three times.

The Chicago, Milwaukee and St. Paul line reported that their lines had jumped from 1,412 miles to 3,775 miles between 1879 and 1880. Some of this is new track. Much of it is a consolidation of very small feeder railroads with 10 to 20 miles of tracks.

Today, May 26, 1880, the North Western Railway, West Wisconsin, St. Croix and Lake Superior, St. Paul and Sioux City, and the Chicago, St. Paul and Minneapolis Railway merged into the Chicago, St. Paul, Minneapolis and Omaha Railway. This merger will help pump money and equipment into the line from Hudson to Bayfield.

At the half-way point to Bayfield, the town of Chandler, the railroads have put up fourteen saloons, two gambling houses, six hotels, and a roundhouse and depot. They would not do that if they did not expect to complete the line shortly.

Much of the need for rail service has been driven by the lumber industry. There are some very big lumber mills along the route, and with all the lumber they ship, it helps pay for expansion. Chandler will be the rail crossing that will support trains coming from Duluth/Superior in the northwest, and Bayfield in the north, to St. Paul on the major east-west tracks, and Madison in the south. The rail lines make a big "X" merging at Chandler. They estimate having up to twenty passenger trains per day going through the rail yard.

Bayfield's Secret Notebook

The lack of towns in-between Chandler and Bayfield has slowed development. Much of the area is wooded or bogs.

Wednesday, June 12, 1881, it was announced that the Omaha Road was starting the work on the final tracks from Cable toward Bayfield. No completion date was given. Several bridges still need to be built.

We have entered the high society mode in Stillwater. The Grand Opera House opened this year. It is as grand as any in St. Paul. It will give people some diversion during the long winters. Kathryn was excited about its opening. She attended the opening presentation, which was a dress-up affair and Kathryn's shop was busy for months making elegant dresses for the affair.

Tuesday, May 16, 1882. The paper says that Cadwallader Colden Washburn, who was one of the first founders of mills in Minneapolis, and the man that was laying out the city of Washburn, in Wisconsin, died yesterday. He started both lumber and grain mills in Minneapolis and made a fortune on the grain mill and was the governor of Wisconsin for two years, 1872-1874.

When I read the article, I was surprised to see that he was a prominent investor in the local railroad. He was using his fortune to direct the development of Washburn, hoping to make the town the major stop for shipping and the railroad. Now, I am hoping that this will not lead to another delay of the railroad.

My son Chris is fifteen this year. He has matured into a strong man like his father. He is very good at school. I asked him the other day what he plans on doing when he is older. Chris said he would like to manage a business when he gets older. I have recognized that he is starting to notice that the girls have been trying to get his attention. Soon, he will be chasing after them. Kathryn has talked to me about that. We need to sit down and have a discussion with him.

David Fabio

I would like to have him marry someone from a good family someday.

Wednesday, October 11, 1882, one more merger. The Chicago and North Western Railway has purchased the Chicago, St. Paul and Minneapolis Railway. This merges more tracks onto the line through Wisconsin. With one railroad carrying the cargo, it will be much simpler for businesses to ship goods. They have also given a completion target of July of next year for the line from Hudson to Bayfield.

If they complete the line on time, Wilhelm and I will need to start planning. How will we ship the gold? Better yet, whom do we ship it to? **I still have not heard from Lewis Patterson in some time.** It has been years. I am very concerned about it. We will see if we get another letter between now and July.

Bayfield's Secret Notebook

Chapter 39

Trains a Comin'

Sunday, July 1, 1883. I saw an article in the paper that the railroad has announced it has completed a track from Spooner to Bayfield. They are also moving the rail hub from Chandler to Spooner due to the source of better quality water. The water consumed by the locomotives requires good water for steam, or else plating of the boiler will occur. The water in Chandler was found to cause problems for the steam locomotives. The buildings; hotels, saloons, roundtable, depot, and other services are to be moved to the new location. One more frustrating delay before they can start normal shipments.

Limited rail service to Bayfield is expected to start later this fall, when maintenance facilities for the locomotives are finished. Passenger service will start next year when the depots are completed. It will take some time to complete the supporting services facilities needed at all the cities on the route, including fuel and water stops, depots and side tracks.

It appears that sometime after the first of the year, I may be able to ship the gold.

Still no letters from Lewis Patterson. Surely, he has seen the news that the rail line has been completed to Bayfield.

David Fabio

Another problem has surfaced. It was reported in the newspaper that the legislature has established the State Board of Corrections and Charities. The charter of this organization will be to investigate various state institutions, provide advice on improving their operations, and prevent irregularities in their management. Each institution is required to have a Board of Managers. In short; the prison will have inspections. I hope they will not require the moving of guards on a regular basis. Victor Lawson has been a strong partner at the prison. I will check with Victor to see what changes he expects at the prison due to this new law.

Tuesday, July 3, 1883. Wilhelm and I discussed moving the gold. We have decided that we will need some help when it is removed from the prison. We will need to do it quickly without anyone seeing us in the cave. I suggested to him, "We should move the gold in two stages. During the winter, when it is cold, we could take it out of the prison. To keep the cave from freezing, any maintenance work would require having the doors closed. This would give us the time to remove the boards, take the gold out of the storage spaces, and replace the boards with new boards, without anyone watching us through the open door.

"Then, we could stash the gold under some of the old boards and haul it back to Wilhelm's basement. From there, we could build some boxes that would hold eight bars each. It would take ten boxes to hold all of the gold. They would be too heavy for any one person lift and steal, and just right for shipping."

Wilhelm listened to my idea and agreed. "It makes good sense. Of course, that is unless we get a letter from your mystery person telling us to keep the gold."

I told him I did not think that was going to happen.

We decided on sometime in February for the move. The ground would be frozen so the heavy wagon would not leave deeper tracks than it should, and will hide the fact that there are gold bricks onboard.

Bayfield's Secret Notebook

I will have one of the companies that makes wooden boxes for the breweries make some boxes special for me.

I am still concerned as to how to contact Lewis Patterson, or his people. This needs to be coordinated. If they still exist, they need to know when we are going to ship the gold. We need to know where to bring it and whom to give it to. That date is coming closer. If we do not hear from him, what do we do? If we get to Bayfield and no one is there to accept it, do we wait for them? How long? What if they never show up? Do we haul it back or leave it up in Bayfield?

The possibilities are way too many. I fear it may upset our family life. If no one is in Bayfield, I may have to live up there for a year or two waiting for directions. What will Kathryn want to do? Will she move up there with me? She will have to sell her business to her partner.

Chris is getting older, but I am not sure I want him to take the risk and go with us on the train. If anything happens and someone found out about the gold, I am not sure what might surprise us. He will want to go along, if I tell him what we are doing. It is going to be hard to keep this a secret. If we move, he will have to change schools and leave his friends.

What about Wilhelm? I will need his help moving the gold. If he is away from his job very long, it may cause problems. Will he want to move to Bayfield if no one meets the train?

Finally, I may have to sell my business or find a partner. If we get to Bayfield and no one is there to meet us, I cannot stay in Bayfield and manage my distribution business in Stillwater. Someone will have to be here to manage my business.

Chapter 40

Bayfield

Saturday, December 15, 1883. I was talking to the railroad officials. They told me that the excitement of the railroad being extended to Bayfield has brought a boom of construction to the town. The completion of tracks, depot, roundhouse, and multiple sidings required for the end of the rail line in an existing town, took planning and a lot of work. Even into the winter snow season, the work has continued at a slower pace until the spring thaw arrives. Tracks have been laid on piers out in the water, and along the edge of town, to service the fishing, lumber and shipping businesses.

Sixteen miles south of town, down the same track, Washburn was building its depot. It is not scheduled to be finished until late in the summer of 1884. Multiple tracks have been planned for the lumber industry, the stone quarries, and for picking up cargo from the ships arriving on Lake Superior.

Everything looks like it is a "go" for shipping my boxes this following spring. It is time to sit down with Kathryn and Wilhelm, to discuss a plan of action. I think I will wait until we get the gold into the basement to talk about the "what if."

Bayfield's Secret Notebook

Wednesday, January 30, 1884. **Disaster!** Five days ago, the prison caught fire. I am still evaluating the situation. The entire facility burned.

Three weeks earlier, the Northwestern Car Company shop, which was inside the prison walls and only 50-feet from the cell blocks, had a large fire. They had used a combination of prison labor and skilled craftsmen to manufacture railroad cars in the buildings. The fire was reported to have started in their finishing shop and created a huge blaze that destroyed the building, which was over 300 feet long and was four stories high.

Like the earlier fire, the current fire started in one of their shops and spread to the prison. The fire broke out about 11:45 pm. The whole town was awakened by the sounds of the fire bell. Stillwater is starting to respond quickly to fires after the last one. Within an hour, the river valley was thick in black smoke from the fire. Wilhelm and I walked down to see what had happened. As we made the corner of the road, we could see the glow of flames lighting up the cliffs surrounding the prison. There was a sickening smell in the air.

All the prisoners had been taken out into the yard, where they were kept under guard as the fire department fought the flames. Apparently, the fire broke out in another of the prisoner manufacturing buildings, and the whole facility was soon consumed in smoke and fire. Warden Reed had contacted the Governor's office to request the State Militia be called out to assist in guarding and moving the convicts. Fortunately, many of the militia were from Stillwater. They formed a chain gang with the convicts, all 330 of them. They were not dressed for the cold January weather, but the heat of the fire in the confined hollow kept them from freezing.

The governor requested that a pumper and fire squad from St. Paul respond to the fire and assist Stillwater's fire department. They were loaded on a railroad car and arrived in less than an hour. By then, the fire was out of control and once again, the prison lost a work building. The fire destroyed the warden's office and guard's offices. It did not spare anything that had something burnable in it, including all the prison records. It was reported that the front wall of the prison collapsed into the street.

One prisoner was apparently missed when they went cell by cell to get the prisoners out. It took some heroic effort for one of the men from Company K of the militia – George Dodd of Stillwater, to enter the inferno and find the man in the smoke. A few moments later and he probably would not have made it out alive.

Governor Hubbard arrived later that Saturday morning to assess the damages. The manufacturing building was a complete loss. Most of the rest of the prison had damage as well. He arranged for the prisoners to be housed in a foundry nearby, until plans could be made for finding jails to temporarily house the inmates, while rebuilding the prison. The militia will help guard them in the meanwhile. Surprisingly, none of the convicts escaped. Rumors had it that a couple of them had tried.

After a lot of discussion between the governor and the warden, they decided they needed to find temporary locations for the convicts rather than keeping them in local warehouses. To keep from having them escape from a poorly built local jail, the Younger brothers and a couple other high profile convicts may be sent to a prison in Wisconsin where they have better security. The rest will be sent to county jails in the surrounding towns including St. Paul and Minneapolis. To find housing for over 300 convicts in already full jails will be a difficult task.

Wilhelm had walked down there with me. After we observed what had happened, he turned and said, "You better change your plans. As I look at it, you are not going to get the bricks out of there for some time."

He was right. The prison officials would be going all over the place for weeks looking for information and anything they could salvage.

Bayfield's Secret Notebook

Between the two fires, there had been significant damage. Then, a team would come in to tear down the remaining portions of the construction building before they could rebuild them. Anyone going in the caves and working on them would stand out like a sore thumb.

I suggested to Wilhelm that we needed to get to Victor. We need to have him remove the food stored in the cave before it rots and draws attention.

We found Victor later that day. He was still shaken from all the activities of the night before. He was worried about his job. It might take months to rebuild the prison. What would he do in the meanwhile?

We told him that the money we were paying him for guarding the cave would continue, but there was one problem. He needed to convince the warden to empty the food from the caves so that it did not spoil before they had a new prison built.

"I can handle that," he told us.

The next day, Victor had a crew of people empty the caves. It only took a few minutes and he locked up the gate after he showed the other guards that it was empty. We only wished that we could have taken the gold out at the same time.

Saturday, March 8, 1884. Work on the prison buildings got underway fairly quickly after the fire.

Following an official inspection, suggestions were made for fire safety. All the fancy woodwork in the offices would not be connected directly with the other areas of the prison. It had been a source of fuel for the fire. The work buildings would also be separated and safety reviews would be conducted periodically. They wanted to make sure that the new building would not suffer the same fate as the previous ones.

As soon as the review was finished, and the legislature provided the funds, the rebuilding commenced.

David Fabio

The prison cells were damaged by smoke and water. The administrative parts needed major work after all the woodwork fueled the fire in that area. As a result, some of the convicts were moved back fairly quickly to their cells. They provided some of the labor needed to clean up the prison. As work progressed, each week more prisoners were brought back to the prison. Many of them were used as labor, to help rebuild parts of the building.

When the work buildings are finished and all of the minor damage is repaired, they will start to bring back the high profile convicts. The Younger brothers are being held in the Washington County Jail in Stillwater.

Saturday, March 22, 1884. The prison has been rebuilt, and they are moving prisoners back into the newly improved prison. There is still some parts under construction, however the cells, a modified kitchen and administration buildings are operational. They will be adding on to the facility, and they are working on the wall that goes around part of the back half of the buildings. The hollow has limestone cliffs. The new wall will prevent the dirt and sand on the hillside from washing in to the prison.

Wilhelm and I have been discussing our options. It is time to remove the gold. They are about to use the food storage caves again, and there is ample distraction from the construction people. If they continue making a wall all the way round the sides of the prison, eventually they may disrupt the caves.

We talked to Victor, and told him that we were uneasy about leaving the gold in the new prison. With all the inspections required, we felt we needed to find a better place to store it. I told him of our plan.

Victor said he would arrange for an inspection of the cave by Wilhelm, where he would tell them there is some wood rot from the moisture and this would be a good time to replace a few boards before they started storing food in the cave. With all the notable prisoners still housed away from the prison, security will be minimal.

They will get a group of people to replace a dozen boards and remove the bricks. The wagon will leave deep tracks. However, with all the construction wagons, it will probably go unnoticed. Now, the question before them was who would do the work. I did not want any more people than necessary to know what they were doing. Someone was sure to talk to someone at the wrong time.

It would take four to six people to move the boards and bricks without looking tired and taking too long. So far, we had Victor, Wilhelm and me.

Chris is strong, and has lots of energy. I decided it was time to ask his help. Kathryn will not be happy with this decision, because it brings him into all the discussions we need to make later this year. He is mature enough that I do not feel that he would idly tell someone about the gold. Four strong people could do the job in about an hour.

I returned home and talked to Kathryn about my decision. She agreed that it was better to use Chris than to bring in another outsider to help. Later in the day, we sat down and told Chris about our plans.

We did not tell him where the gold came from. We used the same excuse Wilhelm had told Victor Lawson earlier, it had been the payment for the distillery I used to own. It was the safest place we could find to store it.

Meanwhile, Victor talked to the warden about an inspection of the caves. Since they had not been used for some time, they needed to be inspected.

Wednesday, March 26, 1884. Wilhelm's inspection of the caves had revealed no evident problems with the roof of the caves. However, he told them there were a few boards that were showing signs of weakness from the moisture in the floor and must be replaced. The next day, Wilhelm borrowed a horse and wagon from the brewery, and a group of men, Johan, Chris and Wilhelm, under the supervision of Victor Lawson, went in to replace a dozen rotting floorboards.

We made quick work of the job. The old boards were removed and holes marked and drilled in the replacement boards. Then, the four of us moved the eighty bricks silently to the wagon. We then placed the "rotten" boards on top, locked up the cave and left as calmly as we arrived. Our nervousness decreased as we left the prison gate.

We were lucky. The frost is not out of the ground, especially in the shaded hollow the prison sits in. The wagon did not leave deep ruts where we worked. Even on the roads in town, nothing showed. If we had to wait another couple of weeks, and the road would have turned to mud.

The horse strained slightly as it pulled the load the half mile to Wilhelm's house. The wagon was much heavier than it should have been with only a dozen boards in it.

When we reached the house, we quickly unloaded the boards behind his house, hauled the bricks into the basement, and then returned the wagon. The job was done. No one had suspected a thing.

I was glad I had included Chris in the job. It was obvious that his youth was a plus over our older bodies when it came to moving the heavy bricks.

I thanked Victor for all his help these past years. What I had thought would be only a couple years, ended up eighteen and a half years. Then, I gave him a case of whiskey and $25 for his help the past week.

I hoped that he had saved his money wisely. The money he had earned over the years would make a great payment on the new house his wife desired. It was slightly over $3300.

Wednesday, July 9, 1884. It is time to make plans to move the gold to Bayfield. I have talked to the railroad people about shipping a cargo to Bayfield. If we ship it by rail, we can ship from Stillwater to Hudson. Then it needs to be transferred to a train from Hudson to Spooner. Most likely, it will need to be transferred to another train that will take it the rest of the way to Bayfield.

I am concerned that the boxes might break open if handled roughly. With all the transfers, there are too many chances something might happen.

I talked to an old friend that I knew who was a scheduler at the railroad. I asked him what it would cost to have a private car, which would take me from Stillwater to Bayfield with some whiskey samples. He looked at me and said, "Depends on how good that whiskey is. If a couple cases got lost on the trip, you might find that an extra caboose would be a great way to travel the rails. You could watch your stock in private and not be bothered. We tend to ship those around every once and a while when we get too many at one location."

The deal was cut. I would have to be flexible as to my schedule. However, he would arrange for an extra caboose that would be hauled on a freight from Stillwater to Bayfield. Since it was a freight train, the car would probably be reassigned to a train in Hudson, and again in Spooner. He could not guarantee how long the stops would take.

Now, it was time to put the plan on the table for the family. This was not going to be an easy decision for any of us.

Chapter 41

The Trip North

Friday, September 19, 1884. This has been an exciting year in Stillwater. The town is booming. The population has increased to 13,700 people. They built a big roller rink in town this year, and the Stillwater professional baseball team has had a fantastic summer. It is part of the Northwestern League. With everything going on, and the town expanding, it makes it hard to decide if we should stay in Stillwater or move.

The town has also grown in saloons. A few years ago, we had 26. This year I counted 57, mostly along Main Street and Second Street. This has been a concern of Kathryn's. She is not as confident walking home at night from the shop as she was a few years ago. It has been good for Wilhelm, as there has been a constant demand for beer and whiskey. The businesses he helps are doing very well.

We had some long discussions yesterday about our future. I realize that this is probably one of the hardest decisions my family has had to make, since arriving in Stillwater.

Next week, the caboose will arrive that will haul the boxes filled with gold to Bayfield. There will be a few other boxes filled with

Bayfield's Secret Notebook

whiskey that can be used, if necessary, at the transfer points to make sure our plans stay intact.

Kathryn is concerned. Chris wants to accompany us to Bayfield. Wilhelm will accompany me as well. He will return to Stillwater once the gold is secure in Bayfield. Kathryn is concerned that Chris may want to stay with me until I can get the gold to whomever it is that is going to meet me. Since we do not have a schedule or name of a person, this may be a while. I told her that Chris is almost eighteen. He needs to start building on the experiences that will shape the rest of his life. I would like to leave him in Stillwater with Kathryn, but I know that he will fight me on this decision.

We have spent many hours discussing the options.

I have found a person to handle my business. He used to work with distribution at a brewery in St. Paul, and is knowledgeable of the towns and saloons in the area. I have been training him for a couple weeks. I told him that I wanted to check out the possibilities along the new train lines in Wisconsin.

Monday, September 29, 1884. Tomorrow, we leave for Bayfield. Later tonight, Wilhelm will borrow the horse and wagon one more time to haul the gold to the awaiting caboose, which is sitting on the railroad spur by the southern train depot. The northern train depot is near our house; however, this track leads to White Bear Lake. The other train line will take us to Hudson. There has been talk about building a "Union" depot so that both railroads could use the same depot. Progress and common sense seems awful slow at times.

Chris will help us move the crates. I will spend the night on the caboose to make sure it does not leave without us.

It was decided that both Chris and Wilhelm will accompany me to Bayfield. He will make good company and it will be safer than leaving him in Stillwater to answer questions as to where we went. If we are not met in Bayfield, we will decide at that point if Chris goes back with Wilhelm or not.

I spent a number of hours talking with Kathryn. She told me that she could take care of herself for the next few weeks. She just wants me to be careful.

Tuesday, September 30, 1884. Chris and Wilhelm joined me at the caboose about 9:00 am. Kathryn came with and made me guarantee that everyone would stay safe and come back soon. I felt bad when she left. I had no way of knowing what was in store for us. If we ran into trouble, she had two businesses to run and enough money to get her through any tough times.

The caboose had seats for four people along with benches that pulled out for sleeping. Between the seats on each side was a small table for the brakeman to write his report on. There were also two fold down seats, one on each side of the car above the regular seat, which would allow the brakeman to watch the train through windows high above the rest of the caboose, in the cupola on top the car. It would give quite a view. All in all, it was not too bad for a couple days travel.

About 10:30 am, a train backed up and the brakeman connected us up to several lumber cars destined for Hudson. Our trip was about to commence. We had some food in the caboose along with something to drink. We should be okay.

The brakeman joined us in the caboose for the short trip to Hudson. It did not take very long. Half of the time was spent on a siding, waiting for a westbound train to cross the bridge over the St. Croix River at Hudson. When we arrived at the yard in Hudson, the brakeman wished us luck and detached the cars from the engine.

We sat there for several hours until another brakeman knocked on the door. He introduced himself and told us that he would be connecting us to the late freight heading for Spooner. It would leave about 6:00 pm. The brakeman told us they would have two cabooses on the train, and he would be riding in the one behind us. If we needed anything, we could wave at the door and he would help us out. It was his job to watch both sides of the train for problems with the bearings on the wheels and sparks from any breakdowns. Also, if they needed to pick up any cars on the way, he would disconnect the cabooses, add the cars on the sidings, and then reconnect the train. He told us to expect to have to stop for water a few times along the route. If we got off, do not stray far. When the engineer blew the whistle, we would be starting very soon.

We stayed in the car and ate a meal of some sausage, cheese, and bread.

At 6:10 pm, we were connected to a string of ten flatcars and four boxcars ready for the trip to Spooner. We felt a jar as the engine backed into the first car and sent a jolt down the rest of the train. When the cars were connected to the engine and the brakeman had checked to see that all the manual brakes were off on all the cars, we started to roll down the tracks.

We could feel the switch tracks as we weaved through the yard and out onto the main line. We traveled for almost an hour before we found ourselves on a siding waiting for a southbound train to go by. As we sat there, we could hear our engine. It sounded like it was belching steam. The weather was plenty warm today and we had the windows open on the caboose.

It did not take long for the other train to come. As it passed us at full speed, it felt as though the wind from the other train was trying to push our small caboose over. My journal was blown off the small table. Soon, we were back on the main line.

After stopping twice at small towns to pick up additional cars, we pulled into Spooner about midnight. The cars were broken apart

David Fabio

based on their destinations, and we said goodbye to the brakeman. We had no idea when the next train would pick up our car.

Wednesday, October 1, 1884. We stayed in the yard all night and most of the next day. I checked with a yardman, and he told me that they had some problems with rain the day before up by Bayfield. He thought it would be later in the afternoon before they put together a train heading north. The yardman checked and came back about twenty minutes later. They would be putting together a train to Washburn shortly. We would be on it. From there, it depended on the condition of the tracks.

About 5:00 pm, we rolled out of the Spooner yard heading for Washburn. We had plenty of warning that allowed each of us to make a trip to the depot to use the facilities, wash our faces and pick up some food for the next leg of the trip before we left.

We traveled over several bridges. Usually, the engineer would slow the train when approaching the bridge to make sure there were no obstructions. I looked out the window, while going over one of them. All I could see was a very long drop with a small river under the bridge. There were no railings in case the train jumped the tracks. But then again, no railing would catch the weight of a train.

It seemed that the farther north we traveled, the slower the train was going. Perhaps it was due to the condition of the tracks. Out in the middle of no-where, the tracks were not as smooth as they were closer to the towns. The maintenance of the tracks seemed to diminish the further we got from Spooner.

Finally, the train pulled into Washburn and we were pulled onto a siding. The engine detached, and was connected to a short set of cars heading south. Within a few minutes, it was leaving for Spooner. It was time to get a good night's sleep and see what tomorrow brings. The storms had returned, and we listened to the patter of the rain on the wooden roof of the caboose most of the night.

Thursday, October 2, 1884. We are still waiting for the tracks north of here to be cleared. The storm last night had blown down some additional trees between Washburn and Bayfield. We have been told that it will be afternoon before we can complete our trip.

Since we knew we were not leaving this morning, we were allowed to use the freight yard facilities. We walked over to a small café for breakfast. The yardman said he would keep a watch on our car to make sure that no one went onboard. Apparently, a couple of need-to-know people were told that a friend of the shipping manager of the railroad was taking some samples to Bayfield, and was allowed to use the caboose. In a way, I was glad. It was nice for all of us to be able to get away from the car for a short time. The seats in the caboose were not as comfortable as one would wish.

In the afternoon, the yardman told me that they were still working on the track. He thought they were almost done, and he was putting together a small supply train to haul railroad ties and pilings up to Bayfield. If we wanted to, he could attach our car to the local. They may have to stop a few times to cut wood, but we would eventually get there. He told us that it might be more enjoyable than sitting in the rail yard all day with the sunlight beating down on the roof of our car.

I thanked him and went back to the caboose.

I decided it was time to update my journal.

*****

Chapter 42

The Crossing

Stan told Barbara and Vivian, "The journal stopped at that point. There were no more entries. It looks like we hit a sudden end to the story."

"Were there any other rumors or hints as to whether or not the gold made it all the way back to England?" Vivian asked.

"That is not the type of thing that gets printed in the paper, would be my guess," Stan answered. "I doubt that England has ever publically admitted to supplying money to the Confederacy. The only proof we have has been the discovery of gold in sunken ships. These were sunk near the end of the war and were attempting to sail to England or France. The rumors existed for years after the war.

"Because of that, I did not make a lot of effort digging for news from the English Parliament.

"However, when I was looking into articles written in 1884 from the area, I did run into one interesting item that seems to fall close to the right date. It was an article from the New York Times. It talked about a train crash. Here, I have a copy of the article, take a look."

Bayfield's Secret Notebook

Stan showed them a copy of the article he found on the Internet.

The following article was printed in the New York Times, October 3, 1884.

A CONSTRUCTION TRAIN WRECKED
TWO MEN KILLED AND SEVERAL SERIOUSLY IF NOT FATALLY INJURED.

Bayfield, Wis., Oct. 2. - A railroad accident happened three miles south of this village at Pike's Creek, this afternoon, by which town men were killed and several injured. A construction train with three flat cars loaded with piles and accompanied by 22 men left Washburn after dinner to repair a washout half a mile south of this point. The train was running about 15 miles an hour when it struck a washout just north of the Pikes creek bridge, and the engine and tender plunged headlong into it. All the hands were riding on the tender and in the cab of the engine at the time of the accident, and as the engine made the fatal plunge one of the rails ran up through the boiler and the firebox, letting the steam and water escape into the cab and tender, scalding the men in a fearful manner. The Masonic Lodge of this city was conducting a funeral a short distance from the scene of the accident and immediately repaired to the spot. The sight was sickening. Men with the flesh hanging in shreds from their faces, bands and bodies were lying on the grass or among the ruins. One man was found dead, his skull crushed, and otherwise mangled. The work of gathering up the wounded and hunting up the missing was prosccuted with diligence. A message was sent to Washburn for a special train, which arrived shortly after. Dr. Hannum dressed the wounds of the sufferers as best he could, and accompanied them to Washburn.

The following is a list of men on the train, with the extent of their injuries: C.H. Hunt, badly hurt; Fred Hunt, badly scalded; C.

G. Anderson, foot hurt; A. Johnson, uninjured; J. Dunham, side hurt; A.L. Johnson, dead; Frank Conlin, dead; F. Barred, slightly hurt; A. Anderson, badly scalded; K. McCoy, conductor, badly scalded; J.J. Barrington, engineer, badly scalded; E.S. Ford, brakeman, not hurt; S. Morris, fireman, badly scalded; Mr. Birt, badly scalded; P. Nelson, badly scalded; William Mack, leg and arm broken; P. Wooley, not seriously hurt; M. McCarty, badly scalded; E. Ottabe, badly scalded.

It is thought that many of the scalded will die. The washout and wreck will delay trains on this end of the line for several days.

"I started thinking about the possibilities, Stan told them. "What if this was the train on which they were shipping the gold. It does not mention any other cars, but what if that was intentional. The writer for the New York Times was not at the scene of the accident back then. He was probably sent information on the crash and wrote it up. It brings up interesting possibilities.

"What if there was another car on that train?"

"I figured it might be hard to find anyone alive that knew about the crash. All the people there would have died by now along with most of their children. Perhaps someone had heard rumors, but those may have been forgotten by now also.

Bayfield's Secret Notebook

"However, I did find some information on the tracks in the area. It just happens that there is a pulp spur just down the track that was used for shipping small logs that were going to be made into paper. Now, here is where you might have to use your imagination, but let's suppose the gold car was on that train. That might explain why most of the crew was riding in the hopper.

"What if the gold was in the caboose along with our group of people guarding it? With the crash, even the people in the caboose would have been thrown around violently, and possibly injured. Their injuries were probably not as severe as those near the engine, who were scalded with the steam. Nevertheless, even at fifteen miles per hour, a sudden stop would send everything flying.

"When the Masons from the funeral heard the crash and ran to the scene, they would have tended the severely injured first. Someone had to ride a horse back to Washburn to get help, and send the other train with medical assistance. That would take time.

"Suppose they discovered the injured people in the caboose, and somehow discovered the gold? Whether they found out about the gold or not, the people in the caboose would not want it sitting there when all the rescue people showed up to help the crew and fix the tracks.

"Here is my 'what if.'"

"The Masons seem to end up in lots of theory movies lately. I'm not sure why. Here, they were definitely on the scene according to this newspaper article.

"Let's remember, the Masons were a group of men that joined this fraternity, that worked to provide a better society, and they were sworn to a lot of secrecy. They were in many of the powerful places of history, and according to my notes, many of the top figures in Bayfield and Washburn were Masons. This is according to the logs I looked at that came from the Masonic Lodges.

"Let's suppose that either they saw the gold, or were told about something important in the caboose that had to be moved. Would you move eighty bricks of gold, and hide them in the woods for a week until everyone repaired the railroad? Probably not.

"With that side spur only a few hundred yards down the track, that led to a secluded area for loading logs on flatcars; on the flat tracks in that area, it would only take a few people to unhook the car, flip the switch track, and push it onto the siding. It would have been totally hidden in there. Even if the caboose was right in the open, with all the gross carnage, most people would not have seen it or paid attention to it, even if it was painted pink.

"When the emergency train arrived, they would have seen the train with the three flat cars, just like the article states. With all the gruesome discoveries, they would not have looked around for anything else. I'm sure the repair crew would have had the same experience. The caboose would have stayed hidden. Only a couple people on the train that were not badly hurt would know.

"That brought up another question I had. Why weren't all the people on the train hurt? Even if you were not scalded by the steam, after being thrown into the engine or into the ditch, you had to be extremely lucky not to break something.

"Were some people riding in another car? Or, were people paid off, originally, to secretly get the special car to Bayfield, and knew about this all along? That might be a reason for not saying anything.

"When the track was cleared, the crews had to haul the engine and cars away. That would take some time since the engine was not light and the repair crew did not have the equipment they have now. Then, someone had to remove the bent tracks and destroyed ties before they brought in the straight tracks and ties.

"Suppose one of the work crews was asked to pick up the stray caboose that was on the spur and haul it to Bayfield or Washburn. The caboose would probably be unnoticed by anyone in town since it was pulled on the end of a repair train.

"Once in Bayfield or Washburn, the contents could be unloaded and moved to a safe location.

"I found this artists rendition of the Pike's Creek crossing.

David Fabio

Crossing Pike's Creek

"I just keep going back to thinking what it would have been like in the caboose. The occupants would have been looking out the window, enjoying the view of the lake at that point of the trip. Johan, Chris or Wilhelm were probably straining to see if they could see Bayfield up the shoreline. Then, without their knowing what was happening, the engine slides off the track and into the ditch next to the tracks.

"The caboose would have lurched forward for a second, and then as the couplings between the cars tightened, it would have come to an instant stop. If the train had been going faster, I am sure all the cars would have left the tracks.

"If anyone was standing, while looking out the small window, they would have been thrown into the wall or to the floor. If there had been three people in the caboose, one of them might have been in the seat that faced backward. That might have protected that person unless something was thrown against them. If they were sitting, they would be thrown forward from their seats.

"I had been thinking of heading up there and walking the tracks in that area, but then I remembered that they tore out all the tracks from Spooner north. The rails were all salvaged for the price of steel. All you could probably see is the old railroad bed, and maybe a spike or two.

"I just wish I knew what really happened."

Chapter 43

Missing

"So, where did the story go from there? You must have some clues from your research?" Barbara asked.

Vivian and Barbara sat there absorbed in the story. It seemed hard to believe that after all that time and energy; the gold would have just disappeared.

"There are a number of possibilities," Stan mentioned. "I figured that I could trace the names back from Jean's friend in the Bayfield area, Olivia, and come from the other direction looking for Johan and Wilhelm. I tried tracing the lineage to see if that would give me a clue.

"I did find a marriage license with Chris Volker's name on it. He was married in Bayfield in 1888, to a woman who listed her previous address as Stillwater, Minnesota. So perhaps he went back for someone he knew, or perhaps he went back immediately and returned at a later date. I do not know. However, this was the strongest clue; it did place him in the Bayfield area.

"They had a daughter in 1892, Helen, who was married in 1925 to Floyd Engler. From this marriage, Olivia, whom we met with the notebooks, was born in 1929.

"Unfortunately, I can not find any records that indicate any of them had purchased businesses or large tracks of land other than Olivia. She had purchased the bed and breakfast in Bayfield. I wish that Olivia was more responsive so we could ask more questions about her past. I still hope that Jean Larson at the inn will be able to get a few more pieces to the puzzle from her."

"Now I wish we had stayed a little longer in Bayfield and tried talking to her again," Barbara said.

Vivian stepped in, "You were lucky to get the information you did. Stan, what other possibilities did you look at?"

"One thing that crossed my mind was a robbery. However, the only one that knew that Johan had gold was Victor Lawson. He probably did not know they were taking it to Bayfield, Wisconsin. Plus, if he wanted to steal it, he could have done it when it was in the prison. He could have arranged for a convenient accident involving Johan's family. Therefore, I ruled him out.

"The group of Masons keep popping back in my head. What if they did find the gold? There are a whole lot of possibilities there. One of them could have taken it and become rich. If you look at the group from Washburn and Bayfield, there are a number of people that would fit that definition. Then again, they might have had to split the gold. You could split the gold several ways and still end up with a lot of money for 1884."

"How much money are we talking about?" Barbara asked.

"With the price of gold back then locked by the government at $32 a troy ounce, about one million, twenty-four thousand dollars would be a close approximation. In today's dollars, almost sixty million dollars. I'm guessing Lewis Patterson was going to give Johan the twenty-four thousand for his work. That was a small fortune back then."

"That's enough to start a treasure hunt," Barbara replied.

"Think you could keep that a secret all these years?" Stan asked her. "If it still existed, would you be able to keep it secret, or keep from spending it?"

Barbara rolled her eyes. "Remember, they could have sold a couple businesses, and a house, and gotten money for that as well. They could have lived on that for a long time. They may not have used the gold for years, or perhaps someone did meet them in Bayfield."

"Possibly," Stan told her. "I have no record of Wilhelm after that date, either. That is the strange part. Why did they disappear?"

"What about your friends the Masons?" Vivian asked.

"Well, the mid to late 1800's were a tremendous time of business development. When I searched the public records, I noticed that Pike's name comes up a lot. The accident happened right near his place. He ends up investing a lot of money in his lumber business, in a quarry he just started, and was a leading contributor to development in Bayfield, which included installing a water system and electric lights for the town.

"There is also a man named Knight who started a lumber mill north of Bayfield at this time.

"When you look at Washburn, 1884 is about the time that many of the big stone buildings started going up. Did all that money come from Mr. Washburn or did they need another source of money to finish the project after his death?

"Oh, I forgot, someone donated the land that the current fish hatchery sits on, and a fisherman named Jim Chapman becomes the game warden in charge of it. The gift of land for a public trust was a first of a kind donation. If you look at those buildings, they were not cheap either.

"All of these men could have prospered from the money, or the Masons could have used it collectively for their communities. Those were only three of the prominent Masons who were probably at the funeral. That is, if they ever did get their fingers on it."

"Any way of proving any of that?" Vivian asked.

"Nope. The trail went up in smoke," Stan answered. "I could find no evidence that any of the men ran into money, or that either town got an instant windfall. I would leave it as a remote option.

"Then, there is the other possibility. What if they made it to Bayfield and met the representative from Canada?" he stated.

"Did you check to see if any steamers came in from Canada?" Barbara asked.

"Yes, but that is no help. Remember, the one line in the journal, way back. 'They have people that go back and forth from Canada who could take the money back.' It could have been a resident of Bayfield, or one of the islands. It could be someone on a steamer, or perhaps on a schooner, that could easily slip into port, and out again without all that black smoke. With all the boilers blowing up on ships during that period, I would put my mark on a schooner."

"Well, Bayfield is still a hotbed for sailing," Barbara mentioned. "So, any other ideas?"

"Still looking at the puzzles. Who was Lewis Patterson, and who was his associate that left the notes? Was it the same person? The only clues written in the journal about people who got off the boat with Johan, was Kathryn Bell. Did she know more than she let on? I have a hard time finding clues about her previous history. What about her uncle? His name disappeared real fast from the conversations in the journal.

Bayfield's Secret Notebook

"No, I am running out of ideas. I even checked for breweries in the area to see if they started a brewery after moving to Bayfield. Most of them were in the town of Steven's Point.

"I thought I might call Jean Larson tomorrow and see if there was anything she might have forgotten, or that Olivia might have mentioned after we left. She said she would keep us informed. I guess I promised the same. Maybe she will have some remote clue that will give us a place to look.

"I still cannot figure out where Johan, Kathryn and Wilhelm went. It is as though they just disappeared."

"What if they changed their names?" Vivian responded. "That would make them hard for you to track and anyone else looking for them."

Barbara and Vivian told Stan that they were glad they heard the story. It still made an interesting tale. It was unfortunate that it was one without a definite ending.

Chapter 44

Final Good-Byes

The next day, Stan gave Miss Jean Larson a call. She had just checked out her last guest, and was glad to hear from Stan.

"Stan, I was wondering what happened to you. Figured you found the gold and were off on the other side of the world," she jested.

"If I did, I would have taken you with," he replied.

He asked Jean, "Have you gotten any other pieces of the puzzle from Olivia in your visits to her place?"

"No, unfortunately she has slipped a lot in her memory. I think she is slowly losing it. Remember, that was why I asked you to come up and visit her when you did. The last time I was there, I had to remind her several times, who I was. How about you, did you find the pieces that fit the puzzle?"

"Yes, and no." He told her the story the best he could on the phone.

"My, that is interesting. When you get it in print, you will have to send me a book so I can read the whole thing," she told Stan.

Bayfield's Secret Notebook

"For as long as you knew her, did she ever show signs of spending money?" Stan asked.

"Just on the bed and breakfast. You know they are a money pit. No, I can't think of her spending any great sums of money. Are you coming up here any time soon? It is just not the same without you solving problems in the area."

"Thanks. Is your deputy still dropping in every morning with the daily report?"

"Just like clockwork," she answered. "Want me to say hi to him from you?"

"Please do. I know Barbara and I will be getting up that way after we are married. Maybe you can find another mystery that can keep me busy."

"Just give me time," she answered. She knew that Stan would try to get up that way as soon as he could. She would just have to wait.

Barbara came in after Stan finished talking to Jean. "Is your girl friend doing okay?"

"Yes, she said to say hi. She wants us to come up that way."

"Stan, I know you did a lot of research, however, I was just looking at my computer. Did you know that there was a 'Steamboat Island' in the Apostle Islands?

"Apparently, there was a small island next to a bigger island in the rough shape of a steamboat. In 1901, there was a big storm on the lake. From what I read, it was one of those that Lake Superior is famous for. When it was over, everything above water on the small island was gone. The waves had eroded the crumbling rocks to the point that they finally gave way to the pounding, leaving nothing but a sandy shoal.

"At one point, both islands had been called Steamboat Island. Then, after some time, the smaller one was called Little Steamboat Island. Eventually, they renamed the larger island Eagle Island after some eagles started nesting there. Eagle Island is just north of the peninsula, by Sand Point. Remember going around that island when we had my boat up there? The missing island was renamed Eagle Island shoal. That was on our map also.

"Didn't you mention that the journal had a note, back when he was in Kentucky, that he was to meet a steamboat? What if the "t" was missing? Maybe it meant meet 'at' Steamboat."

Stan replied, "Vivian, interested in a little cruise on Lake Superior to Steamboat Island? A little sea-sickness from the big lake might be worth finding the sixty million dollars."

"Not even for sixty million," she answered.

Chapter 45

Last Visit

Over the next month, Stan and Barbara had a lot of time to talk about plans for their wedding. The one thing Barbara was having a problem with was keeping Stan's mind on their wedding and not totally committed to the incomplete notebook.

As the next few months went quickly, it did not take long for the last signs of winter to disappear, and the buds to open out on the apple trees in the orchard. The view of hundreds of apple trees in full bloom would let anyone know spring was here.

Soon, the barn would need to be changed over to a wedding hall.

For their honeymoon, Barbara got her wish, to stay in her favorite room at the Chateau in Bayfield.
Stan spent a couple afternoons over at the inn, talking to Jean about wild theories concerning the disappearance of Johan, Kathryn and Wilhelm. Before they left town to head back to Illinois, they took one last drive up to Sand Point and gazed out at Eagle Island.

"You will never know," Barbara told Stan.

When the newlyweds got home, there was a message on their phone. It was from Jean Larson.

"Stan, I was over at Olivia's today. We were helping her move to an extended care home so they could watch over her. When we went to move the set of eagle bookends Barbara admired during your visit to Olivia's apartment, I noticed that they were extremely heavy.

"They are probably lead-filled to keep the books from moving them. Never-the-less, I was wondering, how heavy is gold?"

Stan was silent as he listened to the message. Had they overlooked something after all? With all his research, he never did investigate Olivia's place. At the time, it probably would not have been proper. Stan assumed that Jean had searched everything that was there when she helped Olivia move to Washburn. Now he wondered what else had they missed. Had the real clues been thrown in the trash?

He called Jean Larson. "Jean, I just got your message. You say the bookends are extremely heavy?"

"Yes, I was surprised when I picked one up to put it in a box. It was much heavier than any other bookend I had ever moved. I realize they usually plug bookends to weigh them down and prevent books from pushing them on the shelves, but these are real heavy."

"What about the rest of her belongings, what happened to them?" he asked.

"Oh, we are still boxing things up. They are still at her apartment, with the exception of the things we brought to the home for her," Jean replied. "Eventually, I will haul them here to my place."

Stan had just gotten back home, but he realized the last chance to solve this might be in Bayfield or Washburn. "Think I can come back up and look through things, just to make sure we did not miss any other clues?" Stan asked. "That was the one place I did not get a chance to investigate. We overlooked it when Olivia was having problems with her memory. I wonder if we missed anything else when she moved to Washburn."

"I think I may have a room open. Although, with gold fever running through town, I might get filled up quickly," she joked. "I asked Deputy Miller to look at the bookend today. He said he was no expert, but the bookend was definitely heavier than it needed to be. He was surprised it did not cause the shelf to sag."

"Jean, whatever you do, don't let any of this information out. Even Deputy Miller needs to keep this under his hat until we figure it out. If it gets out, any information available out there will disappear instantly."

"Don't worry, so far we have a lid on it. Let me know when you want to come back," she told him.

"How about noon tomorrow?" he answered. "Time is running out on our clues."

"See you tomorrow," Jean answered.

Stan told Barbara about the phone call, and the fact that he had promised Jean he would drive back up in the morning.

"I'll be ready when you are," Barbara answered. She was not about to miss any endings to this mystery. Besides, she had more experience with gold treasures than Stan. At least she knew the specific gravity of gold.

First thing the next morning, they were back in the car heading for Bayfield. It was as though they were starting to memorize every curve in the road. Barbara was going to have to suffer through staying at Jean's inn. Stan just chuckled at the idea that she would not get her private Jacuzzi. Actually, the inn was very nice, just not as fancy.

They pulled into Bayfield a little before noon, and met Jean at the front desk.

"My, my, you two look familiar. Are you here for a room or to buy the place?" Jean asked.

Stan looked around, and saw that no one was in the lobby. "Does a set of bookends come with the place?" he answered.

Jean smiled, and led them into the kitchen area. "All the guests are out enjoying the sunny day. I suppose you want to look at this before we go any further." She reached into a cabinet and pulled out one of the eagle bookends.

When Stan reached out to look at it, he almost dropped it. It really was heavy. He handed it to Barbara to feel.

"That's over twenty pounds," she told Jean.

"Like I said, could be lead, or could be something else. I did not attempt to break into it."

They laid it on the table and looked at it.

"Jean, do you have a mixing bowl big enough to put this thing totally in?" Barbara asked.

"I think I do."

"Good, we will need the bowl, a measuring cup, and a scale. I think we can answer our questions without damaging it."

Jean got out a large mixing bowl big enough for the eagle bookend to fit inside. Then she found a measuring cup that measured in fine numbers. "What are you going to do?" she asked.

"Well, normally we would fill the bowl with water, and then put the eagle into it. Any water that poured over the sides would be captured and we could weigh the water to get the volume of the object. That's what we would do in a lab. Here, I think we will do it the opposite direction. We will put the eagle into the bowl, fill it up with water, then take it out carefully without spilling the water.

"Then, we can fill the bowl back up using the measuring cup to see how much water is needed to fill the void. By weighing the eagle on a scale, and knowing how much water we needed, I can calculate the mass of the eagle. It may be off slightly, if it is not solid gold, however, I think we can guess within some margin of error if it is lead or gold."

It did not take long to do the test. When they were finished, Barbara smiled and turned to Stan, "Too heavy for lead. The outside must be real thin; it comes in close to the number for gold. If my guess is right, you may have almost twenty pounds of gold in each eagle."

Jean sat back in her chair and stared at the eagle bookend. "So the story was real," she said.

Stan shook his head. "Between the notebooks and these eagles, I would say it would be hard to disagree."

They looked over the eagles for any markings on them. They could see that there was a slight mark on the bottom of the bookends; however, it was so slight that they could not make out what it was.

"Do you want to look at the rest of the things we packed up at Olivia's?" Jean asked.

"Yes, very much so," Stan answered.

Jean led them back to an office area she had in the back of the inn. "When we found the eagles, I called Deputy Miller and asked him if he would help me move some boxes. We filled his truck and the back of my car with everything Olivia had in her townhouse. I brought it back here for safety. Figured when we were through, I could take it someplace."

"Good thinking," Barbara told her. "Is this all of it?"

"Yes, except for a couple items we took to Olivia's room. If you would like, we can go visit her tomorrow and check that as well."

"Sounds like a plan, I think we have a few hours of work here today."

David Fabio

They spent the rest of the afternoon looking through boxes. They had been so intent that they forgot all about lunch. When 6:00 came along, Barbara suggested that she could go out and pick up some sandwiches. It sounded like a good idea.

After a snack, Stan and Barbara spent the rest of the evening looking through boxes. Nothing was overlooked. Jean excused herself from the hunt when the bell rang at the front desk. Her customers were coming in for the evening.

By 11:00 pm, everyone was exhausted. If there was a hint in the boxes, they had missed it. They had gone through every box looking for any piece of paper or artifact that would give them the slightest hint of the past. So far, nothing.

They gave up the search and got a good night sleep. Tomorrow would bring another day.

Jean suggested that they have a late breakfast – say 9:30am. By that time, the other guests would have been fed and out enjoying the day. They could spend time talking while eating.

The night seemed to go by as if it were just minutes. Both Stan and Barbara were so tired from all the traveling and searching, they fell asleep the second their heads hit the pillows. In fact, if it wasn't for the sun shining through the rounded window in the corner of the room, they might have missed breakfast.

When they went downstairs, they were met by Deputy Miller. "Well, about time the two of you woke up. I thought Jean and I were going to have to solve this one by ourselves."

Stan chuckled, "I was wondering if you were going to join us for breakfast," he told Deputy Miller.

Bayfield's Secret Notebook

"Had to give Jean the county report. Besides, I would not miss this one for the world. It is fun to see an investigation that I do not have to write a report about."

They sat down for breakfast and talked about Olivia's belongings, and what Jean remembered from the first time she helped Olivia move. It had been several months, and most of that move was simply putting things in boxes. That was until she had seen the notebooks.

Stan asked if Deputy Miller could run a search on the markings on the eagle if they could figure it out. He could probably slip the markings into some other case he was looking at, and say he was checking to see if they had been part of some stolen property, or something.

"Well, the sheriff would probably say that it was improper use of government funds. But, since he probably owes you a couple favors, I think we can run the trademarks if you can figure them out."

"Thanks, I'm sure your offices have a better database than looking through the Internet trying to find the source of a couple scribble marks," Stan told him.

They sat and enjoyed Jean's cooking while discussing the options. When they were done, Deputy Miller said good-bye and headed north of town, while the rest of them headed to the care center in Washburn where Olivia was staying. They wanted to make sure that there were no clues on anything Jean had brought to the care center.

The sixteen-mile drive to Washburn seemed like it took a lot longer than the last time. They arrived just before mealtime as the people were starting to get lunches delivered to their rooms. Olivia had a corner room. So far, she did not have a roommate. The building had a couple empty rooms, and it gave her a chance to have a private room.

Jean went into Olivia's room first. She figured that it would reduce some of the confusion if she went in ahead of the rest.

"Olivia, hi, this is Jean Larson. How are you today?"

Olivia turned and stared at Jean. It was as if she was trying to remember where she knew her.

"Olivia, do you remember me? I own the Lamp Post Inn Bed and Breakfast in Bayfield, and I helped you move to your new room. It is a wonderful room, I hope you like it."

Olivia stared at her. "I remember Bayfield. What a nice town. Do you still live there?"

"Yes, I still have the bed and breakfast. I brought along a couple friends to see you. They visited you last fall at your house. Do you remember Barbara and Stan?" Jean motioned Barbara and Stan to come into the room.

"Are they friends of yours?" Olivia asked.

"Yes, they came with me to see you and say hi to you."

"That's nice," Olivia replied. "I like company. You say they are friends of yours?"

Stan and Barbara could see the difference between last fall and now. Olivia was definitely more confused now than she was the last time they talked.

Jean spent the next ten minutes gently talking to Olivia about things in their past. She was hoping that something would trigger a link and bring Olivia back to reality. So far, the link seemed to be just out of reach.

They tried to see if Olivia could remember anything about her childhood or life before she bought her bed and breakfast. Barbara had suggested that sometimes people could remember things about their past, while not remembering anything about the past few years. They did not want to push and tire her out, but they realized it might be the last chance they had to find any links to the past.

Bayfield's Secret Notebook

Barbara looked around the room, and asked Olivia about the things she had there. Olivia did not seem to remember many of the objects, but it gave Barbara a chance to pick up each item and handle them, while asking Olivia.

Stan saw what she was doing and offered to put the objects back on the shelves. So far, nothing seemed out of the ordinary.

When they had checked out everything on Olivia's shelves, and found nothing, they visited for a while and then offered to turn on Olivia's television for her before they left.

When the television came on, Olivia looked at it and told Jean, "Did I ever tell you that I used to sail on boats like that?"

Jean looked in amazement. The television station was showing an old movie. The show was about a family that was sailing in the ocean.

"Olivia, when did you go sailing?" Jean asked.

"I do not remember. I was young. I remember watching the big white sail. It felt so good to feel the wind in my hair. My mother would tell me that it would take hours to get the knots out of my hair. She told me to wear a hat. But, when I did, it blew off. I lost my favorite hat."

Barbara and Stan were shocked. Olivia had locked onto a memory. Now, if they could keep her there.

"Was it a fancy hat?" Barbara asked.

"It was my favorite hat for keeping the sun off me," she replied. "It was a white hat with a rim that went all the way around. I remember seeing it in the water, behind the boat. It just floated there. My father told me that by the time he could have turned the boat around, it would have sunk. Sailboats cannot turn like powerboats. So, I watched my favorite hat disappear in the waves behind the boat. I bought a new one, but it was not the same as my old one."

"Your father and mother were in the boat with you?" Jean asked.

"Yes, we would visit someone on one of the islands. I remember going over there several times."

"Do you remember the name of the island?" Stan asked.

"No, I remember seeing a lighthouse. I could see it at night. You think we could go sailing sometime?" Olivia asked.

"Do you remember if the lighthouse was on the same island as your friends?" Barbara asked.

"I do not remember."

Jean motioned that she was going to go out of the room for a minute. She wanted to find a book on lighthouses in the lobby and see if Olivia might recognize one of them.

When she returned, she showed Olivia a few of the local lighthouses hoping it would get a response. Olivia could not remember which one it was.

Barbara asked Olivia if she could remember anything else about her family.

"I do not remember. I used to have a diary. Jean do you know where my diary is?"

"Sorry Olivia, I have not seen it," Jean answered. "Did you write in it every day?"

"Yes, just like my grandfather. You know, he kept a diary too. I read his one day. Then, I decided to write one also."

"Were all of his writings in the two journals?" Stan asked.

"Yes, have you seen them? He had very good handwriting. My father told me that the books were too fragile and would not let me read them after that. He was afraid the pages would rip."

"Do you remember anything about them?" Barbara asked.

"It was too long ago. I remember he was in a war. Did you keep a diary?"

Barbara replied, "Yes, I guess all girls like to keep a diary. It helps us remember the good things when we were young."

Bayfield's Secret Notebook

Stan looked at Barbara. That's one book he wanted to see.

"Do you remember your grandfather Chris?" Jean asked.

"Yes, he was a tall man, with white hair. He walked with a limp."

Jean asked her, "Do you remember why he walked with a limp?"

"He told me he had an accident when he was young. He broke his leg. He said that I need to be careful. I was always careful that I did not break my leg. He was a nice man. I wish I could remember him better. Jean, did you ever meet him?" Olivia asked.

"No, I never did. Do you know what he did for a job?" Jean asked.

"I remember that he had an island. He sold some trees to someone. That is about all I remember."

Jean was amazed that she had gotten that much information out of Olivia. It gave Stan some leads.

"Olivia, do you remember your eagle bookends?" Barbara asked.

"Yes, I got them when I was little. They were so heavy I could not lift them until I was older. I remember my father getting them from the island. He put them and an old Bible in a box and brought it back in the sailboat."

"Did your father say anything about the eagles or the Bible?" Stan asked.

"He told me that the eagles would protect all my books. He told me to keep them forever. That's what I did. Jean, do you know where my eagles are?"

"Olivia, I have them at my house for you. I will keep them safe," Jean told her.

"Oh, that's good. My father would be upset with me if I lost them. You know he told me to keep them."

"Did Chris ever talk about his father or mother?" Barbara asked.

"No, I never met them. I was too young. Did you ever meet them?" she asked.

"No, I wish I had. It would be nice to meet them and hear their story," Barbara told Olivia.

"My father said he wrote down the family history in the Bible. Did your parents do that too?"

Jean rolled her eyes. Family Bible. She remembered some old books that they had taken out of Olivia's bed and breakfast. Was one of those her missing family Bible? How could they have missed that when she moved? At the time, Olivia just wanted Jean to get rid of the boxes in her basement. It was only by accident that she discovered the old journals. If it were not for the old leather covers, she would have never even looked at them. Now, her mind raced with the idea that there had been a family Bible in the boxes.

The rest of the time they spent with Olivia, she did not come up with any information other than what they already knew. The trip was a success. She had dropped just enough hints that they might be able to put a few more pieces to the puzzle.

They left Olivia's room and told her that they would visit her again.

On the way back, Stan asked Jean if she had any idea what happened to the boxes of books Olivia had asked her to dispose of.

Jean sat and thought a while. "You know, I remember taking a few to the library. They were just some common books that Olivia had purchased at the stores and read in the last few years. None of these were valuable, but I figured someone could enjoy reading them.

"There were a few that I thought might have some value. Some of the older books, a couple Dickens's books, and a couple by Edgar Allen Poe, I remember taking them to the used bookstore in town. I do not remember seeing a Bible in the stack. However, I did not pack all the books. A friend of mine helped me. It is possible that the Bible had an old worn out binding and we did not realize it was a Bible. I just do not know for sure. The other option, Olivia may have given it to someone else before the move.

"You think the missing links are in the books?"

Stan nodded his head. "I think that may be the clue we needed. Too bad we did not know that last fall. They may be anywhere by now. We got some good leads though. I think we'll pursue the island possibilities.

"Also, I remembered something from when I was up here writing my other book. You said that in the old days, people used to make up titles for new people coming to Bayfield. Remember that? People were given titles like Baron, or General. What if Johan, Kathryn, and Wilhelm had titles made up for them, by the local people. No one would know if they had a title or not. No one would know if they came from money or not. They might have taken the act a step farther and changed their last name also."

The group arrived back in Bayfield just in time for Jean to handle the evening rush of reservations. She had one customer coming in that evening.

Barbara offered to go get some takeout from a restaurant for the three of them to eat. That way, they could sit and quietly talk about everything they knew.

Tomorrow, Stan and Barbara would pursue the idea that Olivia's grandfather, Chris, had lived on one of the islands.

Chapter 46

Islands

Stan and Barbara chased down the idea that Olivia's relatives had lived on one of the Apostle Islands. They had a general description of Chris, and were hoping that somewhere in someone's writings they may have mentioned a person named Chris who fit the time period.

It was interesting that Olivia knew that Chris had a limp, which happened when he was young. Since it was not in the notebooks, Stan wondered if it could have happened when they brought the gold to Bayfield. Maybe his hunch that they had been on the train, during the tragic accident was correct. He could have suffered a problem from such an accident.

Trying to find a person with a limp a hundred years ago is difficult even in the best of conditions. The only thing they had going for them was the fact that many people, who lived in the area for over 70-years, still lived there.

Stan and Barbara talked to many of the older residents of the area, trying to get a lead. They did have a couple other leads. Olivia mentioned that Chris might have owned an island, and that he sold some trees. Whether he owned an island or just some property, selling the

Bayfield's Secret Notebook

trees may have left a record somewhere or a memory with one of the old-timers of the area.

There were a few people that "sort of" had a recollection of someone on one of the islands who resembled the description, but no one could link him to an exact island, or remember a last name.

In Stan's earlier research, he remembered that birch trees were sold to the woodworking industry and to the military during one of the wars for aircraft wings. That might offer a clue. If it had been general trees sold to the mills for paper, unless it was a big track of trees, it might not be in any record books.

The birch trees sold to the Army/Air Force would have been in the late 1930's to 1940's, before high-speed planes were developed. The tight grain of the birch trees grown out on the Lake Superior islands had the superior lightweight strength needed for aircraft wings. That would put Chris in his 60's at the time. It barely fell within the period. The problem would be getting the purchase agreements from the military. The lumber mills might be an easier place to pursue it. The wood would have been shipped to a mill in Wisconsin that specialized in handling birch for woodworking.

The other locations for timber might be harder to track. Unless they had been recorded by the county, they could have been shipped by boat or rail almost any place, or sent to the local lumber mills.

Stan started by talking to the purchasing departments of the mills in a fifty-mile radius of Bayfield. He hoped that someone would remember a purchase from one of the islands from a man named Chris. It was a long shot, but so had everything else been. He did not come up with anyone who remembered a Chris. However, he did come up with a list of about twelve purchases of wood from the islands, dating back to the 1920's that had been recorded in their ledgers.

David Fabio

Barbara went after the mills that specialized in birch trees and did work for the government in secret, back in the late 1930's. Surprisingly, since birch was no longer used in aircraft, she was given the names and dates of the purchases, including which islands the wood came from.

Between them, they had a number of names and places to check out. If they could find an old-timer from one of the listed islands, maybe they would remember the person listed and either confirm or deny it was their man.

It took the next four days to run down all the leads they had come up with after talking to the lumber mill managers. When they were done, they had four purchases that were still on the table. The others had been systematically eliminated from the list.

The last four were proving it was hard to find people who knew about the sale or the person that sold it. They had four purchases, from three islands. It was better than the twenty-two islands in the Apostle Islands, but it was still a shot-in-the-dark. Heading to all four of the islands from Bayfield, you would have to pass by one of the lighthouses Olivia remembered from her sailing days. It was still possible.

Jean was still bothered by the fact that she might have given away the secret without even knowing there was something in a book. Even though it had been a long time, she decided to walk over to the used-book store in town, What Goes 'Round, and ask the owners if they remembered any of the books, and better yet, did they still have any of them.

The people who worked there knew their books. It was even possible that they might remember if anyone local purchased one of the books. Jean wished that she had a full list of books that were in the boxes.

Bayfield's Secret Notebook

When she got to the bookstore, the owner and one of the clerks were doing an inventory of the books on the shelves. Jean asked if they remembered when she brought in a couple boxes of books last fall, including books by Dickens and Edgar Allen Poe. She was surprised when they told her they remembered them.

"I remember those," the owner told her, "they were in great shape. In fact, we had a bet between us as to how long they would stay on the shelf, before we sold them. I remember, because I lost the bet."

The clerk had a big smile on his face. "That's right," he replied.

"Do you remember if there were any papers in the books? Perhaps some loose pieces of paper stuck between the pages?"

The owner replied, "Sorry, I do not remember any. Did you lose something?"

"A friend of mine might have. I do not know. She thought there might have been some information stuck in the books," Jean told them. "Do you remember who purchased them by chance?"

"Yes, I think Mary purchased the Dickens books. She loves to read when she is in town. You can ask her. I think she said she was going to be at her restaurant south of town, today. The other books by Poe had been sold separately to people who came in the shop. That's how I lost the bet. I thought it would go as a collection."

"Well, I'll check with Mary to see if there was anything in the books," Jean told them. "There is also the possibility that there was an old Bible from the late 1800's in the box. Would you remember seeing it?"

The owner thought for a second, "I remember that one. It was a really old looking German Bible with a leather binding."

"Do you know what happened to it?" Jean asked with a cringe.

"Actually, I do. When we get one of these really old Bibles in, that are in good condition, I usually sell them to a bookstore in Stillwater, Minnesota. They specialize in old religious books. I was busy that day so I brought it home. I forgot about it, until you mentioned the age of the Bible. It must be in the office at home some place. Want me to check?"

"Please, if you would. It would mean a lot to a friend of mine."

The owner promised they would call her later that evening if they still had the Bible.

When Jean got back to the inn, she could hardly wait until Stan and Barbara got back to tell them the results of her search. The Bible had been written in German. Because of this, it was probably the reason it was missed when packing up Olivia's bookshelf. Had it said "Holy Bible" on the cover, they would have spotted it.

Barbara and Stan got back to the inn about 8:00 pm. They were exhausted from talking to people all day. They had to hire a boat to get to the last island to talk to a person who lived there for 80-years.

He had been avoiding their phone calls, figuring that they had been trying to sell something. Finally, Stan and Barbara figured the only way they could eliminate the lead was to go out there and talk to the individual in person.

"It's about time you got here," Jean greeted them. "Just about gave up on you."

"Sorry, I forgot to check in every other hour," Stan snarled. "What's so important?"

"Thought you might like to know I got a lead on the books."

That got Stan's attention. His spirits lifted as he asked Jean for the details.

When she finished telling him about her visit to the bookstore, the phone rang. It was the owner of the bookstore. The Bible was still at their house. They wanted to know if Jean wanted to come over and pick it up or if they should bring it to the bookstore.

Bayfield's Secret Notebook

"I'll be right there," Jean told them. She turned and asked Stan and Barbara to watch the counter. You know the drill. Anyone calls; you can book them in, or tell them to call me back in an hour.

Jean was gone for only 35-minutes. When she came back through the door, she had a large, old German language Bible in her arms. "Anyone want to do some reading tonight?" she asked.

The bookstore owner gave her Olivia's Bible without charging her, figuring that she wanted it back. It would have fetched a couple hundred dollars on the open market.

Johan's German language Bible

When they opened the Bible, they discovered several pages of writing that matched the writing in the journals. It appeared that Johan had removed them to protect what they contained. Johan had done the job so skillfully that Stan had not realized some pages were missing.

There were also some pages in a second handwriting, it was Chris's. He had added information to the pages his father had written.

Bayfield's Secret Notebook

The three of them spent the next four hours reading the notes and discussing them. It was after midnight when they looked at a clock. No one had cared what time it was.

Stan was right. Johan had written about the accident.

We were riding in the back car of the train, along with the brakeman and one other person who was riding with us in the caboose. Wilhelm was discussing the view of Lake Superior and which of the islands were visible, when all of a sudden the train jerked forward and then came to an immediate stop. Those of us that were not seated were sent flying.

I was sitting at the small table on the right side of the caboose. When the train suddenly stopped, I bruised my ribs on the table in front of me. Wilhelm, bruised his shoulder.

Chris was less fortunate. He was standing, looking over us at the lake. He went flying down the center aisle of the caboose coming to rest on the floor on top our crates. The two crew members landed on top of him. Right away, we realized that he had broken his leg.

When we looked out of the caboose to see what was happening, we saw a huge cloud of steam rising from the engine. Then we saw it, the engine was upright but pointed down into the ditch next to the tracks. That was why we came to such an immediate stop. The men that were riding on the tender behind the engine were burned badly or busted up something terrible from the accident.

I stayed with Chris while the rest went to help the injured. I found a couple of branches nearby and made a splint for his leg, using some rags to tie the splint and stabilize it to reduce the pain. When Wilhelm came back to the caboose and told me about the horrible story of the others, I joined him in trying to help some of the severely injured. We used the remaining liquor we had with us to help reduce their pain. I cannot even write about some of the injuries.

There was a funeral at a cemetery nearby. A number of Masons were burying one of their members. When they saw the accident, they came running. After seeing the mutilated crew, one of them set off on horseback for Washburn to get help.

When we had done all we could to help, I got the men that were riding in the caboose with us to unhook the car and help us push it back a hundred yards onto a pulp siding. I did not want people looking in the caboose, so I told the men that helped us push it off the main track; I would send them a case of whiskey if they did not tell anyone that the caboose had been attached to the train. They agreed to keep it quiet.

When the rescue train arrived from Washburn, they did not even see the caboose sitting fifty feet off the main tracks. Everyone's attention was on the train wreck and the injured.

The severely injured were loaded on the train and taken back to Washburn, along with several of the crew members that had died instantly when the hot steam melted the skin from their bodies. Those on the rescue train did not even notice the caboose. After all they had seen, they were not looking at the scenery.

We stayed in the caboose. With all the severely injured, we knew that the doctors would be busy with them first. Chris's injured leg would wait. We figured that a repair train would be dispatched immediately, and we could get a ride to Bayfield.

A repair train arrived from Bayfield just as the other train pulled out for Washburn with the injured. They must have been experienced at train derailments. It did not take them long to figure out what had to be done first.

When the disabled engine was righted and repairs on the track and rail bed were complete, our caboose was pulled into Bayfield by the repair train the next day.

Chris's leg was examined by a doctor in Bayfield, who re-broke the partially set leg and attempted to set it properly. Unfortunately, when he was done, one leg was slightly shorter than the other. The doctor's alignment of the bones were not correct and Chris had to settle for a limp.

After they fixed Chris's leg, we stayed at a hotel near the lake, while he was healing.

The next morning, we heard someone knock on our door. When we opened the door, an older man introduced himself, and said that he had been waiting for twenty years to meet me. It was the man Lewis Patterson had said would meet me in Bayfield.

After a brief meeting to confirm who he was, Wilhelm and I showed him where the crates were stored containing the gold.

For all my efforts that had taken me from Kentucky to Wisconsin, I was given two golden eagle bookends, which he said I could sell or keep as long as I wanted, along with $20,000. It was my payment for the treasure I had been protecting all these years.

The man removed the crates containing the gold and we never saw him again. We never asked around town if anyone knew the man. We decided that it would be best if all the secrets were maintained.

We spent the next week in Bayfield, before returning to Stillwater. Kathryn was relieved when we all returned, especially after hearing reports about the train accident. She was relieved that the event was over.

That night, Kathryn told me a story I found hard to believe. She was the one Lewis Patterson had hired to watch me. Her uncle was also one of Lewis Patterson's people, and not really her uncle. She never expected to have to stay in Stillwater, and hated the fact that she had not told me earlier.

She told me, "I am terribly sorry, I should have told you a long time ago."

I was taken by surprise. So, that was how Lewis Patterson knew that his money was safe. I wondered why he had not communicated with me over those years.

Bayfield's Secret Notebook

I remembered back, how Kathryn had told me that they had not seen how well she could shoot when the War Eagle had been attacked. At the time, I thought she was joking. Now, I wondered, what if I had decided to keep the money, would she have shot me to bring the gold to Bayfield?

I decided that I would never ask that question.

We talked most of the night.

All three men who had been in Bayfield were impressed with the location, and the rash of building that they observed while they had been there. Stillwater was a booming town. However, Bayfield and Washburn were just starting their development. They decided that this was the place to make their fortunes during the boom.

The next year, Johan sold his business to his partner and moved his family to Bayfield. Wilhelm moved there a year later, after selling his house.

Chris wrote that Johan had fallen in love with the lake. He had bought a boat and they hauled cargo to the islands. Eventually, they found a good deal on some property on Outer Island, and purchased it for an investment. Turned out it was full of birch trees. Eventually, they moved to the island.

Chris had continued to write to a girl he knew from Stillwater. Finally, she said that if he came back to get her, she would marry him. It was six years after their original trip from Stillwater.

The notes stopped at that point in their family history.

The next morning, Jean made breakfast for Stan and Barbara. They were the only people at the inn, with the exception of Deputy Miller.

As Jean went out to answer the phone, Deputy Miller asked a question.

"What are you going to do, with the gold?"

"Good question," Stan answered. "I guess that is between Olivia and Jean. I'm not sure where the possession goes. Olivia does not need the money, and she does not have any relatives we can find. Jean was in charge of all of her possessions."

Jean came back in with a grim face. "That was the care center. They called to let me know that Olivia died shortly after midnight last night. I guess I will have to make some arrangements."

"I guess that answers our question," Deputy Miller stated. "Looks like you just inherited a set of eagles."

Jean was not that excited. "I guess, I would rather have my old friend back," she said.

They sat and reflected on the interesting life Olivia had as they finished breakfast.

Stan and Barbara stayed for the funeral. With a little looking, they found the private burial area on Outer Island, where Olivia's other relatives were buried.

Before Stan and Barbara left for home, Jean told them that she was changing her will.

"Someday, when I die, I am going to leave you a pair of eagles. Until that day, if you want to see them, you will have to stay at the inn. They will be keeping my register company on the shelf, where I can look at them and enjoy all the memories associated with them."

"We'll be back," Stan told her. "Keep the room ready."

They drove back and relayed the long story to Vivian.

Bayfield's Secret Notebook

Final Notes:

The era from the end of the Civil War to the late 1880's was a period of time that saw many changes. The paddlewheelers opened the transportation of goods along the Ohio, Mississippi and Missouri Rivers. Slowly, the railroads became the important link in the system to move people and cargo between locations that were not on the rivers.

During this period, towns like Stillwater evolved from being lumber towns, to manufacturing towns. The territories were becoming part of the industrialized United States. Wealth was starting to show. The need for pleasure shaped another part of history. Baseball, theaters, and dancing appeared in the workweek.

Bayfield and Washburn evolved with the connection of railroads into shipping points on the Great Lakes.

Prisons were often used as a source of cheap labor. The Stillwater Prison was no exception.

Occasionally, well known convicts were sent to prison. Their notoriety probably exceeded the other reasons for remembering convicts at the prison. The Jessie James gang brought notoriety to the Stillwater Prison.

Bob Younger died in the Stillwater prison on September 16, 1889, from tuberculosis. He never did get his freedom.

It was thought that Cole and Jim Younger spent a number of additional years in prison due to their history with the Quantrill Raiders and the Confederacy. They were finally paroled on July 10, 1901.

Jim Younger committed suicide after his release on October 19, 1902.

Cole Younger was a model prisoner. When he got out, he lectured and toured with Frank James in a Wild West Show. He claimed in a book he wrote that he was a Confederate avenger and had only committed one crime – he robbed the Northfield bank. On August 21,

David Fabio

1912, he became a Christian and repented his criminal past. He died February 18, 1915.

The split between the North and the South resulted in deep problems in our society, which took many years to heal. It was caused by greed and power, and the resulting attitudes survived in our nation because of the hatreds developed during the war. Just like the Hatfield's and McCoy's, after time some people forgot why they had been feuding, it was just the way it was.

Just as it took generations for the people's hearts to heal, it took just as long for the political feelings between the nations to heal. Relationships, broken before the revolutionary war, were rekindled in the War of 1812, and once again in the Civil War. The support from England and France to the Confederacy is well documented. The attempts of the Confederacy to repay them from the Confederate Treasury, is where mystery novels are born. Millions of dollars of Confederate gold was unaccounted for by the end of the war.

It is not known how much repayment ever reached the shores of England or France. It is known that the Confederacy tried several methods to repay the countries for their efforts.

Bayfield's Secret Notebook

For those readers interested in information about riverboats of the period, the following books were used for reference:

Paddle Steamers by Kim Watson
Paddlewheels on the Upper Mississippi 1823-1854 by Nancy and Robert Goodman
Steamboats on the St. Croix by Anita Buck
Steamboating on the Upper Mississippi by William

About the Author

David Fabio is the author of two youth adventure novels – The Hidden Passage and The Second Summer.

He has also written a historical fiction novel for youth centered on life on the Mississippi River – Tales from a River's Bend.

Now, his eight other mystery novels – Search and Seizure, Secret of the Apostle Islands, Bayfield's Secret Notebook, Water Pressure, The Spot on the Wall, The Missing Jewels, Meadow House, and The Ship challenge the reader's imagination.

He is an educator, photographer, and an outdoor enthusiast. His love for nature and learning about the outdoors is evident in many of his writings.

Suggested other mysteries by the author:

Search and Seizure – a suspense mystery about scientific research, espionage, and murder.

When a researcher is killed and another shanghaied, attempts to uncover the killer and solve the mystery by FBI Agent Lawson leads to unexpected places.

Secret of the Apostle Islands – the mystery of a lost sailboat, last seen in the Apostle Islands.

When a woman's husband goes missing, the story leads to adventure, romance, and intrigue in solving the case.

Bayfield's Secret Notebook – a historical fiction.

A long time hidden notebook is discovered that tells about its writer's involvement in the Confederacy's attempt to return gold to England at the end of the war.

The story leads from Kentucky to the Mississippi River, leading to Stillwater, Minnesota and eventually Bayfield, Wisconsin.

David Fabio

Water Pressure – when the state wants to pump water from Lake Superior to supply the major cities, because the rivers are contaminated, the mystery starts.

An international water conference leads to a murder mystery. It is up to Martin Berman and Tracy Saunders to follow up the leads given to their television stations along with the help of FBI Agent Mark Lawson.

This book involves mystery, romance and murder. Locations include: Minneapolis, St. Paul, Grand Marais, Duluth, Williston, and other towns.

The Spot on the Wall – an action fiction.

When two old friends team up to work for a corporation that designs surveillance equipment, imaginations in technology go to work.

This book involves competition, imagination, high technology, mystery, kidnapping, and the FBI.

Located in Minnesota.

Bayfield's Secret Notebook

The Lost Jewels – an action fiction.

The a long lost relative's mysterious letter turns up talking about imminent danger and jewels, leading to a quest to solve the old mystery.

Locations include: Davenport Iowa, Kansas City Missouri, Alliance, North Platte and Kearney Nebraska

Meadow House – a historical fiction.

In the midst of a fictional story lies the interesting historical past of a small town in Minnesota – Marine on St. Croix. Why did a future President visit this community?

Locations include: Marine on St. Croix, St Cloud, and Stillwater, Minnesota.

The Ship – a mystery action fiction.

In this murder/mystery, set in the area around Lake Superior, FBI agent Mark Lawson attempts to solve two murders while investigating a smuggling operation.

Locations include: Two Harbors and Duluth Minnesota, Superior Wisconsin Hong Kong, and North Korea.

Made in the USA
Columbia, SC
28 June 2018